The Other Murder

The Other
Murder

Kevin G. Chapman

Other novels and stories by Kevin G. Chapman

The Mike Stoneman Thriller Series

Righteous Assassin (Mike Stoneman #1)
Deadly Enterprise (Mike Stoneman #2)
Lethal Voyage (Mike Stoneman #3)
Fatal Infraction (Mike Stoneman #4)
Perilous Gambit (Mike Stoneman #5)
Fool Me Twice (A Mike Stoneman Short Story)

Stand-alone Novels

Dead Winner
A Legacy of One
Identity Crisis: A Rick LaBlonde Mystery

Short Stories

The Car, the Dog & the Girl

Visit me at www.KevinGChapman.com

For Sharon, who is the queen of the "B" plot. All my love.

"An error does not become truth by reason of multiplied propaganda, nor does truth become error because nobody sees it."

– Mahatma Gandhi

"In seeking truth, you have to get both sides of a story."

– Walter Cronkite

Chapter 1 — Friday in the Park

Friday

JAVIER HEARD A SCREAM.

He was heading home after leaving the basketball court at Sixth Avenue and 3rd Street. His pick-up team had won three straight games. He could have remained on the court for another, but he had promised his mom he would be home by nine o'clock. His boss at the supermarket wanted him stocking shelves by six a.m. and didn't permit late arrivals. He took his usual route, cutting through Washington Square Park on his way to the NYCHA apartment building on 6th Street, between Avenue C and the FDR Drive. The courts in the park along the East River were closer to home, but the college scouts only watched the Sixth Avenue games, where the best street players dazzled spectators.

The scream stopped him as he trotted along a paved path curving between the trees, thick with fragrant spring blossoms. Looking left, he tried to convince himself that the sound might not have been a cry of distress—and that it might not have been from a woman. People yelled for all kinds of reasons. A dropped cell phone or a mean Tweet could prompt one. He resolved to ignore it and keep going. He needed to make sure his little brother got to bed before his mom got home from working the evening shift at the hospital. Spring pollen hung in the still air, leaving a pungent smell that mixed with the Italian sausages languishing on a rolling food cart's grill a few hundred feet to the south.

Two strides later, he heard it again—this time louder and more clearly a cry of pain and fear, almost certainly from a girl. His mother would be unhappy if he was late. She would also be unhappy if he ignored a cry for help. She had a mantra, repeated often enough to be part of Javier's psyche:

A person is defined by the actions they take and by the actions they choose not to take

He made a sharp left down a dirt path. His shoulder bag containing his hoops gear swung in a wide arc around his body. He made his way through some thick bushes toward the sound.

* * *

JOE MALONE HEARD THE BANG from inside his guard house. It was barely a shed, plopped down at the southwest corner of Washington Square Park. Joe, working for New York University that Friday evening, was moonlighting from his regular gig as a security guard at the Citi Bank on Church Street. He had put in his twenty years at the NYPD and was supposed to be enjoying his retirement while working the cushy bank assignment he had lined up years earlier. Divorcing his wife had left him with an account balance requiring supplemental income. If he were still on the force, he would have had enough seniority to pick his shift and assignment. Retiring had been his worst decision. Well, maybe not as bad as leaving his wife for a woman who dumped him six months later. Now, he had to make another decision.

He knew that sound. A gunshot has a specific aural texture and echoes off the surrounding buildings, even when it comes through the trees. Most New Yorkers would ignore it, even if they knew what it was. That's the nature of city life. Don't get involved. Cops think differently; and deep down, Joe was still a cop.

The inside of the park, however, was not his jurisdiction. The university wanted him in his little shack on the sidewalk, to make the students feel safe as they strolled up and down the cobbled sidewalks between the bars and clubs and restaurants. If there was a fight or a purse-snatching on the street, he was expected to emerge from his shelter and take action. The wrought-iron barrier separating the park from the sidewalk was his boundary. Joe was supposed to leave the dark shadows under the city-owned trees to the NYPD. If something was happening inside the park, university security was supposed to call 9-1-1. Those were his orders.

Joe was lousy at following orders. He slid off his chair and stretched his back as he wandered out of the shed and tipped his head up, listening in case there was another shot. He could hear a truck speeding up Sixth Avenue a block away, and the buzzing chatter of happy and drunk college students. The ambient noise drowned out any sounds coming from the park. The lights on the street gave way to shadows on the far side of the fence. Nothing. No second shot.

He dialed the local police precinct and spoke to the desk sergeant. "This is Joe Malone, NYU Security at 4th and MacDougal. I have a probable gunshot inside Washington Square Park, likely to my north. Please send a unit over to check it out . . . Yes, I know the difference between weapons fire and a car backfiring. I'm retired NYPD. Just send a car."

He punched END and again tilted his head, listening. Nothing. The precinct dispatcher would eventually put out a call for a squad car, but it would take a few minutes, at least.

"Fuck it." Joe walked through the gap in the fence, pulling out his two-foot-long tactical flashlight that also served as a Billy club. He walked along a smooth, paved path, still listening. The street sounds were muffled here, behind layers of shrubs and trees. The pool of brightness from his flashlight filled in the shadows. He left the pavement, following a dirt path toward what he knew was a clearing around the Hangman's Elm. Joe had no clue how the tree got its name, but assumed criminals were actually hanged there in olden times. It was a spot where people gathered in the daylight for picnics and where New Yorkers who preferred not to be seen came to score some weed—or more—after dark.

Joe wasn't interested in busting a small-time drug dealer or their customers, but he figured the shot he heard had come from this direction. The clearing was as good a place to start as any. Another bang caught his attention. It was farther away, toward the east: different, but likely another gunshot. He swung his light around to confirm there was no potentially hostile person in the clearing. Emerging through a gap in a line of thick forsythia bushes where the path narrowed, Joe shone his light at the Hangman's Elm.

He saw a flash of purple and a dark shape on the ground. He walked toward it, shining the light all around the silent dirt, trampled by hundreds of New York feet. When he was close enough to be sure of what he was seeing, he rushed forward. It was a girl. On the ground. Not moving. He knelt in the dust, not worrying about what evidence he might be trampling. Sticking the flashlight under an arm, he reached out and nudged her, in case she was just sleeping. She wasn't. He rolled her onto her back. His eyes jumped to the dark hole in her forehead. She wasn't going to need an ambulance.

Chapter 2 — Dream Job

HANNAH'S PHONE BLASTED the opening bars of "Takin' Care of Business" at nine-fifteen Friday night. She was on a date—a first date. Not wanting to appear too anxious, she wore a conservative green dress with a high neckline and half-sleeves. Hannah's brown hair, which she usually kept in a ponytail, hung in loose curls around her shoulders.

"I'm really sorry, but this is my boss. I need to answer." She was already halfway out of her chair. Hannah had mostly talked about her job during cocktails and dinner, so her date, Erik, should not have been surprised. She had described the job as exciting and challenging, but also requiring long and unpredictable hours. She could be called to cover a breaking news story at any time. Her explanation was proving itself all too true.

"We're not sure who the victim is, but the report is a young female." David Butler's voice carried excitement and urgency. "Terry is down there with a van. He was shooting background video of a climate change roundtable with John Kerry, a Saudi prince and the Chinese vice president when he got a tip about this shooting. We're a little light tonight, so let's see if there's any link between the climate conference and this dead girl."

It was the kind of breaking story Hannah lived for. Dave was her managing editor, so she had to take orders from him. But he knew how to push her buttons and make her *want* to drop everything and rush to the scene.

"I'm sending William Wilson. Try not to piss him off too much. We want to do a live shot for eleven o'clock. First segment. Can you get there?"

"Absolutely." Hannah's response carried more excitement and emotion than any of her conversation at the dinner table with Erik.

"You're not my first choice, Hawthorne, but nobody else is available. Don't give me another Lower East Side Baby. Got it?"

Hannah cringed and bit her tongue. It was useless arguing with Dave that the Lower East Side Baby debacle wasn't her fault. The witness she put on camera two months earlier claimed he saw the baby's mother in the window before the child fell. Hannah had no way of verifying it. After Hannah put him on camera, a reporter from *The New York Post* discovered the witness on a security camera at the critical time, outside a strip club ten blocks away. The network was embarrassed. The witness turned out to be the woman's ex-husband and had a grudge. The injured child was not his. It was a mess.

"I won't let you down, Sir." She ended the call and hurried back to the table, making her excuses and giving Erik a peck on the cheek. "This is my life. Like I told you, it's exciting, but sometimes inconvenient. Can we try again?" She grabbed her sweater, blew him an air kiss, and hustled away. Erik sat in disbelief for a moment before reaching across the tiny table to stab a bit of Hannah's abandoned crème brulé.

Hannah waited on the Sixth Avenue curb outside Possa Notte and lit a cigarette. She hadn't wanted to endanger a first date by smoking in front of Erik, but now she was working. As soon as an empty yellow cab pulled over, she tossed the butt and climbed in.

* * *

ONE HOUR AND FORTY MINUTES LATER, Hannah walked down the cobbled sidewalk along the north side of Washington Square Park, holding the elbow of a young woman in a pink sweatsuit and matching flip-flops. The girl, Petra Burroughs, was the former roommate of the shooting victim, Angelica Monroe. Petra's brown hair was pinned up with a plastic claw clip. She had no makeup and looked like she was ready for bed.

Hannah guided Petra through the growing obstacle course of broadcast media equipment. Since the initial police calls about a shooting in Washington Square Park, a swarm of media had descended on the area. Black power cables snaked across the sidewalk every ten feet, connecting portable generators to aluminum spiders with flood-light eyes that illuminated the eerie scene. Hannah and Petra passed several broadcast vans before arriving where her cameraman and driver, Terry, had staked out a position.

Unlike most of the other media vehicles, the white American Cable News van was emblazoned with the corporate name and logo. The company's executives had decided that, even after the near-riots targeting journalists after the George Floyd murder, the young network's branding was more important than the risks to its reporters. Terry, the first media member on the scene, had grabbed a location on the curb next to an access path into the park under a streetlight. Any extra light for a camera shot was gold for a nighttime live report.

Hannah had wheedled the victim's identity out of a university security guard named Joe Malone, who found the body. Hannah implied that she could get Joe an on-camera interview. A shy smile and a hundred-dollar cash payment, for a copy of Joe's cell phone picture of the crime scene, convinced Joe to give up

Angelica Monroe's name. Hannah then worked Instagram and Twitter to find photos of Angelica. There were plenty, one of which included Petra, whose name was tagged. Paydirt. It would have been a better story if Angelica was somehow linked to the climate conference. Still, the brutal murder of an attractive young woman in the middle of Manhattan was juicy—as long as she could come up with a witness to put in front of the ACN camera.

Petra was, naturally, skeptical when Hannah contacted her via social media. However, Hannah's youth and her own online photos and portfolio broke down Petra's resistance after the seventh message. When Hannah arrived at Petra's dorm room, the girl was reluctant to talk about Angelica. "I was, like, only her roommate. And that was last year. It's not like I knew her that well. I'm . . . really not the best person."

Hannah was not going to lose this witness. "Don't be modest. You lived with her for a year. You can certainly tell our viewers how crushed you are about losing her at nineteen. I'm sure she was a good friend and a kind person, right?"

Petra fidgeted, clasping her hands behind her back. She avoided making eye contact. Hannah couldn't be sure if her reluctance was trepidation about being on camera or something else.

She didn't have time to psychoanalyze the girl. "Look, right now everybody is speculating about Angelica and what happened. You will be the first person who knew her to go on camera. You don't get many chances to be the star witness. Can I count on you?"

"Can I change into something nicer, and put on some make-up?"

"You look great just as you are," Hannah lied. She wanted the girl to look natural, even disheveled. Speed was the name of the game. The first interview was, by definition, the best one. "We need to hurry if we're going to make it in time for the eleven o'clock top story. Just grab a sweatshirt, in case you get chilly."

As they walked past a barrier of yellow crime scene tape, Hannah prepped Petra for her on-camera appearance. "Our reporter, William Wilson, is a wonderful guy. You'll like him. He'll lead you through the interview, so don't worry. We want you to talk about Angelica. It's a tragedy. We want our viewers to know her through you. You'll explain what a wonderful person she is— was—and about your feelings now that you know she is so suddenly gone. It must be awful, knowing a classmate could be murdered only steps away from your dorm."

Hannah stopped talking long enough to gauge Petra's demeanor and mood. The girl's eyes looked like golf balls, with dime-sized black pupils. Panic. Hannah wanted sadness. She changed her approach and asked Petra whether Angelica had a boyfriend.

"Um, I haven't really hung out much with Angie this school year. She lives in a dorm up by Union Square and we don't have any classes together. She had a guy last spring named Tony, but I haven't seen him on Angie's Instagram lately, so he's probably not around anymore."

Hannah escorted Petra around two black-and-white police cruisers, both with their blue and red lights twirling. They stopped at the ACN interview location, where Terry had marked a huge X on the sidewalk stones with red duct tape. Behind the mark, a four-foot-high iron fence made a perfect background for the live shot, the trees beyond draped with crime scene tape.

Hannah stood on the red mark with Petra, consoling her and building up her confidence about being on camera. When Terry gave the signal, William Wilson emerged from the ACN van and walked to the mark, while Terry focused the HD camera, mounted on a tripod. The flood lights brightened as Wilson stepped into the illumination, smiling and holding a wireless microphone.

Hannah stepped aside, giving Petra a raised thumb of support. Her phone vibrated. "Hey," she answered, knowing from the caller ID that David Butler was on the other end.

"Are you ready? We want a buck-thirty at two past eleven."

"All set, Boss. Did you get my notes?"

"Yeah. Nice work. How the hell did you get the dead girl's roommate?"

"I'm just that good. And she's last year's roommate. Let's get the lead-in right."

"Fine. Fine. We have it. You're sure she's legit?"

Hannah bit her lip. "Yes. It's based on photos on Angelica Monroe's Instagram."

"Who?"

Hannah sighed. "The dead girl. Don't worry, the witness is solid."

"Tell William to tape a second segment after you're done live. We want two minutes for the overnight. You got any other witnesses?"

Hannah held the phone away from her ear, slowly counting to five. It was a technique one of her journalism school professors taught her to avoid blurting out something she would regret later. "No, Boss, I've been fully occupied securing you the scoop of the night. It may take me another half hour to get an interview with the killer." The silence on the other side of the call, rather than a burst of laughter, signaled that her sarcasm was not properly appreciated. "But I'll keep digging, as soon as we finish the live segment."

"OK. You did good tonight, Kid. Keep it up." The line went dead. Hannah smiled, despite being pissed off. She hated that it made her so happy to get a small nugget of recognition from Butler.

When Hannah looked up, the red light atop the huge black camera in front of Terry flashed. William Wilson thanked the studio anchor and launched into Petra's interview. As Hannah had hoped, Petra looked like she had been ready for bed, but agreed to be interviewed in her night clothes because she was so mortified by her friend's tragic death. She told the camera how Angie loved animals and wanted to be a veterinarian. When asked to recall her favorite memory of Angelica, Petra's tears flowed like a spring rain. Through her obvious grief, Petra said Angie was popular and a friend to everyone. She could not understand how anyone would want to hurt her. It was gold.

After the live interview ended, Terry and William held Petra in place, then launched into a series of questions that could be edited together later into the longer piece. When the questions ended, Terry hustled Petra inside the van on the pretext of giving her a downloaded copy of her interview. The goal was to keep her under wraps so the other reporters and producers couldn't grab her for a copy-cat spot. Hannah remained outside with William, who unbuttoned his dress shirt and pulled his necktie down three inches.

"That was fantastic! You got us the absolute best interview. I'm sure there wasn't a dry eye in the studio. This Angelica girl is as tragic as it gets." He stepped toward Hannah with his hands spread wide, angling for a hug.

Hannah extended a hand, holding him at bay. "Don't seem too happy that she's dead, William. The people want to see you cry, not pop the champagne."

Wilson pushed through her outstretched arm and grabbed her shoulders with his manicured hands. He leaned in to kiss her as her elbow bent. She turned her head and winced as he planted his lips on her cheek, then released his grip and turned away with a smile. Hannah thought about tripping him as punishment for the unwanted kiss, but recalled Dave's admonition that she should not piss off the network's most popular field reporter. Wilson walked around the front of the van and disappeared beyond.

After escorting Petra back to her dorm, Hannah waved at several colleagues from the local network affiliates. They flashed expressions conveying congratulations, admiration, jealousy, and contempt all at once.

Back at the van, Terry sat in a folding camp chair, smoking a cigarette. "Can I bum one?" Hannah held out her left hand without waiting for a response. It was a familiar dance.

Terry bumped his pack and offered the extended butt, saying, "You should quit."

"I know. Thanks." She used her own lighter. She had half a pack in her bag inside the van, but smoking Terry's didn't count against her self-imposed limit of five per day.

"You going home?" Terry asked between drags.

"Not sure. You?"

Terry blew out a perfect foot-wide smoke ring that drifted toward the crime scene tape attached to the iron fence. "I'm gonna stay. This location is too good to give up. Butler gave me permission for the overtime. He said the morning show will want a shot, even if there's no update."

Hannah nodded. Terry was dedicated, and he was right about the prime location. If they moved the van, three others would battle for the turf. It was best to dig in. Parking regulations would not be enforced as long as the media was there.

Hannah surveyed the scene. Two reporters from other networks stood in pools of bright light doing live reports. They were so close to each other they had to angle their cameras in order to avoid having their neighbors in the shot. She counted six news vans parked along the street, five with their satellite dish antennae extended skyward.

A middle-aged man wearing a faded blue sports jacket and a dark-haired woman in a jacket and slacks combo ducked under the yellow tape, accompanied by two uniformed officers. They moved along the iron fence, then turned right, into the park. "Those are the detectives," she said in Terry's direction. She stepped toward the park entrance, but was stopped by two officers who held out their palms without speaking. The press was not allowed behind the tape while the investigation was ongoing.

Hannah returned to the van. It was nearing midnight, but the scene was still buzzing with activity. There were more reporters than cops. "I think I'll stick around a while and see if the detectives come back."

"Suit yourself." Terry tossed his spent cigarette on the pavement and crushed it out with a clunky black shoe. "I'm going to try to get some sleep while I can."

"Great." Hannah gave him a pat on the shoulder. "Fantastic work today."

Terry grunted as he disappeared inside the van, which was equipped with a hammock and a mini-fridge. She shook her head slowly, marveling at the feeding frenzy all around her. She needed a big story to make her boss forget about the Lower East Side Baby. She snuffed out her butt and sat down in Terry's abandoned canvas chair, then mumbled to herself, "This is going to be great."

Chapter 3 — Step Right Up

DETECTIVE ANDREW "DRU" COOK ducked under the streamer of yellow crime-scene ribbon. He glanced back to make sure his partner, Mariana Vega, made it through behind him. Dru had been a homicide detective for seven years and was increasingly annoyed when calls came in on a Friday night. It was certain to ruin his weekend.

Dru liked to think he didn't look like a cop. His athletic six-foot frame attracted admiring glances. He still had a full head of wavy hair, although he had to admit that what was once Norse-god-blond had darkened through his twenties. Now, at age thirty-six, it was at best sandy-brown. Still, he had the blue eyes and light skin of his Scandinavian ancestors.

The area around Washington Square Park was buzzing with an intensity unusual for a Friday at nearly midnight—and that was saying something. The New York University area, like much of Manhattan, normally got busier as the hour got later. Mariana had parked two blocks away because of the news vans blocking all the normal no-parking spots cops usually occupied. With several dozen reporters and at least eight camera crews encircling their crime scene, this figured to be a long night.

The two detectives each pulled out blue latex gloves and prepared for the initial look at their stiff. Dru wore a faded blue sport jacket. Mariana's tailored blazer was a dark maroon above her black slacks. Her long, dark hair was tied back in a neat ponytail, leaving her face unobstructed.

Two uniformed officers stood guard at the entrance into the park. One had a cigarette dangling from his mouth.

"Put that shit out!" Dru snapped. "You're on duty."

The officer dropped the butt and crushed it into the ground with a black boot.

Mariana turned her head slightly and mumbled, "Geez, Dru, give a cop a break. Just because you're trying to quit doesn't mean everyone else has to."

"Smoking on duty is against regulations."

"When did that ever stop *you*?" Mariana raised one manicured eyebrow.

Dru and Mariana walked slowly down the paved path, curving through the landscaping toward the big tree known as the Hangman's Elm. When the pavement curved left, they ducked under more yellow tape onto the grass. They knew to take their time when traversing a fresh crime scene.

They emerged past a line of azalea bushes into the clearing around the huge elm. Mariana turned to her right, surveying more crime-scene ribbon wrapped around protruding branches and bushes in the absence of anything else to which it could be affixed. She couldn't help but think of the song her mother loved about yellow ribbons and old oak trees.

Mariana stood six inches shorter than her slightly more senior partner. A light-skinned Dominican with slender legs and mysterious dark eyes, she looked like anything but a cop. After nine years on the force and four working homicide, the veteran beat cops had learned not to underestimate her small package.

A uniformed officer stood between them and the big Elm tree, waiting. Four portable light stands, each with three large aluminum pans reflecting the light from halogen bulbs, made the clearing as bright as a movie set.

"Hey, Hernandez," Dru called out. "You in charge here?" Officer Emmanuel Hernandez nodded. He had a boyish brown face below short-cropped black hair, buzzed above both ears. Dru had worked with him before and was glad he had a competent officer in charge of the scene. "Good. What've we got?"

Hernandez gave a quick rundown to the newly arrived detectives. "The victim is identified as Angelica Monroe, sophomore, nineteen. Looks like a gunshot." A lumpy white sheet lay under the Hangman's Elm on the packed dirt. One large light, resembling a grotesquely oversized desk lamp on a bent goose-neck arm, illuminated the corpse.

The assistant medical examiner was packing up her gear in a green duffle bag, looking like a dental hygienist who had completed a tooth cleaning. An EMT crew stood idly by beyond the big tree, ready to remove the body as soon as the detectives finished their inspection. Hernandez explained that the university security guard who found Angelica searched her purse and found an NYU identification card. The responding officers had already contacted campus security and were securing her dorm room, several blocks to the north.

"Good," Dru interrupted the narrative. "We'll check there when we're done here." Dru then took a few paces toward the covered body and called to the Assistant ME. "Natalie! We have a cause of death?"

"Detective," she sighed, "you know I can't give you that at the scene." Natalie Or, a slender Asian woman in her early thirties with long black hair tied in a bun, put a bony hand on her hip and glared at Dru. They had worked on the same crime scenes many times. Without an autopsy, she could not give any definitive answers and they didn't want to be quoted to the press prematurely. Despite the caution tape and a phalanx of officers surrounding the scene, an intrepid reporter could be lurking in the shadows, waiting for such juicy information.

"I know. The university security guard and Officer Hernandez here both say gunshot. Can you at least confirm the likelihood for me?"

Natalie pressed her lips together until they formed a pink line and rolled her eyes. "Fine, I'll say there appears to be a gunshot to the head. Large caliber. I see no obvious alternative causes of death. Yet." She turned away and grabbed her bag. "Now, if you will excuse me, it's a busy night and I have another corpse to inspect." She walked toward the park exit.

Dru nodded in sympathy. He knew there was another body waiting for her on the other side of the park. Two for the price of one. She didn't even need to move her wagon from its parking space. He wondered whether she had secured a closer spot than Mariana.

Then he turned back to Hernandez. "Sorry, Hernandez. I cut you off before you were finished."

"Understandable, Sir." He continued the rundown in an efficient monotone. "The victim had a large purse containing a plastic baggie with what I estimate to be one ounce of weed and $500 in cash. Also an iPhone, which is locked."

"So, not a robbery," Dru observed.

"A drug buy gone bad?" Mariana suggested.

"Why would a dealer shoot his customer and not take the cash?"

Mariana shrugged. "Somebody trying to steal the weed after the buy?"

"Why not take the weed and the money? And why would she fight back enough to get shot?"

Hernandez, who had been listening intently, asked, "Should we let the press know about these details?"

Dru put a hand on the officer's shoulder. "Hernandez, you know better than that. The press is never our friend. They want any details they can get out of us, but anything we say will only hurt the investigation. Say nothing. No cop has ever cracked a case by sharing information with the press at a crime scene."

"OK," Hernandez replied, properly schooled. Hernandez then finished his recitation of the important information. The responding officers had bagged blood found near the body and a small amount from the ground about twenty feet away. They also recovered a silver-grey shoulder bag with the logo of Emirates Airlines, which had been on the ground near some bushes on the perimeter of the clearing around the tree. After following standard safety protocol, they had opened it and found a pair of Air Jordan basketball shoes and a basketball jersey. The jersey was damp and sweaty, as if recently worn. There was no identification in the bag, but the sneakers had the initials "JE" written in black ink under the Nike logo.

"Good work, Hernandez. We'll get you promoted to detective yet," Dru smiled. Hernandez bowed his head in acknowledgement, but didn't comment.

Dru and Mariana slowly walked the scene. When they reached the body, Dru motioned for Mariana to remove the sheet. The body's most significant attribute was a dark hole above the left eye. It was easily identifiable as the likely cause of death, even without confirmation from Natalie. Angelica's purple top, which looked like silk, was torn off one shoulder. The corpse showed scratches and bruises, consistent with an assault. Two fingernails on her right hand were jaggedly broken.

Mariana extracted a tongue depressor from a pocket and lifted the dead girl's skirt. "Natalie will do a rape review when they get the body back to the morgue, but her underwear looks to be intact. If it was a sexual assault, it doesn't look like it got far." Nothing else around the body caught their attention.

They next inspected the athletic bag, which was waiting a few feet from the body. Inside, the basketball jersey was less sweaty than Hernandez described, but the passage of time explained the change. The bag could be significant, but Dru had no idea how.

Dru and Mariana both pulled out flashlights and slowly patrolled the area. Despite the artificial lights, the detectives liked to provide their own illumination, since there were always shadows and hidden places at a nighttime murder scene. They were already assuming a murder. College students didn't shoot themselves in the foreheads with nonexistent guns.

Five minutes later, Mariana called out, "Hey, Dru. Take a look at this." She was standing near the edge of the clearing, next to some thick bushes. On the ground to her left, two yellow flags marked the place where the responding officers had found the Emirates Airlines bag. When Dru joined his partner, Mariana directed her flashlight beam to the ground next to a forsythia bush, thick with new spring leaves and the last remnants of yellow blossoms. In the pool of light, Dru saw the object of Mariana's attention, a small detached branch sporting four shoots of green leaves. "Had to come from that bush, pushed forward by somebody coming through from the back side."

Dru nodded his agreement. "You think the bag?"

"Probably. Somebody came through here, then dropped the bag."

"The girl?" Dru asked.

"Not likely. Sweaty basketball gear? We can check the sneaker size against her foot, but I doubt it."

"The killer?"

Mariana looked around, as if the bushes would speak to her. "Maybe. Could have seen her, or followed her, then dropped his bag to attack her. Then ran off afterward, leaving the bag behind."

"Maybe," Dru said slowly, not convinced. "It would explain the bag. But why not take it with you after you kill her?"

"The bag could belong to a bystander."

Dru cocked his head to the side. "If so, where is he?"

Mariana shrugged. "Ran away?"

"And left his bag? Those are Jordans. He must have been in a big hurry."

"It's just a possibility," Mariana said. "Could be another buyer, waiting their turn?"

After another ten minutes of meticulous searching, Dru and Mariana rejoined Hernandez next to the elm tree. The EMT crew had removed the body, leaving only small yellow markers behind.

Dru asked, "Any luck finding a witness?"

"None so far."

"What about the guy who found the body?"

"The security guard? Name's Joe Malone. Says he's former NYPD. We sent him back to his guardhouse at the corner of 4th & MacDougal. He was being a pest. He'll be there until two o'clock. We told him not to leave until he talked to you."

Dru and Mariana exchanged a glance, then Mariana shrugged. "Might as well get it over with. What else do we have?"

Hernandez pointed to the east. "There was another murder on the far side of the park, a Hispanic male. Shot once in the chest. A bloody knife was recovered at the scene. At least, that's what I heard. We have two teams of officers over there handling the scene. One's a buddy of mine and gave me the details."

"Any time of death on that one?" Dru asked.

"Not sure."

Dru looked at Mariana. "Could be a connection?"

"Maybe. We should check to see if the dead guy fits the shoes from our bag."

"You have a Cinderella complex, Mariana. Anybody ever tell you that?"

"Fuck you."

Dru chuckled as he turned away toward the path back to the exterior perimeter of the park. "Let's go. Nothing else for us here. Let's take a stroll over to see who's working the other stiff. Then we'll talk to the security guard and then check the girl's dorm room."

"Oh, boy," Mariana replied sarcastically as they walked briskly away from the Hangman's Elm, toward the street and the bright lights of the television camera crews. They ducked under the yellow tape and walked east. After several hundred yards, they reentered the park and walked along an internal path to the far northeastern corner.

They reached a wide swath of grass crisscrossed by dirt paths. Even after midnight, the unusually warm April air was comfortable. An ambulance, lights on but without a siren, pulled up on the narrow, paved path.

Dru spotted detective George Mason, standing alongside two uniformed officers. He called out, "They're still sending your ass to the dog cases, eh?"

"I'll take 'em," George replied with a chuckle. "You can have the spotlights."

Mariana playfully punched George on the right shoulder. "We got a circus over on the other side of the park. Where are your film crews?"

"Nowhere," George said. "We got a Latino teen here, dead with a gunshot in the chest. Nothing those vultures care about."

Dru asked, "You get a bullet?"

"Nah. Embedded in the body. Looks like small caliber."

"Hmm," Dru grunted an acknowledgement. "We'll see if there's any connection to our NYU undergrad. If it's the same gun, we may have something to investigate."

"Yours also small caliber?"

"No, actually. Ours looks like a howitzer. But you never know. Any ID on the kid?"

"None." George moved toward the body, holding out an arm to welcome Dru and Mariana to his crime scene. "We've got nothing else here besides the knife." Dru pointed to the evidence bag on the grass next to the covered corpse's head. George nodded. The bag held a long knife, its blade extended and bearing dark stains.

"Prints?"

"The forensics team collected some, then bagged the knife. The body has no obvious cuts, so it looks like the kid made the mistake of bringing a knife to a gunfight."

"Anything else of note over here?" Dru asked while walking around the body, examining the trampled grass with his flashlight. The floodlights here were half as bright as those illuminating the Hangman's Elm. "Any witnesses?"

"No. The after-dark regulars aren't in a hurry to talk to us. Until we have an ID on the kid, there's not much else to do."

"Yeah," Dru mumbled, "we're lucky. We have an ID, and now we have a dorm room to search. We should go."

"Sure. You go stand in front of the cameras," George said with a chuckle, "I'll close my case before you."

"Yeah, you're probably right." Dru turned and tapped Mariana on the arm. "Let's go talk to Joe Malone."

* * *

THE LITTLE GUARD SHACK wasn't large enough to contain three people, so Dru and Mariana asked Joe Malone to step outside for their interview. Joe was happy to oblige.

"I knew I heard a gunshot," he volunteered. "It definitely came from the north, so I made the call to check it out."

"Slow down, Joe." Dru held up an open palm. "Let's do this one step at a time. First, do you remember seeing the girl earlier in the evening?"

Joe, who was bouncing on the balls of his feet, became still as he contemplated the question. "I don't think so. I certainly don't specifically recall."

"OK," Dru continued, "So, you heard a shot. How long between hearing the shot and finding the body?"

"Lemme see," Joe looked at the sky. "I waited a minute to see if there was another shot, then I called the precinct and asked them to send a squad car. The dispatcher didn't seem to take me very seriously, which is why I decided to go in myself. I went in cautiously, so, maybe six or seven minutes."

"When you got to the clearing, did you see anyone there, besides the girl?"

"No," Joe immediately replied. "I swept my light all around the area. There was nobody."

Mariana then cut in. "Did you hear anything, like somebody running away, or shouting?"

"I heard another shot," Joe offered. "It was farther away, off to the east."

"The other murder," Mariana made eye contact with Dru.

"That's good information," Dru took back the lead. "So, you found the girl. Did you move her?"

"Sure. I had to check if she was alive, so I rolled her over. She was face-down when I got there. As soon as I got a look at her head, I saw the shot, so it was pretty obvious she was gone."

"And you checked her wallet?"

"Yeah," Joe dropped his head, suddenly not as enthusiastic. "I know I should have left it for the responding officers. But I was a cop for twenty years, so I know how to manage a crime scene. I worked the Righteous Assassin murders, you know."

"Really?" Mariana responded without considering how she was interrupting Dru's questioning.

"Sure." Joe snapped back to his animated self. "I was at the scene when Slick Mick Gallata got snuffed."

Dru looked at Mariana while replying to Joe. "That must have been exciting, but let's stick to the present. Did you remove anything from her purse?"

"No. No way. I saw her NYU ID, so I pulled it out to see who she was. I figured it would aid any investigation to have an ID on her."

"Did you identify anything else of significance at the crime scene?"

"No. I told everything to the responding officers."

"OK, Joe. Thank you." Dru turned away.

"Wait," Joe raised his voice. "Don't you want to hear my theory about what happened?"

Dru turned his head. "If we have any additional questions, we'll let you know. Detective Vega will give you a card. Please send her a text so we know how to get you if we need you."

Mariana extended a business card, which Joe took, looking annoyed. Without any additional conversation, the two detectives walked toward their parked sedan. Angelica's dorm room was far enough away that they should take the car. "Looks like we're going to run up some overtime this weekend," Dru mumbled.

* * *

A HALF-HOUR LATER, Dru and Mariana left Angelica's dorm building, leaving two uniforms behind to finish taking an inventory. A clumsily hidden space in a bin under her bed contained two smaller plastic bins with remnants of marijuana and three pre-rolled joints. The hangers in her small closet contained some fashionable dresses and tops, with similarly high-end shoes on the floor. They had her phone, but could not access it without an unlock code. They found nothing else of significance in the room.

On the walk back to the car, Mariana said, "You figure the weed is our connection?"

"Maybe. She could have been meeting her supplier. She either had a heavy habit or was buying for more than one person. Hard to figure why the guy would shoot his customer."

"You assume a guy?" Mariana opened the car door and slid into the driver's seat.

When Dru had buckled up, he replied. "Women don't generally carry cannons. You saw the hole in the girl's head."

"True enough. But you know what the old man taught us. Never assume anything. Keep all possibilities in play until the evidence rules them out."

"Who are you now, Mike Stoneman?" The two detectives had both spent time under the wing of the department's most senior homicide detective. Dru wished Stoneman, or any other detective, had drawn this case.

"I wish." Mariana rolled down her window, enjoying the warm air of spring in New York. It had been a cold winter and she wanted to enjoy the fresh breeze. She pulled into traffic without another word. Neither asked what the other had planned for the weekend. It didn't matter.

Chapter 4 — Distant Lights

PAULO RICHARDSON SAT on a threadbare sofa in front of a huge silver box. It perched on an aluminum and glass table in his studio apartment on Manhattan's Lower East Side. The hulking unit was a Mitsubishi 42-inch CRT High-Definition television, and had been state of the art in 1986. Paulo had recognized it as likely still functional and enlisted three buddies to help him drag it up to his apartment after somebody left it out with the trash.

Paulo, knobby knees tucked under his wiry frame, nibbled at a plate of rice and beans with sausage while he watched the ten o'clock news. His impassive brown face, accented by a wispy goatee, split its attention between the food and the anchor, in her green dress with a cut-out slashing from her shoulder to mid-breast like a wound from a broadsword. He could not understand why the wardrobe people at the station picked such inappropriate attire for their news anchor. She looked like a nightclub date awaited her immediately after the broadcast and she didn't want to change.

Paulo wore boxer shorts, an aging NYU t-shirt, and white athletic socks with blue and red stripes at the ankles. Clear, brown eyes hovered under a mop of disheveled black hair he tried unsuccessfully to tame each morning with a comb.

At thirty, he still felt like a journalism school student, even though he had been writing for the *Lower East Side Tribune* for six years. None of his colleagues had been at the tiny neighborhood paper as long, and many who started after him had long since moved up to more established publishers. "Paper" was a colloquialism, since it published only online. The *LES Trib*, as the staff called it, was near the bottom of the ladder for a Columbia Journalism School graduate. He knew that, but couldn't bring himself to leave. It was his neighborhood. There were important stories to write, stories that mattered to the local residents and merchants. He had convinced himself he could make a difference. That was why he took the job in the first place, despite credentials that would have landed him a much more prestigious gig.

Next to him on the sofa, a battered laptop computer sat with its lid open. Two paragraphs of text waited patiently for Paulo to return to his typing. He was in no hurry. The story was routine and, like so many, depressing. Another local business had announced a bankruptcy filing. The owner hoped to keep his combination dry cleaner and laundromat open while he negotiated with creditors, but the prospects weren't good. If Mr. Liu had a better credit score, he might have found a bank willing to extend him a loan. The immigrant from Malaysia had no connections through a golf club to help him. He would likely have to liquidate to satisfy his debts. That was how Paulo saw it, another minority entrepreneur struggling to stay afloat after the Covid-19 pandemic and trying to contribute to the local economy, succumbing to unavoidable circumstances. No government bail-out would save him. He was small and could easily be allowed to fail. Paulo was not in a hurry to finish the story.

The television news was mostly drivel, until the anchor teased her audience with a promise of "breaking news" concerning a shooting in Washington Square Park. As the station went to commercial, Paulo put down his fork, unfolded his awkwardly long legs, and padded to his west-facing window. He used a napkin to clean his wire-framed glasses. He could see the reflection of flashing blue and red lights beyond the end of 6th Street. Another bit of senseless violence, probably another illegal gun. It was a familiar tale.

He turned away from the window when the news anchor came back on, still wearing her green party dress. He knew the network had to save enough time for weather and sports, so there would not be much to say. They went live to a reporter standing on the sidewalk outside the park. She exhibited a full mouth of brilliantly white teeth when the anchor threw it to her with the banal lead of, "What's happening out there?"

The field reporter, wearing a tight black dress with a low neckline, started talking—another woman whose wardrobe was appropriate for the red carpet at the Oscars, but not for an urban crime scene. She had nothing to report. The police would only confirm one victim, a young woman whose identity had not been released. Maybe the police didn't know. Reports from unnamed sources called it a shooting. That was all she could say.

Only one thing was absolutely certain, Paulo thought. The dead woman in the park was White. The TV reporter hadn't said so, but the attention level for this story was way too high for the victim to be a person of color.

"Back to you, Candice," she chirped, flashing another smile as if a casting agent were watching.

Paulo snapped off the television. His gaze fell briefly on his laptop and the unfinished story waiting for his attention. For a moment, he considered putting on shoes and hustling over to the park. He dismissed the thought. There were probably a dozen reporters and several camera crews digging out anything meaningful. But tomorrow there might be something for him.

He went back to his laptop and banged out the rest of the depressing bankruptcy story. He tried to humanize Mr. Liu and make his readers understand that the system was stacked against him. Paulo stopped short of advocating for the city government to make low-interest loans available to failing small businesses on the same terms that the feds provided liquidity to large banks and manufacturers. But the message was carefully woven between the lines. He was pleased with the final draft and sent it to his editor a few minutes before midnight.

Outside the window, the distant red and blue lights still flashed. He flipped on the television and navigated to New York One. The 24-hour news channel ran on a loop after midnight. It was rough and superficial, but tended to be reasonably accurate. The shooting in Washington Square Park was the lead story. The victim now had an identity: Angelica Monroe, a White girl from Westchester County and a sophomore at NYU.

"Knew it," he mumbled to nobody.

After a minute of talking that shed no new light on the facts, the anchor introduced a replay of an interview credited to American Cable News, with a young woman named Petra. She said she was the victim's freshman roommate. Petra had no insight into the murder, but extoled the virtues of the dead girl and cried when asked how she felt about a brutal murder so close to her university sanctuary.

Paulo turned off the set when the broadcast switched to a secondary story. He had no doubt that Angelica Monroe was a tragic casualty of the city's violent personality. Nobody deserved to be shot to death at nineteen. It was a big story. Guns, murder, a young, White victim: all the attributes of a media feeding frenzy. He should probably stay out of it.

As he brushed his teeth, Paulo mentally reviewed the stories on his work-in-progress report. Clarence, his boss and the only editor at the *LES Trib*, insisted on a report every Friday. Today's sheet included the bankruptcy story he had just filed and three story ideas on which he had not done any significant reporting. There was always breaking news to cover, but his readers mostly wanted in-depth pieces. That was what got Paulo excited about being a journalist. At the moment, he didn't have any stories in his head that would keep him up late. Maybe after the police made an arrest in the park shooting, there would be something to dig into. Maybe.

As he meandered toward sleep, his mind kept returning to the female news anchor's silly party dress. That was mainstream journalism. His stories were marginal news from a low-rent online paper.

Tell that to Mr. Liu, he thought.

Chapter 5 — The Circus Is in Town

Saturday

SATURDAY MORNING, Mariana walked into the bullpen at the precinct house on 94th Street and saw Dru emerging from their captain's office. Edward "Sully" Sullivan was seldom in the office on a Saturday, and never at eight o'clock. Clearly, the Angelica Monroe case had caught the attention of the NYPD's top leadership.

"Couldn't wait for me?"

"Sorry." Dru motioned for Mariana to follow him toward the stairs. "Sully surprised me and pulled me in as soon as I got here. He apparently got an earful from the commissioner at seven this morning. We're all hands on deck on the Monroe murder. We're also now assigned to the other murder from last night."

"The Latino kid?"

"Yeah. We still don't have an ID on him. We may not get it before Monday unless we think it's connected to the girl."

Mariana stopped halfway down the first flight. "Spare no resources for the White girl, huh?"

"Don't," Dru paused, but kept walking. Over his shoulder, he said, "Sully's doing what he's told. Take it up with the commissioner."

They took an unmarked sedan from the motor pool on the theory that they might need to drive to Westchester to talk with the dead girl's parents.

"Where's that on our priority list?" Mariana asked.

"Pretty low. The media has already done the research for us."

After the American Cable News broadcast had divulged Angelica Monroe's name, the media swarm scrambled to find background on the dead girl. During the drive downtown, Dru summarized a folder of notes cobbled together from online news sites.

"Angelica Monroe was the oldest of three children. The family lives in West Harrison, Westchester County. Her high school yearbook is available online, so we have photos of Angelica and basic information. She was on the volleyball team, in the *a cappella* choir, the National Honor Society, and wrote for the school newspaper. She wasn't the homecoming queen or the class president, but from all appearances was smart, pretty, and athletic. Her father is an accountant for a big pharmaceutical company with headquarters in White Plains. Nothing on the mom. Not much detail yet on the father, but seems like a pretty typical upper-middle-class family. No wonder NYU wanted her."

"Anything on her college classes or activities?" Mariana honked as a biker swished past her while they were stopped at a red light.

"Not yet. There's a bunch of images from her Instagram and Twitter accounts." Dru held up several print-outs so Mariana could sneak glances as they crawled through rush-hour traffic. The photos showed a pristine smiling face, with an aquiline nose, high cheekbones, and bright eyes decorated with makeup and long, thick lashes. She was not quite a model, but attractive and always wearing flattering clothes.

"Did you see the morning news?"

Dru grunted. "Yeah. Quite a circus. I'll give them credit for getting their information quickly. I'm sure the mayor and the commissioner were watching, too. It was the top story on Good Morning America. Angelica Monroe is America's tragic sweetheart."

As they neared Washington Square Park, Mariana once again parked two blocks away from where the police command post had been set up the night before. The news vans were locked in the same places along the north side of the park. Walking from their sedan, Mariana counted eight satellite dish towers, swaying in the breeze above the tree line like oversized sunflowers seeking the day's first rays. At the base of the telescoping spires, the vehicles sat nose-to-nose as their crews jockeyed for the best angle to light the morning remote broadcasts. The twenty-four-hour news dragon needed continuous feeding, Mariana thought.

Video crews had descended on the Hangman's Elm, which had been deemed fully inspected and was no longer cordoned off. One pair of uniformed officers stood watch over the clearing around the tree, keeping order as the journalists maneuvered to be the next in line to tape a segment on the exact spot where Angelica Monroe was murdered. A makeshift memorial had sprung up at the base of the majestic tree. The small pile of bouquets and stuffed animals provided an emotional background for the cameras and talking heads.

Dru and Mariana approached the corner of Washington Square North and MacDougal Streets at nine o'clock. Three black-and-white squad cars crowded around the corner, double-parked with their lights flashing. Eight uniformed officers stood around the lead car, talking and sipping coffees. One of the officers waved a hand holding a cigarette toward Dru as they approached.

Mariana grabbed Dru's elbow to stop him before they got within speaking distance. "I'm not complaining about the weekend overtime, but how are we going to find productive assignments for so many officers? You have some master plan you haven't shared with me?"

"Yes. It's called looking busy." Dru stopped on the sidewalk, still twenty feet from their posse of uniforms. "The captain is going to get a call today from the commissioner's communications director, after *she* gets a call from the deputy mayor. They're going to want to know what's happening in the investigation, and they will each be able to tell their people that we have a squad of eight officers and two detectives combing the park and interviewing witnesses in a Herculean effort to solve this awful crime as quickly as possible. It doesn't matter if we find any useful information, as long as we look incredibly busy."

Mariana tilted her head toward the blue sky, dotted with satellite dishes. "We had two officers working a double-murder when we found Floyd Merriman."

"Yeah, but there weren't any camera crews on that one." Dru took a step forward, but stopped when he felt Mariana grab his jacket sleeve.

"Since when does the press decide what resources are assigned to an investigation?"

Dru turned and held up an index finger, as if ready to emphasize a point, but lowered it as he took a long breath. "I'm not making the decisions, OK? And neither is Sully. Don't be mad at me. We've got a job to do. You can file another complaint when we're done."

She said nothing while Dru pulled away and approached the waiting officers.

"All right, folks. Put out the cigarettes and put down the coffee and listen up." Dru separated the eight officers into two groups. Pointing at the cluster closest to the street, he leaned in, keeping his voice down since there were reporters ten yards away. "You two teams are going to interview students, starting with the girl's dorm building. The goal is to trace her movements in the hours leading up to nine o'clock last night. If we're lucky, someone will be able to shed some light on why she was in the park after dark, and whether she was alone."

Turning to the two officer pairs closer to the park, Dru pointed east. "The other two teams will canvas the park. Talk to the vendors and the regulars who hang around during the day. Somebody might have seen the girl." He pulled an envelope out of his jacket pocket and handed out photocopied pictures of Angelica Monroe to all eight officers; a pretty, smiling one from Instagram. "Her face is all over the news and the internet already, but use these to make sure you get a real ID. See if you can find somebody who saw her last night."

He then pulled out another envelope and handed out another set of images to the two park teams. This one showed the lifeless face of a teenage boy. It was washed out by the camera's flash. A red splotch marred his left cheek around the eye socket. "While you're talking to people, show 'em this one, too. The kid was shot and killed over on the east side, beyond the fountain. We're not sure if it was before or after the Monroe girl. If anybody recognizes him, let us know. We don't have an ID yet. We're working both cases and he might be connected, somehow. Any questions?"

Nobody spoke.

"Fine. Meet back here at four o'clock. If you find anything significant, radio it in to us. Let's get moving."

Dru and Mariana were officially assigned both cases, since they were going to be working the same vicinity anyway. "It'd be nice to have a better picture of the dead boy," Mariana said with a tinge of sadness. "It's like the brown boy is just a stiff and the White girl is a movie star."

"Yeah. It would be nice, but until we have an ID and can get a family photo of him, we go with what we've got.

He and Mariana walked six blocks east to a stocky three-story building on Washington Place that housed the offices of NYU security. The lobby guard, in a uniform intended to evoke the look of an NYPD officer, was expecting them. The guard passed them quickly to a harried-looking middle-aged woman, who introduced herself as the weekend manager, Joline Maxwell. She escorted them down one floor to a windowless basement where two younger officers in much less impressive uniforms sat behind work stations in front of a massive wall of flat-screen video monitors.

Maxwell explained that the university security system included 264 cameras located around the sprawling downtown area that NYU liked to call its "campus," but which everyone else called the NYU "area". All the university buildings were on city streets, without any enclosed space dedicated only to the school. The campus stretched ten blocks to the north of Washington Square Park and five to the south. Sometimes two or three university buildings were adjacent to each other, but most were surrounded by privately owned offices, businesses, and apartment buildings.

In such a spread-out environment, the security force relied on video surveillance and quick-response teams rather than having live guards in every location. Students on work-study jobs, she explained, supplemented the uniformed officers by serving as front door security at dorms, libraries, and classroom buildings.

They had call buttons that would summon an officer within two minutes. That was the claim. Dru and Mariana both doubted the practical reality. Most of the officers were part-time, including some moonlighting active police, some retired cops, and some professional security guards engaged through third-party providers.

At Maxwell's direction, a desk jockey named Carlos began rolling video they had already culled from the night before. The two detectives watched on the largest wall monitor, giving instructions to stop or rewind the action. The system was not sophisticated enough to zoom in on sections of the picture, or to provide computer enhancements of blurry images. Such were the creations of the FBI, imaginative television writers, and maybe Disneyland. In the real world, even a relatively well-endowed school like NYU had low-end security cameras that could be cheaply replaced when broken or vandalized.

"There she is." Carlos used a red laser pointer to identify an image from the lobby of Angelica's dorm at 5:23 p.m. Friday. The girl walked inside, flashed her ID card to the student "guard" at the door, then disappeared toward what Carlos said was the bank of elevators for the building. He cut to a clip from 6:33, when a woman wearing a dark, long-sleeved top left the building. The overhead camera, focused on the door, caught only her back. She was alone, clutching a large purse under her left arm. They saw the figure turn left, south, outside the door.

Carlos efficiently queued up the next clip, eleven minutes later. The woman rounded a corner and walked down a sidewalk, toward the next camera, then vanished as she walked underneath the elevated sentry.

"Where is that?" Dru asked.

"Corner of 8th and MacDougal," Carlos replied quickly while navigating his mouse around two monitors.

"Do we know where she's going?" Mariana pointed toward the screen, as if she could swipe her finger and make the next image appear.

"Yeah, I think so," Carlos mumbled as he punched some keys on his console. The next image was a more distant view of a street after dark, with numerous pedestrians traversing the sidewalk on both sides. Lights from storefronts and streetlights cast pools of light on the concrete pathways. The neon marquee of a jazz club beckoned to passersby to stop and look.

"That's 3rd Street," Mariana called out. "I recognize the Blue Note."

"Right," Carlos confirmed. The digital time stamp on the image read 7:43:23 and counted up the seconds in the screen's lower-left corner. "There! See her walking west on the north side of the street?" Carlos again flashed his red dot on the image to direct the detectives' eyes.

Dru and Mariana squinted and both confirmed they saw the figure, in the same outfit with the same purse. She turned and entered a doorway halfway between MacDougal and the far end of the block, which they knew was Sixth Avenue.

Dru asked, "Do you know what that door is, where she went in?"

"I'm pretty sure it's a bar called The Scampering Squirrel. It's a popular hang-out for students."

"She's underage to be in a bar," Mariana pointed out, knowing the reality of university-area bars, which rarely asked for ID lest their business tumble.

"Well, she was in there for about an hour," Carlos responded. "The last clip I have is at eight thirty-five." He called up an image from the same camera. They watched as the woman approached, now facing the camera. She was accompanied by a male, dressed in blue jeans and a New York Mets t-shirt, moving east. Angelica's companion had light-colored hair and was several inches taller than her. He looked to be White, although the image was not clear. His face, while visible to the camera, was too far away to make out. As they watched the couple come closer to the camera, their faces came more into focus, although neither face was fully recognizable.

"Can you get us a still shot of him, as good an image of his face as we can get?" Dru directed, without saying please.

"Yeah, sure. Gimme a second." Carlos paused the video and clicked his mouse a few times, causing a large square to appear on the monitor around the two faces. "Should come out in a minute," he said. "The printer will need to warm up first."

"Is that the last shot you have of her?" Dru squinted at the blurry image still on the screen.

"It's the last good one. They turn north at the corner and walk north, but we only have their backs in that shot."

"North on McDougal—toward the park, right?" Mariana again pointed at the wall monitor.

"That's right. The camera at 4th Street isn't working. We have a repair order in for it, but we've got the street covered from 3rd and 6th, so it's not a priority. I checked the 6th Street camera looking south, but she's not there."

"Must have gone into the park, which we already knew," Dru said into Mariana's ear.

"Yeah," their tech responded, as if Dru were talking to him. "Unfortunately, we don't have any cameras inside the park. It's not our property."

"Any ID on Angelica's boyfriend?" Mariana asked.

"No. We don't have facial recognition software or anything like that."

Mariana turned to Dru. "Maybe one of her friends will recognize the guy, especially if they know he left that bar with her last night."

Dru agreed and turned to Maxwell. "So, the video puts her time of death sometime between eight-forty and nine-oh-two, when your guard found her under the big tree."

"The Hangman's Elm," Maxwell confirmed. "That's right."

"OK, that's a pretty narrow window. Mare, as soon as we have a digital image, send a text to all the officers out working the park and the dorms and let them know the window and that they are now also looking for anyone who might be able to ID the guy."

* * *

WHEN THE BRIGHT SUNSHINE hit Mariana's eyes after being underground for over an hour, she pulled dark glasses from her inside jacket pocket. Dru squinted at his phone. They were both copied on an email from the medical examiner's office. "We have at least a preliminary autopsy," Dru reported. They sat on a low concrete wall separating the security building from the sidewalk. Nearby, a blue pole labeled "EMERGENCY" with a call button and a blue light at the top stood ready to flash its beacon to summon help for a distressed NYU student.

"Fastest autopsy on a Saturday ever," Mariana muttered.

"It's good for us. Don't bitch. It's not the first time a high-profile case got special attention."

Mariana read aloud from her phone's screen. "'Cause of death: gunshot to the head.' Tell us something we couldn't figure out ourselves," Mariana turned her head to see Dru concentrating on his own screen.

"There were defensive wounds, which suggests a struggle."

"Yeah, for sure. I remember those fingernails. But no tissue under her nails, so no DNA to sample."

"Seems odd, though." Dru looked up to make eye contact with his partner. "The shot in the head seems like an execution. How was there a struggle and then that kind of kill shot?"

"Maybe she lost the struggle?"

"Clearly." Dru slipped the phone back into his hip pocket.

"At least she put up a fight," Mariana mused.

Dru stretched his arms toward the sky and stood up. "C'mon. Let's go question some scared-shitless college students."

Chapter 6 — The Greatest Show on Earth

HANNAH SLEPT IN THE VAN Friday night. Terry gave up the tiny hammock and took the driver's seat, reclined back as far as it would go. The cops were not giving out tickets, since the whole street was cordoned off and the media crews were scrambling around all night. A bang on the outside of the van at five-thirty a.m. roused them both. When Hannah opened the sliding door, Judy Johnson's smiling face greeted her. More importantly, Judy held a tray with three cups of coffee and a McDonald's bag. The aroma of egg McMuffins and hash browns overcame the stink of sweat and dirty socks wafting out from the cramped van interior.

"You are an absolute angel," Hannah said, reaching for a coffee.

"Get me an interview like the one William Wilson got last night and I'll buy you breakfast every morning." Judy sat down in the canvas chair still standing sentry over their interview space outside the van. The morning sun had not yet peeked above the eastern horizon, leaving the park in a pre-dawn glow.

Hannah and Terry made a circuit around the media encampment. They used the bathroom in a nearby library building that had become the *de facto* media rest stop, then returned to find Judy touching up her make-up, getting ready for her seven o'clock shot. She was in full make-up and wore a shiny lavender dress that hugged her curves and contrasted with her hazel eyes. Her auburn hair was pinned up carefully to stay out of her face until she was ready to let it loose before her air time. Judy had not eaten any of the food she brought, but did sip a coffee, leaving bright red lipstick stains on the edge of her plastic lid.

While Terry set up Judy's shot and waited for the cue from the studio, Hannah walked again around the perimeter of the media bivouac. She listened in to a reporter practicing his delivery for an upcoming live report next to the ABC7 van. The talking head had nothing new to report since the night before, which made Hannah grin. A few fellow producers with whom she had good relationships told her about the rumors flying between the media members. Half were based on actual information wheedled from the uniformed officers who still surrounded the crime scene. The other half were wild speculation or intentionally planted false leads, as the hyper-competitive journalists tried to send their colleagues on wild goose chases.

"There's only so much story, and carving it up ten ways is difficult," Trish Halston from WPIX observed.

"What you need is an expert who can come in and give a proprietary opinion," Hannah suggested.

"An expert on what?" Trish threw back her head and looked at a helicopter circling above the scene, as if an aerial shot of a dark Washington Square Park was going to shine some unique light on Angelica Monroe's murder. "If we had enough information to know what we need an expert on, we'd have a story." She stopped and stared Hannah in the eye. "And who did you pay off to get her name last night?"

Hannah shrugged and turned away, a tiny smile curling the corner of her naked lips. Putting on makeup on a location shoot was not a priority.

Walking back toward the ACN broadcast location, Hannah noticed Paulo Richardson, a print reporter she recognized. He had worked the Lower East Side Baby story, and had written an article after the ACN interview with the now-discredited witness. Paulo's story was a fair piece, blaming the witness for lying and noting that ACN had no way of knowing. He and Hannah had crossed paths a few times, but had not spoken since Hannah's embarrassing blunder.

She positioned herself behind Richardson while he finished talking to an elderly man holding a white Maltese puppy in his arms. She tried not to obviously eavesdrop on the discussion, but quickly figured out that the old man was talking about what he saw in the park long before Angelica's murder. He railed about the drugs that were bought and sold and the unsavory characters who congregated in the park at night, making it dangerous for a local resident like him to safely walk his dog.

When Paulo wrapped up, Hannah tapped him on the shoulder.

"Hey, Hannah." Paulo immediately recognized her and smiled.

"Nice to see you, Paulo. I haven't had a chance to thank you personally for your piece about Mr. Berrubi after the whole Lower East Side Baby thing."

"No thanks needed. It wasn't your fault."

"Can you tell that to my editor?"

"If you recall, everyone else covering the thing bit on his story just like you."

"Yeah, I know. But I was the one who surfaced him. We got the story first, which is all that matters, right? We can't get 'em all perfect."

"Maybe not for you television guys," Paulo responded with a twinkle in his eye. "We real reporters need to do better. We have an annoying habit of getting corroboration and checking our facts before we publish."

They shared an awkward laugh. Hannah put a hand on Paulo's shirt sleeve. "I hope your boss went easy on you. At least you got to follow up and keep reporting on it. I got yelled at and then shipped off on another crap assignment."

"Was that you last night—the roommate?" Paulo's question seemed innocent enough, but Hannah suspected there was a hidden sub-question about whether she properly did her homework before presenting Petra Burroughs to the world on ACN's broadcast.

Hannah suppressed a smile. "Yeah. We got a good one. I had corroboration from Angelica's Instagram account that they were friends."

"You got a white whale. Don't be modest." Paulo reached out and put a hand gently on her shoulder. "You're good, Hannah. You give me a tip right now and I'll treat it as the freaking gospel."

Hannah put a hand on top of Paulo's, then stepped back. "I'll make sure you get to watch my next scoop. What about you? Anything juicy you can share?"

"Nothing on your Angelica. You're the front-runner on that one. But did you know there was another murder last night in the park?"

Now Hannah was interested. She stepped forward, so Paulo could whisper in her ear if he wanted to. "I did not know about that. Was it nearby?"

"It was on the east side, so a few blocks away, but it was about the same time as the girl. The cops don't have an ID on the victim yet. I'm told he was late teens and Latino. Not much else yet."

"You think it could have a connection to Angelica?"

"No way to know. Maybe. Nobody over here seems very interested. You want me to keep you updated on developments?"

"Hell yeah!" Hannah playfully shoved Paulo in the chest, sending him staggering back a few feet.

Once he regained his balance, Paulo broke into a broad smile and laughed. "OK. We'll keep each other advised. We each get the first report, then we share. Deal?"

"Deal," Hannah smiled back. She liked Paulo. She had seen him around the edges of a few stories in Lower Manhattan and respected him. He seemed to genuinely care about his little neighborhood paper and the people in his community. She admired Paulo, but at the same time wondered why he wasn't more ambitious. All she wanted was to get away from ACN and jump to a better job. "If I come across anything on the other murder, I'll pass it to you. I doubt my boss will want to cover it."

"Thanks. Text me." Paulo turned and walked down the sidewalk toward the NYU dorms. Hannah resumed her path back to the ACN news van.

Chapter 7 — In the Midway

PAULO SPENT FIVE HOURS prowling the NYU vicinity and Washington Square Park. He immediately regretted not sleeping later. His two objectives were to find a local angle on the Angelica Monroe murder and to dig up some information about what he had come to call "the other murder." Uncovering anything new on the Monroe case was a needle in a haystack with dozens of other reporters on the same scent. But he knew he was the only one seriously digging into the other murder.

Paulo had a contact at the city's EMT dispatch office named Patricia Suggs, who clued him in that two crews had been sent the night before to Washington Square Park and that both reported their victims as dead on the scene. Both were taken straight to the morgue. One, he already knew, was Angelica Monroe. His contact was not able—or willing—to provide any further details about Angelica's cause of death or physical condition, despite Paulo's begging.

The other corpse was an unidentified Latino male eighteen to twenty years old. The preliminary cause of death was a gunshot wound to the chest. Since Patricia had no gag order on that case from her superiors, she confided that the dead kid had been beaten up pretty good before he was shot.

Paulo wanted to establish whether there was any connection between the two incidents. He also wanted to know more about the male victim.

Despite conducting a half-dozen interviews, Paulo uncovered no new information on either murder. He was twelve hours behind the reporters who had been on the scene since the night before, and he had no resources. As much as he hoped for a magical break, he knew that great reporting was always built on hard work and research. His editor wanted the local angle on things. Angelica Monroe had no connections to the Lower East Side. The only potential hook would be if the killer—or the victim—was a local resident. So far, the cops showed no inclination toward announcing any arrests.

The coincidence of a second murder in the park on the same night was stuck in Paulo's head. He spoke to an officer who was looking for potential witnesses to the Angelica Monroe murder. The officer said he had no reason to believe there was any connection between the two cases. Just a coincidence. Paulo didn't believe in coincidences.

Since the officers in the park were not providing any help, Paulo decided to change venues. It was nearing noon and he had skipped breakfast, so he headed to Al's Diner. The polished steel exterior had been standing at the corner of 7th Street and Avenue A since before Paulo could remember. It served the neighborhood well-prepared and inexpensive food, gave jobs to the local teens, and gave the scraps to the homeless. Alexander Temetka owned the diner. "Big Al" knew everyone and treated his patrons like an extended family. He was a throwback to when the Lower East Side was a village. Big Al was in his seventies now and the locals wondered what would happen when he could no longer run the joint. Paulo ate there often, and he knew that many local cops also frequented Al's.

Taking a seat at the counter, Paulo ordered the soup and sandwich special and a coffee. He was mostly finished when three officers he knew well came in and seated themselves in a large booth in the corner. Paulo left a generous tip under his plate and took his coffee over to join his friends.

"Hey, Jodi." He smiled and scooted into the worn faux-leather seat.

"That's Officer Jodi to you, Mr. Richardson." Jodi Wresh, like Paulo, had grown up on the Lower East Side. Jodi did a stint in the Navy, then came home and became a cop. They remained friends, even after Jodi got engaged to a guy Paulo thought wasn't good enough for her. The other two cops at the table were Rico Espinoza and Bill Walsh. Both men were the same age as Jodi. Rico was short and stocky, while Bill was a tall beanpole, like Paulo.

"Fine. Fine," Paulo made eye contact and exchanged nods with the other officers. Their crisp blue uniforms contrasted with Paulo's jeans, black t-shirt, and slightly threadbare sport jacket. "I'm glad I bumped into you."

"Looks like you were staking us out," Bill quipped.

Paulo did not respond to the good-natured dig. "I've been trying to track down information on a murder last night in Washington Square Park."

"Sure, bro," Rico said, "you and every other reporter on the planet. What makes you think we know anything?"

"And why would we tell you if we did?" Jodi slid a few inches away from Paulo.

"No. Not Angelica Monroe. The other one. The Latino kid found on the east side."

"Oh, yeah," Jodi sighed. "Estrada. That's a real tragedy. Did you know Javier? He worked at Snyder's grocery on Fifth."

Paulo moved to reach for the pen and note pad in his jacket pocket, but held himself back. He had to rely on memory during these off-the-record conversations. "Javier Estrada? The ballplayer from Prep?"

"We're off the record, right?" Bill asked.

"Sure. Like always. You guys know nothing gets attributed to you."

Rico exchanged glances with his fellow officers, then gave Paulo a quick summary. "Yeah. The hoops star from Prep. He had a gunshot wound in his chest. His mother filed a missing person report when the kid didn't come home after a basketball game last night. It hadn't been twenty-four hours, but the desk sergeant took the information and it matched up once the ME had prints from the body. There was a blood-stained knife on the ground nearby with his prints. Javier had a juvenile record, so he was in the system."

Paulo fought himself to stay quiet and not interject questions.

Jodi picked up the narrative from Rico. "His mother works as a nurse's aide at St. Mary's hospital, where my mom works. His mom told my mom that Javier had scholarship offers from a few D2 colleges, but he was hoping to get an offer from a D1 school."

"So, any theories about what he was doing in the park that got him killed?"

Rico held up a wagging finger. "No, man. We got the ID only an hour ago. I'm not sure the detectives have even notified his mother yet. You gotta keep this to yourself until then."

"That's cool," Paulo held out his coffee cup, as if swearing on his daily caffeine. "But I want to make sure this story doesn't get lost in the tsunami of coverage on the Monroe girl. You need to let me know when the ID can go public. I'll embargo it until then, but don't let this kid be a nameless shooting victim. It sounds like he has a story that needs to be told."

"I'm down with that," Rico responded. "This one is right up your journalistic alley. It's nice having somebody competent writing about the neighborhood."

"Only *competent*?" Paulo feigned shock.

"*Barely* competent," Jodi chided. "But we're still happy to have you. I'll call you when the family gets notified."

"Thanks. I owe you one."

"You owe us a dozen," Jodi playfully planted a light punch into Paulo's right shoulder. "We're expecting at least a nice lunch on the tab of our local newspaper."

"OK—OK. Fine. Lunch is on me. Is there anything else you can tell me about Javier's murder? I have another source who says he was beaten pretty badly. Can you confirm that? Or confirm the cause of death?"

"Nah," Rico waved his hand as if swatting an imaginary fly. "Too soon. They took prints from the body, but ain't no way they're processing an autopsy for that kid over the weekend. That shit is reserved for white angels."

"Zip it, Rico," Jodi scolded. Then she turned to Paulo. "That was off the record, Paulo. Right?"

"Sure. I'm not going to compromise my best sources on the force to cast shade on the medical examiner or point out the racism we all know exists. You're cool, Rico."

"Officer Espinoza to you," Jodi tried to maintain a stern expression, but broke into a grin inside of ten seconds. "Seriously, Paulo, we know you have our backs. That's why we share. Nobody told us it was confidential. Hell, nobody on the comms team gives a shit about a dead Latino. So, if you dig up anything, you let us know. And if we hear anything, we'll let you know if we can."

"I'll tell you one thing," Bill Walsh said,-"I'll bet you a steak dinner those are Javier's Jordans in that bag they found. Ow!" Bill jerked backward, then glared at Jodi, who was staring daggers after kicking Bill under the table.

"What bag?" Paulo followed up on the tantalizing but vague reference.

"Never mind," Jodi shot back. "That's also off the record."

"If it's off the record, which is fine with me, then go ahead and tell me what it means. I won't attribute it to anyone."

"Can't do that," Rico put a hand gently on Bill's shoulder, as if holding him down before he made any more comments. "We did get instructions about that. Just leave it be, Paulo."

"Fine." Paulo knew when to back off.

Clearly, the reference to the bag was something very sensitive that the beat cops had been told to keep confidential. "Javier's Jordans" could only be a reference to the dead boy's basketball shoes. Paulo could deduce that the shoes being "in that bag" didn't mean the body bag in which he was carted off. There must have been a bag the police found at the scene. A kid like Javier would want good shoes to play in, but wouldn't want to wear his precious Jordans walking around on the streets, or in the park. He would want to keep them clean and not step in anything, so he'd carry them in a bag. His mom reported that he didn't come home from a basketball game. There was plenty for Paulo to follow up on, even without any more direct information from his cop friends.

"Don't worry. It's all off the record."

All conversation ceased when their waitress Shirley, who had worked at the diner since the first day Paulo had stepped foot in the place with his father, hustled up to the table. They knew that if they failed to give her their undivided attention and order quickly, she would walk away and not return for fifteen minutes. Behind her back, they called her "no-shit Shirley."

Rico ordered steak and eggs, then said, "Thanks, Paulo." The other cops ordered similarly high-end menu items.

When Shirley finished scribbling on her order pad and stalked away, Paulo dug into his wallet, handed Jodi his Visa card, and stood up. "Slip that under my door on your way home tonight, please. I won't be using it again today after this grand feast."

Jodi slid the card into the breast pocket of her uniform shirt. She lived two floors up from Paulo in the same apartment building. Their parents had keys to each other's apartments. "Sure. And thanks."

"And don't leave Shirley more than an eighteen percent tip." Paulo exited to the street and headed back toward the park. He had some useful information, and since he could not interview Javier Estrada's family, coworkers, and neighborhood friends until the cops broke the bad news to his mother, he was going to try to find somebody who knew something about a bag of Jordans.

Chapter 8 — Eye of the Beholder

DRU AND MARIANA WALKED north toward Angelica Monroe's dormitory building. The morning sun glared into Dru's eyes as they traversed the cross-streets. The officers who had been canvassing the building all day had identified four students, all women, who said they were friends with Angelica and acknowledged partying with her.

They set up an investigation space in a music rehearsal room off the building lobby. The area was small but fully enclosed and, presumably, soundproofed. One uniformed officer stood sentry outside while another went to fetch the next witness. Talking in a neutral space, rather than in the women's dorm rooms, figured to make the witnesses less comfortable and more in a hurry to spill their information and get away. It also minimized the chances of a hidden recording device or a roommate.

The first witness was Debbie Cannon, a senior who lived down the hall from Angelica.

"How well did you know Miss Monroe?" Mariana asked casually. She and Dru had decided that Mariana should act as questioner, figuring the young women would be more open with a less threatening female detective.

"We weren't besties or anything," Debbie responded hesitantly. Mariana did not respond, waiting for Debbie to keep

talking. After a fifteen-second pause, the tactic worked. "I mean, we talked in the hallway, and sometimes I hung out in her room. Angie and I went to some of the same parties."

"Did Miss Monroe—Angie—have any enemies? Anyone who might have wanted to hurt her?"

"Hurt her? No. I mean, I heard some girls snarking about how they wished they could afford Angie's shoes. She had some killer shoes. But that's just jealousy. None of them would want to hurt her."

"Did you and Angie ever smoke weed together?"

Debbie pulled her head away from Mariana, clearly surprised. "Hey, I'm over twenty-one. So, it's legal."

"I'm not saying it isn't. Don't worry, we're not trying to bust anyone for underage smoking. Do you know where she got her weed from?"

"No," Debbie shot back immediately. "I never asked, and she never told me."

"But Angie had weed available, right?" Mariana stole a quick glance at Dru.

"Sure she did, and she didn't mind sharing it."

"Did that make her popular?"

Debbie looked toward the door, as if wondering how quickly she could end the interview and escape from the nosy detectives. "Sure. I guess."

"Did other people come to Angie to get their weed?"

"I guess. She always had some."

"Did people buy weed from Angie?"

Debbie's face morphed into panic. "No. At least, not that I ever knew about. And I never bought weed from her."

"We're not suggesting you did, Miss Cannon. We're trying to trace Angie's movements and figure out who might have been with her last night. Do you know if there's anyone she might have been buying from, or who might have been with her?"

"No. I don't know anything about where she got hers from. She seemed to have plenty."

"What about guys? Were there any guys Angie dated or hung out with a lot?"

"There were plenty of guys around when we were out at parties, but nobody she dated very long that I remember."

"Ever seen this guy?" Mariana showed Debbie the grainy photo of the tall man walking down 3rd Street with Angelica shortly before her murder.

Debbie held the photo print close to her eyes, studying the blurry image. After thirty seconds, she handed the photo back. "No. I don't think I know that guy. He doesn't look like anybody I've seen with Angie."

"One last question, Miss Cannon. Do you know where Angie got her money from? You mentioned that she had nice shoes. We've seen photos from her Instagram account where she's wearing some nice clothes, and she had lots of weed to spread around. Must have cost a lot. Did she ever say where the money came from?"

"She said her folks gave her money. I didn't really ask about it, but I remember her saying that to somebody."

Mariana turned to Dru, who shook his head, indicating he had nothing he wanted to ask. "OK. Thank you, Miss Cannon. We appreciate your cooperation. We're in the middle of an investigation that has been getting a lot of attention from the press. We're not going to tell anyone you spoke to us, or that you and Angie smoked pot together. I suggest you keep all this information to yourself. It will help our investigation, and it will keep you off the evening news."

Debbie bobbed her head up and down several times. "Yes. I get it. I'm not saying anything to anybody."

"Great. The officer took your contact information, so if we need to ask you any more questions, we'll reach out. For now, you're free to go."

Debbie exited hurriedly, leaving the door open. Their sentry asked if they wanted the next witness. Dru said they needed a minute first.

"We have any information about Angelica's family situation? If she was a rich kid, spreading around a lot of weed to make herself popular, that would make sense. It wouldn't explain why somebody wanted to shoot her in the head, but it would explain the money and the dope."

"I haven't checked the news much today, so I'm not sure. I saw that her father works for a big drug company in White Plains."

"Well, that could mean money. We'll check it later. Let's talk to the rest of our student witnesses."

Over the next hour, Dru and Mariana interviewed three more dorm residents. They were more reluctant than Debbie to admit that Angelica always had an ample pot supply and enjoyed sharing it. Since the other witnesses were all underage, they feared admitting illegal drug use to a police officer. But, between the lines, their stories about Angie corroborated Debbie's information. None knew of anyone who wanted to hurt Angelica, and none admitted to knowing where she got her supply. None could identify the man in the security camera photo.

When the last student exited the rehearsal room, Dru slumped into the now-empty witness chair and put his feet up on a narrow counter running along the wall. "So, what have we learned?"

"Angelica was well-liked, popular—as long as she had weed to spread around—and had no known enemies or boyfriends. So, not much. If she was dealing, it doesn't seem like any of them knew about it."

"You believe them?"

Mariana leaned back in her plastic chair, rotating her neck to work out the kinks from sitting at attention and taking notes. "I didn't get any indication of deception on those questions. They might not have admitted it if they knew, but I think they were being truthful. They don't know."

"She could have been selling to other people, but not to her friends," Dru suggested.

"Sure. It's possible. But why—and how? She's a suburban girl. How's she going to work up a network of buyers outside her main circle of friends?"

"OK. Let's assume she's just a rich kid who likes weed and likes being the life of the party. She could have been in the park to buy some more. Her supply was tapped out, judging from those bins under her bed. She had a small bag in her purse, but not the kind of supply these girls were telling us about."

"She goes into the park to meet her dealer. If she's been a good customer, why kill her?"

Mariana tilted her head back and looked at the fluorescent lights on the ceiling. "Something goes bad. Maybe she wants a volume discount. Maybe the dealer wants to screw her, but she resists. They struggle. The dealer pulls out a gun, shoots her dead, then runs off."

"Was the dealer playing basketball before meeting Angelica?"

"Maybe. It would explain why he left the bag behind if he shot the girl, then ran. I wonder if she was friendly with any basketball players?"

"Maybe Angelica's parents can shed some light on things." Dru pulled out his phone and checked his messages. "The county sheriffs are at their house, helping the local cops keep the press off their property. The department liaison says we can talk to them today if we get there before six o'clock."

Mariana stood up. "Let's go."

They exited into the lobby and headed for the main door. They saw the student security monitor at the lobby desk, talking to a Black man wearing jeans and a hoodie.

Hoodie Guy was arguing with the desk attendant. "Man, just call up to her for me. Allie Roe. Room 502. She's expecting me."

Mariana stopped, causing Dru to bump into her back as he followed her. "502? That's her room, right?"

"Yeah."

"You think he knows?"

"Let's ask him," Dru replied, reaching for his badge and ID.

Mariana approached the man in the hoodie. It was their normal procedure. The suspect—or witness—was less likely to run from a woman. "Excuse me, Sir, can I ask you why you want to see Angelica Monroe?" While Mariana was speaking, Dru circled around behind the man to block his retreat.

"What? N-nothing. No biggie," the man was flustered by Mariana's question. He spun around and took one step toward the door when he ran smack into Dru's chest.

"Don't be in such a hurry. Maybe we can help each other." Dru held up his badge and grabbed the man by the arm above his elbow with a firm grip, guiding him toward an empty space to the right of the entrance where a droopy potted palm leaned against the wall.

"Hey, man. Let go of me!" The man in the hoodie pulled his arm, trying to break free from Dru's grip without success. "I ain't done nothin'!"

"In a minute. We need to talk with you first. I'm Detective Andrew Cook, NYPD. What's your relationship with Angelica Monroe?"

"Who?"

"The girl in room 502. You were asking about her."

"No, man. Her name is Allie. She's a—a friend of mine." The man's eyes bounced between Mariana, Dru, and the exit door.

"Is that right? Well, how do you know her?"

The man didn't answer.

Mariana broke in with a soothing, motherly tone. "Let's try something easier, huh? What's your name, Sir?"

"I don't have to answer any questions," the man said, seeming to gain some confidence.

"No, Sir. You do not. You know your rights. But, on the other hand, we're investigating a murder and since you are here saying you had an appointment with the dead girl and you're behaving suspiciously, we have probable cause to arrest you and bring you in for fingerprinting and interrogation at the station. If there are any outstanding warrants for you, then you'll be spending the night in the lock-up. If not, then maybe you get released by tonight. Or, you can tell us your name and help us conduct our investigation. What do you think?"

The man stared at Mariana without speaking for half a minute. "Murder? You telling me Allie's dead?"

Dru pulled on the man's elbow, still locked in his grip. "Do you watch TV? Or read the newspapers?"

"No, man. Why would I? It's all fake news, right?"

Dru leaned in close enough to smell marijuana on the man's breath. He looked like he might be over twenty-one, so smelling of weed was not probable cause to presume illegal activity, until they saw some ID. "Here's some real news for you. Angelica Monroe, the girl who lives in 502, was shot dead last night. I'm guessing that if you murdered her, you wouldn't come around here today, so why don't you start by answering the lady's question and telling us your name?"

Their captive decided that cooperation was more attractive than a trip to the station. He produced a driver's license reading Eldin Garfield with an address in the Bronx. He had turned twenty-one in January. Dru gave him back his elbow. Mariana took a photo of the card with her phone and forwarded it to the desk sergeant back at the precinct asking for a quick warrant check. Eldin didn't give up any background about himself, but he admitted that his appointment with "Allie" was supposed to have been the night before, but Allie was a no-show.

"You were going to sell her some weed?" Dru leaned in close and spoke softly.

"Sell? No, man. No. I was going to buy my weed from her."

Dru and Mariana exchanged quick eye contact. "How much was she going to sell you?"

Eldin shuffled his feet and stuffed his hands into his jeans pockets. "You know, a few ounces. For me."

Mariana handed back his driver's license. "You're over twenty-one, Mr. Garfield. You can go to a dispensary and buy your weed legally. Why get it from someone like Allie?"

"Hey, man. You know how it is. Her stuff was good, and cheap, and no taxes. And she's been helping me out for a while, so, like, I'm a loyal guy."

"Is that right?" Dru looked Eldin up and down. "That's admirable, Eldin. Good for you. But, unfortunately, the supply has dried up. So, where were you last night around nine o'clock?"

"What? I—wait, I don't have to answer a question like that."

"No. You don't. Not if you have something to hide."

"I—I got nothin' to hide. But I think I should ask for a lawyer."

Mariana stepped in, pushing Dru back gently. "OK, OK. Let's keep it light. You're not under arrest. But in case we need to contact you again, you need to give us your phone number."

Eldin balked, but eventually provided his number. Mariana dialed it to confirm that Eldin's phone rang when she called. Dru got a text from the precinct confirming that Eldin had no active warrants and no prior convictions.

"You have a nice day," Dru said, stepping aside to leave a clear lane for Eldin to exit the building. He and Mariana watched the back of his purple hoodie turn right and head uptown.

"I'm dying to know where Eldin goes," Dru said, motioning toward the door. He and Mariana hurried up the sidewalk, immediately seeing Eldin's hoodie a block ahead. He didn't look back, seemingly oblivious to the concept that the detectives might follow him.

They gradually closed the gap with their quarry as he stopped at traffic lights, heading east. When Eldin ducked into the entrance to the number 6 subway at Astor Place, the detectives hurried down the stairs, then lingered on the platform until the uptown train arrived. They entered a car behind Eldin's, watching him through the window between cars until he exited at 68th Street.

Eldin's hoodie made following him simple, allowing Dru and Mariana to stay with him through the Manhattan streets until he arrived at Hunter College. He maneuvered to a central quad and took a seat on a wooden bench, pulled out a cell phone, and was lost in whatever messages or websites he was viewing while the detectives found a vantage on a concrete planter where they could sit and still keep Eldin in sight.

After ten minutes, a man wearing a bright purple Hunter College t-shirt approached Eldin and sat down. The two exchanged greetings, then purple t-shirt held out a hand toward

Eldin. They couldn't see well enough to swear the man held cash in his hand, but when Eldin held up his hands and shook his head, the guy quickly put the hand into his pocket. The two men had what seemed to be a heated conversation for a minute, then purple t-shirt got up, gestured toward Eldin with a raised middle finger, and stomped away. Eldin shook his head, reached into a pocket, and lit a cigarette.

Dru nudged Mariana. "I think we've seen enough." Mariana called in for a patrol unit to meet them on Lexington Avenue. On the ride back down to the command post at Washington Square Park, they tried to make sense of what they had learned.

"So, Monroe was Eldin's supplier?" Mariana asked.

"Looks like it. It's consistent with the bins she had hidden in her room. A bit out of character for the innocent victim, eh?"

"Does that explain the money in her purse in the park? She was there to make a buy so she could replenish her supply, which then she re-sells to guys like Eldin. That was a big-ass purse she was toting—too large for a small girl's make-up, huh?"

"It would explain a few things, except $500 doesn't seem like enough. If Angelica was a middle man for other dealers, she'd need more than that to buy a new supply, don't you think?"

"Yeah. The murder could have been a simple robbery. Somebody sees her, figures out she has a bunch of cash. She resists. They struggle. He shoots her, then runs away."

"That doesn't explain why her killer didn't take the money. Who accosts her, kills her, and doesn't rob her?"

"Maybe he did. Maybe she had a couple grand in the purse that the killer snagged, but he missed a few bills."

Dru looked out the window at the passing cityscape. "What about the athletic bag?"

"I'm running out of scenarios," Mariana admitted, while glancing at her phone. "Then again, we might get some help on that."

"What?" Dru pulled out his own phone.

"Says here we got an ID on our other victim. Name is Javier Estrada. He was on the basketball team at Lower East Side Prep. I'm gonna guess those were his Jordans and that was his bag."

"Great. So, why was he at the scene of Monroe's murder, and why did he leave his bag behind, and who killed him?"

Mariana shrugged. "I said we got help. Not answers. Let's get back to the park and see if the uniforms have dug anything up for us. Then we still need to talk to the parents."

Chapter 9 — Change of Direction

LUIS TORRES LEANED AGAINST the smooth, rounded concrete edge of the huge fountain in Washington Square Park. A toothpick protruded from his lips. His thin frame fell short of six feet, but his bony arms and legs were sheathed in sinewy muscle. Luis had dark complexion, inherited from his Puerto Rican father, and Latin features from his Spanish mother. Wearing jeans and a white t-shirt, he could blend in with any New York City surroundings.

The afternoon sun had begun its descent toward the Hudson River, shifting the shadows to the east. The massive circular fountain stood in the absolute center of the park's perfect rectangle, four east-west blocks long by two north-south blocks deep. It was surrounded by an expansive concrete plaza, big enough for a dozen food vendors to work their carts without being within twenty feet of each other. The park was usually teeming with activity, but today the crowd was thinner than normal. A significant percentage of the usual population didn't like being observed so closely by New York's finest.

Uniformed police officers were accosting everyone in the park, looking for potential witnesses who might have been in their same spots the night before. A few food vendors packed up and slipped away before it was their turn for interrogation. The cops weren't asking for proof of citizenship or vendor licenses, but some folks weren't taking any chances. Luis wasn't worried. He calmly told two separate sets of officers that he had not been in the park the night before. He was a practiced liar, including plenty of conversations with cops since he was a teenager. If you couldn't lie well, you spent a lot of time in juvenile hall and your buddies didn't invite you along for activities they didn't want spilled to the police.

While the officers were busy on the far side of the plaza, Luis made eye contact with a youthful-looking man who had been lurking around the edge of the open space. He wore a denim jacket with khaki slacks. His sandy hair blew across his face in the breeze as he approached Luis.

"I got the message," he whispered.

"It's cool to talk normal, Slick. Guys who whisper look like they're tryin'a hide something."

"Yeah. Sure," the man Luis called Slick replied in a more normal, but still hushed voice. "Enrique over by the elm told me to meet you over here. You think it's OK, even with all the, uh, extra people around?"

"No, man. It's not OK. We're goin' somewhere else. We gotta be extra careful, ya know? Just be cool and come with me."

Luis removed his toothpick and flicked it toward the steps leading down from the fountain's outer circle to the water beyond. Without any gesture, Luis strode purposefully away from the fountain, passing under the Washington Square Arch, which was a replica of the *Arc de Triomphe de l'Étoile* in Paris. Slick stayed one stride behind his leader's right shoulder.

They walked three blocks, then turned west on 9th Street, where Luis stopped abruptly and then ducked into a doorway. He walked into the office building without hurrying, across the deserted lobby, past a bank of elevators, and into a men's room marked only by a black stick figure. He held the door, indicating that Slick should enter.

Once inside, Luis stopped. Slick kept his distance. "Alright, Slick. We're a little nervous right now about all the police activity. So, before I take you to see Bull, I need to make sure you're not wearing a wire. Strip down."

"What? You got to be kidding me."

"No big deal, Slick. Just take off your shirt and pants so I can make sure you're clean. No inspection, no meet-up."

Slick scowled while Luis stood passively, waiting. Five minutes later, after Slick got redressed, they exited and turned west. After only a few steps, Luis veered suddenly again, this time into a small café. A bored-looking barista stood behind a coffee bar. She briefly made eye contact with Luis, who kept walking. Slick followed to the rear of the long, narrow space, where Luis stopped and gestured toward an archway protected by a thin, black curtain.

Slick hesitated, looking nervous. Luis held the curtain aside so Slick could see Bull, sitting at a small table with a tall, half-empty glass of beer in front of him. Bull waved him forward as Luis closed the curtain and exited the joint, heading back to the park.

Chapter 10 — Exit This Way

PAULO SPENT THE NEXT HOUR trying to get some information from the police officers working the park. After several failed attempts, he spotted an officer he knew by name. "Yo, Carlos! You got a quick minute?"

Officer Carlos Nunez dropped his head. "Oh, c'mon, Richardson. You know I can't talk to you about this case, man. I'll get my head handed to me."

"No sweat," Paulo came closer, stopping with his shoulder almost touching the officer and looking up. Nunez was a good half-foot taller than Paulo. Carlos was a basketball player. Paulo was hoping for a connection. "I'm not interested in the little White girl. I'm looking into the other murder—Javier Estrada. He was a good kid from the neighborhood. Ballplayer. Worked at Snyder's grocery. Did you know him?"

Carlos looked confused. "You mean the kid on the Lower East Side Prep basketball team? You telling me he was the other murder last night?"

"Yeah, man. Sorry to give you news you didn't have. I just heard he was ID'd a few hours ago. It's a shame. I'm looking for somebody who can help me find his bag and get his Jordans back for the family."

"That was his bag?" Carlos mumbled to himself.

"You know where they found his bag?" Paulo pressed.

Carlos paused—not what Paulo wanted—but then said, "That body was found all the way over on the other side of the park."

"What about the bag?"

Carlos again stood silently, thinking. "Man, I can't say anything about the evidence in the Monroe investigation. It's too hot."

"Yeah. I get it. But can you tell me who I can talk to? The family wants to get Javier's bag back for his funeral."

"Sure. Oh, man, that's so sick. What the hell was the kid doing? Hey, I'm off the record here, right? Don't go getting me in trouble."

"Sure, sure. Off the record. Not that you've told me anything. So, who should I be talking to?"

"The lead detective is named Cook. They got a base camp set up at the northwest corner of the park. He might be there. Don't tell him I sent you, OK?"

"Fine. No problem. And thanks, man." Paulo walked quickly away.

* * *

PAULO STOOD NEXT TO A black-and-white squad car, its blue and red lights flashing continuously. He guessed it was the closest thing to an interrogation room the detectives could manage in their field location. "I'm not asking about the Monroe investigation, Detectives. I'm looking into the Javier Estrada murder."

The two detectives made eye contact, then Dru said, "You got that information awfully quickly, Mr. Richardson. We only got the name a little while ago. I don't suppose you would tell us where you came across it?"

"I'm sorry, Detective. I can't reveal my sources."

"Didn't think so." Dru turned away. "You said you had some information about the Monroe case."

"I think there might be a connection. Javier was a basketball player. His mother reported that he was at a basketball game last night and never made it home. Now we know why. I'm betting he would have had his good shoes in a bag if he was coming home after playing some street ball. If the bag was found near Javier's corpse, there wouldn't be much of a mystery. If the bag was found somewhere near where the Monroe girl was killed, that would suggest Javier was there."

"So, you think Javier Estrada killed Angelica Monroe?" Dru asked.

"Not likely. He's a good kid. Was. If he was heading home from a basketball game, he wasn't stopping to murder a girl he didn't know. And with a gun he was, what? Carrying around in his gym bag? And then somebody else happened to come along and kill him, after beating him up, on the other side of the park? That doesn't sound very likely."

"How do you know he didn't know Angelica Monroe?" Mariana asked.

Paulo held out his hands in surrender. "I guess I can't say for sure. It seems unlikely that he ran in the same social circles as an NYU student from Westchester. But you never know."

"Yeah. You never know," Dru agreed. "First rule of investigations—assume nothing."

"OK. Fine," Paulo conceded, "but it's more likely that somebody else killed them both, which seems like something worth investigating."

"You'd think two veteran homicide detectives would have already figured that out," Dru deadpanned.

"Of course. I mean, I wasn't suggesting that you don't know how to conduct an investigation."

"Good."

"So, you can confirm that the bag containing Javier's Air Jordans was found somewhere near the Monroe murder site?"

"No. But thanks for stopping by. If you have any other information about the case, please give me a call." Dru handed Paulo a business card, then turned away, grabbing Mariana by the arm and leading her back toward the makeshift command post. Paulo stood alone, the blue and red lights reflecting off his glasses.

Chapter 11 — When He's Right

D RU WATCHED PAULO WALK AWAY, then said to his partner, "What do you think?"

"The reporter's right. The JE initials written on the shoes. Has to be the same kid. I'm thinking he was cutting through the park on his way home. He saw something. The killer took him out, probably after killing Monroe. The kid left his bag behind. Maybe they killed him over by the Hangman's Elm and moved his body after, but more likely they migrated over there together and that's where he got shot."

"You're discounting the possibility of a female killer?"

"Yeah. I am. Don't tell anyone."

Dru laughed. "I won't. How does this new information help us?"

"Maybe the kid, Javier, knew the killer? Maybe he was involved somehow?"

"I'll call the ME to expedite the forensics on the bullet that killed Estrada. Natalie said it looked like a small caliber shot, which would be different from the slug that killed Monroe. You think two guns?"

"Obviously. What does it mean?"

"Maybe two shooters? At least it's something. More than we're getting from any of the random potential witnesses here in this park."

"What about the guy on camera with Monroe?"

"Yeah. That's another angle. Which lead do we chase next?"

Mariana looked toward the east. "We still need to talk to the family."

* * *

WHILE THEY WERE ON THE northbound Bruckner Expressway, Dru's phone buzzed with an incoming text. "We got the preliminary ballistics report on Estrada. The slug in his chest was a .22, likely from a small pistol like a Saturday Night Special."

"Odd weapon for a drug dealer," Mariana observed.

"Unless the drug dealer is a nineteen-year-old girl," Dru noted. "It says the bloody knife they found at the scene had only his prints on it. The blood was not his type. Seems like a fight, then a shot. The kid had defensive wounds and appeared to have been beaten up."

"You saying somebody got into a knife fight with the kid, then shot him with a girly gun?" Mariana looked skeptical.

"No, I'm not saying anything. I'm just reading the report. We won't have a full autopsy with lab results until at least tomorrow, but the ME says there was no gunpowder residue on the kid's hands, so he probably isn't our shooter. It says his left ankle was swollen and might have been injured." Dru dialed the desk officer who had been assigned to do a background check on Angelica. He put his phone on speaker so Mariana could hear. "Ellen, you have the background check on Angelica Monroe?"

"Yeah. I do," came the female voice. "I was going to send it in a minute."

"You're on speaker with me and Detective Vega. Please tell us what you have."

"Angelica Monroe has no prior arrests. Well, no arrests at all. She is, however, the registered owner of a .22 caliber pistol as of last October, when she purchased it at a firearms show in Pennsylvania. The gun was not recovered at the scene and was not found in her dorm room. That's all I got, Detective Cook."

"Thanks. I'm not sure what it means, but thanks." He hung up and stuffed the phone into his jacket pocket. "Seems like too much of a coincidence that Monroe owned a .22, which is not accounted for, and Javier Estrada was shot with a .22. I think we can rule out the possibility that Monroe shot Estrada on the other side of the park, then came back to the Hangman's Elm and got herself killed, after which her killer took her little gun but left behind her purse."

"Yeah, easy to rule out that scenario," Mariana agreed. "I'd say it's too damned easy for people to buy guns these days, but in her case, she would pass any background check—not that they do them at gun shows in Pennsylvania."

"It was illegal for her to take it across state lines and be in possession of it in New York City, of course, even if it was legally purchased in another state. But I guess she didn't know, or didn't care."

"I'll make sure we book the corpse for illegal possession," Mariana deadpanned. "I'm thinking that whoever killed Monroe took her gun and used it to kill Estrada."

"Could be. Now all we need to know is who killed Monroe, which is pretty much the point of this investigation."

"No shit?"

Dru shrugged. "Yeah. No shit."

Chapter 12 — Meet the Family

DRU AND MARIANA FINALLY arrived at the well-kept Westchester county residence of the Monroe family. The media horde had laid siege to the quiet street, where a local police unit and one county Sheriff's SUV kept the peace and made sure traffic wasn't obstructed. The Monroe house was decidedly not the most impressive structure on the block, at least from the front.

Dru and Mariana were ushered into a clean but modest living room. Mariana immediately noted that the home's furniture, decorations, and general presentation were inconsistent with Angelica having money to buy the clothes and shoes they found in her dorm room closet.

Charles Monroe, Angelica's father, had not shaved. His bespectacled face and balding head made him look older than the detectives figured him to be, based on his oldest child being nineteen. He explained that he was an accountant for a pharmaceutical company with a satellite office in White Plains. His wife, Rebecca, wore a crisp blue skirt, cream blouse, and two-inch tan pumps. Her light make-up and perfectly combed hair suggested someone who, unlike her husband, was concerned about her appearance for the detectives—or perhaps for the cameras. Rebecca explained that she cared for the kids: Angelica's younger sister, Jessica, who was a junior in high school, and brother Alex, thirteen. Mrs. Monroe said she worked part-time at the local library.

"We were so proud when Angelica got into NYU," Rebecca fought back tears, but maintained her composure without needing a tissue. "And she got a partial scholarship, which allowed us to afford it."

Dru saw Mariana's right eyebrow raise. "What about her social life? Did she have any boyfriends in college?"

Rebecca, who was clearly the spokesperson, replied. "She mentioned a few boys last year, but nothing serious. As far as we know, she didn't have any kind of steady guy."

"Did she have any good friends at school we might talk to?"

"Oh, I don't know about that. Angie was quite popular in high school. She had plenty of friends, but none of her close friends went to NYU. She worked hard in college, although her grades were not as high as we expected last year. In high school, she had a four-point-oh. But I know things were harder for her in college. She also had to work, you know. We're—we were so proud that she found a job and worked to help pay for her expenses."

"Where did she work?" Mariana asked.

"It was a diner, near campus. She was a waitress. She had to work nights and weekends, but that was so helpful for us, because even with the scholarship, NYU is expensive."

"So, the cash she had in her purse, that wasn't money you sent her?" Mariana looked at Mr. Monroe, hoping to draw him into the conversation, but he sat impassively while his wife did all the answering.

"No. We send her a hundred dollars per month, but whatever else she had must have come from her tips. She said she made good tips."

Dru changed the subject suddenly, hoping to get a true response. "Did Angelica smoke marijuana?"

"No!" Mrs. Monroe's voice raised in volume and pitch. "No, I would not allow that."

"So, she never got into any trouble in high school connected to drug use?"

Charles Monroe finally spoke up. "Detective, we're in mourning here. Our baby is dead. Why does it matter?"

Dru's expression softened. "I understand, Sir. I'm very sorry for your loss. No parent should have to bury their child. I'm asking because we're looking for leads that could help us find her killer. She had some cash and a plastic bag of marijuana in her purse. We found a plastic bin with several joints and marijuana residue in her dorm room. If she was buying pot in the park last night, it could be connected to her murder. We're hoping to find somebody who was with her or who knew whom she might have been buying from. I know it's hard to talk about, but if you can point us in the right direction, it might help."

"Dear?" Mr. Monroe turned to his wife.

"No. I'm sorry. She never used drugs when she was living at home. At least, not that I ever knew about. Her friends were all nice kids. If she had drugs in her dorm room—well, I have no idea where they came from."

"I understand. One more thing. Do you know the unlock code for her iPhone?"

Mr. Monroe shook his head. "No. She was on our cell plan, but she didn't ever tell us her code. She wanted to maintain her privacy."

"Fine. Will you give us authorization to let Apple unlock the phone for us? There might be some information that will help the investigation."

"Of course. We'll do anything we can to help."

Mariana told the Monroes to expect a form to authorize access to the phone, which would take several days at least. With nothing more to ask, the detectives said goodbye, after extending more condolences.

* * *

AS THEY LEFT THE MONROE HOME, the assembled reporters pummeled Mariana and Dru with questions. "Why are you here today?" "Is there some new information?" "Do you have any leads?" "Have you found the murder weapon?"

Dru waved off the questions and allowed the local cop to escort them back to their sedan.

Once on the Cross-County Parkway, Mariana said, "It sure would be nice if we could answer any of those damned questions."

Dru grunted and pulled out his phone to check for any updates that had come in while they were interviewing Angelica's parents. "We got the report from Mason about his interview with Javier Estrada's mother."

Mariana exited onto the southbound Bruckner. "We have at least a half-hour. Read it to me."

"He says the mom, Martha, was of course devastated when she got the news. She had reported her son missing because Javier was usually so conscientious about being home on time— let alone not coming home at all—after playing ball. Javier's dad has been gone for years, so Javier helps take care of his two younger siblings while the mom works evening shifts at the hospital. She said Javier always played on the courts on Sixth Avenue on Fridays and he was always home by nine o'clock. Javier was a good boy, she said. He had a job at a local grocery store. He was a good student, stayed out of trouble, and played lots of basketball."

"Did we get the juvenile records on the kid yet?" Mariana asked.

"Not sure. Let me finish this first and then I'll look." Dru took a moment to find his place, then continued. "George says he asked the mom if Javier had gotten into any trouble with the law when he was younger. She denied it at first, but eventually admitted he had gotten mixed up with some rough neighborhood kids and arrested for shoplifting and vandalism."

"Find me a kid from that neighborhood who didn't."

Dru didn't laugh. "The mom said Javier started playing on the school team at Lower East Side Prep in his sophomore year. He was good. The team was in the city public schools championship this year."

"I remember," Mariana broke in. "It was a big upset. That school had never won anything."

"I confess I don't follow the local high school hoops scene," Dru said. "According to the report, Javier had scholarship offers for college. He was apparently still waiting to hear from some D1 schools. That's why he was playing street ball on Friday—to get noticed by the college scouts. His mom confirmed that Javier had a silver Emirates Airlines shoulder bag he carried to the courts so he didn't have to wear his Air Jordans on the sidewalk. She also confirmed the initials on the back of the shoes."

"What about drug use or involvement?" Mariana slowed to turn off the highway onto Riverside Drive.

"I thought you wanted me to read it? Shall I read it to myself and then tell you about it?"

"No, Prick. I apologize for my impudence."

"Your what?"

"Never mind. Just keep reading and I'll keep driving."

"Fine. George says he called the grocery store owner and confirmed that Javier worked there for the last eighteen months.

Hadn't missed a day. Says he's straight as an arrow." Dru paused while scrolling through the rest of the report. "I don't see anything about drug use. Maybe George didn't ask."

"So, nothing to suggest the kid was a drug dealer, or an associate of one. We should talk to the players over at those Sixth Avenue courts, to confirm that Javier was playing ball on Friday and what time he left."

"That makes sense. I don't much doubt the mother's story, but we should get confirmation. We can't make any conclusions without confirmation."

Mariana's hands gripped the wheel so tightly her knuckles turned white. "Sometimes that's true. But not always. Sometimes the witnesses who could provide the confirmation don't want to talk."

"Sometimes they didn't see anything."

"Cut the shit, Dru. I'm sick of you needling me about it, like it was *my* fault and not yours."

"We've been over this. It was not your fault, but it was your *choice*." Dru fixed a stare at the side of Mariana's face. She did not turn away from her driving.

"You should have backed me up. That's what a partner is supposed to do."

Dru turned away and watched a barge chug up the Hudson River. "If I thought it was going to make a difference, I would have. I didn't think accusing the guy of being a racist on top of using excessive force was the right call. I told you that. We need officers to support us. Hell, we can't do our job without them. If we get a reputation for making those kinds of accusations against our uniforms, we might as well move to the suburbs and investigate lost dogs. You know that. I was doing what I thought was best in the long run. I know you want to make captain someday. You can't lead a unit with that kind of reputation. Damn it, Mare, it was best for you, too."

Mariana took the sharp left exit under the George Washington Bridge onto the West Side Highway. "I didn't see it that way, which you knew. I wouldn't have made the report if I didn't think it was important." She fought to control her voice. Yelling would not help. "You're right that I made a choice. I'm thinking about Javier Estrada's mom. Thinking about what kind of shit she's going through. It doesn't matter if her kid was a choir boy or a drug dealer. He's dead at eighteen. No mother deserves that. When the officer who beat up Floyd Merriman loses it again and kills somebody's little boy, I'm going to know I did what I needed to do. But you didn't. You're going to have to live with that."

"I backed you up on the excessive force charge. We agreed on that."

"That's not enough to get the bastard fired!"

Dru continued to scan the river, not turning back toward his partner. This conversation had been coming for two weeks. They both had been avoiding it. He didn't want to create a bigger rift than already existed. "You're right. I'm going to have to live with it. We're both going to have to live with it. Are we good?"

"I'm fine. Just stop bringing it up."

"Fine. It's behind us. Let's see if we can do the right thing for Mrs. Estrada—and Mr. and Mrs. Monroe."

Mariana changed lanes, preparing to turn onto Canal Street. "Let's do that. Did George send through any information about Estrada's juvie record?"

"Yeah." Dru opened a separate email and scanned the contents before speaking. "It's not much, like the mom said. Three arrests: one for petty theft, one for property damage, and one for disorderly conduct. There's a note here about a property crimes detective being involved. Name's Patterson. Ever heard of him?"

"No. I got nothing." Mariana smoothly turned down Fifth Avenue toward Washington Square Park.

"I'll make a note to look him up. Maybe he'll have some insight. In any case, the last arrest was more than two years ago. So, at least since he's been working at the grocery store and making it big on the court, he's got no busts."

"Straight as an arrow," Mariana repeated the grocer's description as she eased into a space marked "no parking anytime" near the corner of 6th Street. "The media circus must have thinned out. I got a much better spot tonight."

"We can only hope." Dru slammed his passenger door and trudged toward the park command post.

Chapter 13 — House of Mirrors

HANNAH KEPT CHASING the tentacles of the Angelica Monroe story, which were spreading out in every possible direction. Of course, she thought, every other print reporter and broadcast producer was doing the same. On a monster like this one, nobody wanted to find themselves on the wrong lead. The pack mentality resulted in every media outlet reporting on everything any other outlet reported.

Two days in, everybody had found witnesses who knew Angelica and who could provide the tears and the human-interest stories about what a wonderful person she was and what a tragedy it was that she was gone. Hannah had nailed that one on the first night. The next logical sources of new information were Angelica's high-school friends and teachers. A parade of news vans descended on the generally sleepy suburban community of West Harrison, searching for new voices and new tales about Angelica. Hannah's network dispatched another team to follow that lemming march.

Hannah stayed in Manhattan, looking for something different. If there wasn't something new to report on, or an arrest, she would get a new assignment. The news cycle was always looking for the next story. Hannah suspected there was still more to the Angelica Monroe murder, but she had to find it quickly.

The angle Hannah latched onto was the mystery man. She interviewed several people who had been questioned by the officers involved in the investigation. They all said the officers showed them a photo from a security camera of a man who was with Angelica the night of her murder. This got Hannah's attention. Getting a copy of that photo, and potentially finding the mystery man, could be the next big scoop.

Hannah had learned early in her cable news career that a portable tripod would fit in her purse. She found that potential witnesses who were reluctant to talk to a producer sometimes opened up like a ripe avocado when they thought they were on air. She could pull out her tripod, extend the telescoping legs, and mount her iPhone into a clip on the top. Then, she would put the witness in front and start questioning. Since she worked for a low-end cable network, the witnesses bought her story that ACN could not afford to send a camera crew with her and that they always used iPhone video on air. It was plausible, and it worked.

With her trusty tripod in her purse, Hannah returned to the guard shack at the southwest corner of the park and security guard Joe Malone, who found Angelica's body.

"I can't tell you anything about the girl's murder," Joe immediately said upon seeing Hannah at his doorless doorway. "I got orders."

"Don't worry, Joe. I understand. You need to keep confidential things to yourself. I'm not going to ask you anything about Friday night or the crime scene. But I want your expert opinion about the police investigation, and whether you have any theories about who might have killed her. You were a cop, right?"

"For twenty years," Joe said proudly.

"So, do you have any opinions?"

"Sure. Yes. I can do that without breaching any confidences." Joe dug out a pocket comb and made an attempt at organizing his thinning hair. Hannah noticed and smiled as she set up her tripod.

"Stand here, with the park behind you. The sun will be in your face." She focused the iPhone camera and pressed the record button. "Don't worry about any introductions, Joe. We'll do a voice-over about who you are. I'll ask you a bunch of questions, then we'll edit them down to your best answers. Take your time. Are you ready?"

Joe cleared his throat and nodded.

"Joe, what's your evaluation of the police investigation so far?"

"I, uh, I think they are covering their bases very thoroughly. They have four teams of uniformed officers and two detectives handling witness identification and interrogation, which is an extraordinary deployment."

"How long should this process continue before they run out of possible witnesses to interview?"

"I would expect today might be the last day for that, at least at this level of intensity." Joe was getting comfortable. His voice, which had been tentative, now exuded confidence and authority.

Hannah gave Joe a silent thumbs-up sign from behind the camera, then asked, "Have the officers had any luck finding the guy who was with Angelica on Friday night?"

"How do you know about that?"

Hannah smiled sweetly at Joe. The camera was rolling. In Hannah's experience, people hated looking stupid on camera and would say anything to fill the void of silence. She said nothing.

"Well, um, we have some security video of Angelica walking down the sidewalk, down there, coming from one of those bars down 3rd Street." He gestured toward the west. "The police think the man might have some information, but they can't find him."

"Is that the photo the officers have been showing to people all around the park?"

"Yeah, have you seen it?"

"I have," Hannah lied, "but I couldn't get a copy. Do you have one?"

Joe looked uncomfortable. "Yeah, I do. They sent one around to all the university security guys so we could be on the lookout for him. I can show you on my phone when we're done with the interview."

"Great!" Hannah gushed.

"But . . . hey, can we turn off the camera?" Joe asked.

"Sure." Hannah pushed the STOP button. "You were great, Joe. Thank you so much."

"Yeah, well, I'm not sure I'm supposed to give you that photo. I could get in trouble. So, you can't use that part. OK?"

"Joe, it's on film. This was an on-the-record interview. I can't just delete it."

The former cop squirmed uncomfortably. "I know, but, hey, I'm tryin' to help you out here. You need to work with me."

Hannah did her best to seem conflicted. "I could say that the photo came from an anonymous source close to the investigation, but then I wouldn't be able to use the video of you talking about it."

"Yeah," Joe eagerly agreed. "That would work. You can still use all the other stuff."

"Show me the photo," Hannah said while she dismounted her iPhone.

"I'm—I'm not sure—"

"I might even be able to get you a small payment to compensate you for your trouble." Hannah recalled that a hundred dollars had loosened Joe's memory about Angelica Monroe's name Friday night.

Joe found the still shot of Angelica and the mystery man on his phone and showed it to Hannah. "This is it. I know it's not a great image. Do you think five hundred dollars would be a fair finder's fee?"

"Two hundred is the best I can offer, Joe. That's the standard rate to pay for a photo or video. I am willing to keep your identity confidential. I can call my boss if you're willing to go on the record."

"No. No. Thanks. Do you have cash on you?"

Hannah dug two hundred-dollar bills from her purse. She had such petty cash exactly for such situations. She then took snapshots of the photo, explaining that Joe wouldn't want to send it to her by text or email, which would leave a trail. He was grateful for Hannah's discretion.

* * *

TEN MINUTES LATER, Hannah walked down 3rd Street with her phone in hand. She needed time to think about how to use the photo in her next segment with William Wilson. She wondered how Dave would react to having the only photo of the mystery man. She also needed a drink and a smoke.

A group of students with backpacks emerged from the doorway of a seedy-looking bar below a neon sign reading *The Scampering Squirrel*. She dug out her precious pack of Virginia Slims and extracted one of her daily ration. While she enjoyed the nicotine rush on the sidewalk, she watched a trickle of patrons entering and exiting the bar. It seemed very much a student hang-out.

She studied the blurry, pixilated image on her phone. Could the mystery man be a fellow student? Not likely. The cops and the NYU security force would have found him by now. A friend of

Angelica's? The cops would have questioned her known friends. Could the man be her killer? She didn't envy the challenge facing the police.

After sucking the last morsel from her smoke, Hannah went inside and took a seat in the center of the bar. She ordered a Stella Artois from the female bartender, who looked barely old enough to serve alcohol. When the tall, bulbous glass branded with the beer's logo arrived, Hannah struck up a conversation. It was before five o'clock and the place was sparsely populated, so they had a few minutes together. Hannah got the definite impression that Jade, the bartender, was hitting on her, which was not unusual. She had been told multiple times that she put out a definite lesbian vibe. She was happy to play the role for a few minutes.

"Hey, did you know the girl who got murdered Friday night, Angelica Monroe?"

Jade put both elbows on the bar and cradled her chin in her cupped hands. "I didn't, like, *know* her, but she did come in here sometimes, so I recognized her picture on TV."

Hannah leaned onto the bar with her forearms and placed her head level with Jade's. "I have some information about the investigation, but it's confidential. Can you keep a secret?"

"Ooooh, I love secrets. And sure, I hear stuff you wouldn't believe here behind the bar. You think I go shooting my mouth off about them? I'd never get a tip." She tittered at her own joke in a high pitch.

"Well," Hannah lowered her volume further and stretched her neck forward, "the cops are looking for a guy who Angelica was with on Friday night, a few minutes before she was killed. A tall, light-haired guy. They were walking down 3rd Street together, toward the park. Heck, they might have been coming from this bar. How about that?" Hannah knew not to actually ask Jade if she knew about the photo or if she ever saw Angelica with a guy fitting the description. She was merely sharing gossip. If Jade knew anything, she would be more likely to give up the information on her own.

"Yeah, I know. Some cops were in here asking everybody if they had seen Angelica with this guy. They had a bad picture from a sidewalk cam."

"Did they interrogate you?"

"They asked me some questions. It's not like they took me into the back room and roughed me up or anything. I told 'em shit. I don't go ratting out my customers, right?"

"Oh, so you *did* know something, but didn't tell the cops? That's pretty ballsy."

"The cops don't scare me." Jade's eyes flicked to the left, down the mostly empty bar, making sure nobody was overhearing them. "Between you and me, I'm gonna miss her because she always had good weed and she liked to spread it around. I know Lars will feel the same way."

"Lars?" Hannah nearly fell off the front of her bar stool in her effort to lean in even farther. She could smell Jade's spicy perfume.

"Yeah. . . . You know . . . the *guy.*"

"You mean the," Hannah lowered her voice to a whisper, "the guy the cops are looking for? You know who he is?"

Jade winked. "Like I said, I hear a lot of things, and I keep 'em to myself. He doesn't need trouble from the cops. All he was doing was buying weed. I mean, c'mon, it's no big deal. He shouldn't get deported over that. He's an amazing guy. He's got one more year of med school. Leave him the fuck alone, right? It's not like he killed Angie."

"Right," Hannah agreed. "The cops think he might know something, like whether she went into the park alone, or if she was meeting someone."

Jade stood straight up, narrowing her eyes and looking sideways at Hannah. "You're not a cop, right?"

"Oh, God, no! I'm sorry. Listen, how about I buy us both a shot of Fireball?"

Jade's suspicious face swelled into a mischievous half-smile. "Comin' right up." She bent over to reach into a mini-fridge behind her as Hannah sat back on her stool, deciding whether to push for any more information.

Jade lined up two shot glasses and poured them to the brim in one motion, splashing some sticky brown liquid on the polished wood. Hannah reached out and took her glass. "To Angelica, may she score all the weed she needs in the afterlife."

"I'll drink to that," Jade lifted the second glass and pounded the shot like the pro she was.

When Hannah swallowed and gently set down her glass, she said, in a whisper, "And to Lars, may the cops never find him."

"Amen." Jade scooped up the glasses and deposited them in some secret bin behind the bar.

Hannah reached into her pants pocket and produced a clip of cash and credit cards. Peeling off two twenty-dollar bills, she tossed them on the bar. "Hey, I have to run, Jade. Will you be here later?"

"I'm here until midnight, baby."

Hannah waved as she moved across the tacky floor and back out into the shadows cast by the sun, falling slowly toward New Jersey. She had some research to do—trying to find a third-year med student named Lars who was not a US citizen. But first, she wanted to have another chat with Petra Burroughs, the roommate from her triumphant Friday night interview. She had pushed

Petra to say nice things about Angelica, but Petra had been a little reluctant. Hannah remembered wondering why at the time, but chalked it up to being nervous about speaking in front of a TV camera. What if Petra's reluctance had a different motivation?

She dug out her phone and found Petra's number. Although she knew Petra would prefer a text, she opted for a call, hoping to catch her off guard. When Petra answered on the second ring, Hannah pumped her fist in the air, drawing sideways glances from a few fellow pedestrians.

"Petra, Hi. Hannah Hawthorne from American Cable News. How are you doing?"

"Um. Fine, I guess. Why are you calling?"

"I wanted to thank you again for the interview you gave us on Friday. You were really great. I have a couple of follow-up questions I'd like to ask you. Can I buy you a drink and talk for a few minutes?"

"Can't you ask me on the phone?" Petra wasn't jumping at the prospect of another interview.

"No. This is something I need to talk about in person. It's kinda personal about Angelica, but it would mean a lot to our reporting." Hannah wheedled Petra for another minute before overcoming the student's reluctance. Petra conceded that she didn't have any plans until later in the evening and agreed to meet at The Scampering Squirrel.

* * *

HANNAH AND PETRA SAT on hard wooden benches in a corner booth. Hannah ignored the disapproving glances from Jade behind the bar. Petra had a cosmopolitan in front of her in a delicate glass with a long, thin stem. Hannah sipped a glass of Stella.

"I'm doing some reporting that comes from other sources. But I can't publish without some corroboration. You don't need to be named. You can be an anonymous source with knowledge of the facts."

"What facts?"

Hannah pulled a steno notebook from her purse. She had written notes for herself and pretended to consult the records of some earlier interviews. "You understand how important it is for us not to mis-report things, right?"

"Sure." Petra shifted on her booth bench and took a sip. "But I'm not sure I want to say anything."

"Fine. Don't say anything. But you can help me by confirming things I think I already know. You don't have to talk. Just nod your head if I have things right, and shake your head if I have it wrong. You can do that, right?"

Petra nodded, but didn't speak, reaching for her half-empty glass.

"Great. The information I have is that Angelica was selling weed—to multiple people."

Petra glanced toward the empty dance floor next to the booth, then nodded silently.

"OK. I'm guessing Angelica was doing it because it made her some money she didn't otherwise have. Would I be right that it started while she was a freshman, and still your roommate?"

Petra's eyes flashed anger, then she nodded firmly.

"Oh, God. Was she selling weed right from your dorm room?"

"No!" Petra blurted out, then hushed her voice. "I wouldn't let her. It was bad enough that she kept her stash in the room, where somebody might think it was mine."

"Right," Hannah soothed, pleased with herself that the ploy of Petra not speaking had lasted only three questions. "Do you know where she got her supply from?"

"No. And I didn't want to know. I wanted her to stop, but she said she couldn't. She was running up some big credit card bills. Did you know that the credit card companies offer us free cards while we're students, just so they can get us hooked on buying things on credit? They are such leeches!"

"I know," Hannah agreed. "In fact, that might make a great story, once I'm finished with this one. Did Angelica pay off her credit card bills with the money she made selling pot?"

"Duh," Petra rolled her eyes. "I heard her telling her parents that she got a job working at a diner. Ha! She never worked at any diner. She bought her Halston dresses and her Gucci handbags with her weed money. Angie once said at a party that her parents were rich and she got tons of spending money from them, which is how she always had such good weed to share. Hey, you're not going to quote me on this, are you?"

"No. No, not at all," Hannah soothed. "This is all completely off the record. I'm not even taking notes." She reflexively patted her iPhone, which was in her hip pocket and had been recording since before Petra arrived. "I'll only use you for verification, without using your name."

Over the next ten minutes, including another round of drinks, Petra vented about how Angelica had "ruined" Petra's freshman year. "Angie was super bummed because she had some friends who had rich parents and they always had money to spend. They went shopping together and went out to clubs in their new clothes. And they all smoked weed. Angie didn't have any money. She even borrowed from me. After a while I wouldn't give her more because she never paid me back. I know it's a cliché that some girls don't know how to manage their money, but for Angie it was really true."

"Why didn't she ask her rich friends for help?" Hannah nudged.

"Ha! Those rich bitches loved to spend daddy's money, but they would freeze you out in a heartbeat if they thought you weren't in their league. I told Angie she should forget them, but she wanted to hang out with the cool kids, you know?"

"I know," Hannah said with conviction. "So, Angie was selling pot to get extra money?"

"Yeah. It had started over the winter break. I went home, and when I got back, Angie had new clothes and shoes in her closet and the room smelled like pot. At first, she denied it, but it wasn't hard to figure out. By spring break, Angie was spending more time peddling dope than studying. Everybody called her 'the girl with the weed,' which made her very popular. Her rich bitch friends loved it."

"How did she explain all her new clothes to her parents?"

"She didn't go home much, and they never visited. She was out all night most weekends. I had to scrub our room with heavy-duty cleaning products to keep the smell from getting into everything."

"I'm sure a lot of students smoked pot, though. Right?" Hannah motioned to their waitress for another cosmopolitan.

"Sure, lots of my friends smoke pot. It wasn't like anybody on the floor was going to rat out Angie to security, but nobody knew what was really going on. I once opened the supply box under her bed. There were dozens of pre-rolled joints and zip-lock baggies of loose weed. She must have been making thousands of dollars a month."

"You're sure you don't know where she got her supply from?"

Petra shook her head. "Once a month or so she would go out late on a Friday night and come back with a big purse that looked heavy. She spent hours in the bathroom with the door shut while I pretended to sleep. I don't know where she got it from."

"What about who she sold it to? Did she sell it to other students here on campus—to the other girls on the floor you said smoked pot?"

"That's the weird thing," Petra said, draining the last drops of scarlet liquid from her glass. "I never saw her sell any of it to anyone in the building. But I did see her get phone calls, sometimes late at night." Petra glanced up as their waitress arrived with a fresh Cosmo.

Hannah was fine with Petra getting drunker and waved off the server's question of whether she wanted another beer. "Let me ask you this, did you ever see Angelica with a tall White guy named Lars, a medical student?"

Petra scrunched her eyebrows together as she thought, carefully sipping away the liquid from the brim of her martini glass. "No, I don't think so."

"OK. Fine. It was worth a shot. What about anybody else she sold to? Did you ever see her meeting with somebody to sell pot?"

"No. It's not like I was spying on her."

"Of course not. I wasn't implying that."

Hannah sensed Petra's information was about exhausted and motioned to their server for the check. She made small-talk with Petra for five more minutes without getting anything useful. Then, Hannah paid the bill and excused herself, walking by the bar on her way out and waving to Jade, who did not return the greeting.

* * *

THE SUN HAD SET by the time Hannah got back to the news van, where Terry was setting up a shot for William Wilson. After the reporter finished talking on camera for forty-five seconds without saying anything new, they went inside the van. Hannah disclosed what she had learned, showing them the blurry photo of the man she now suspected was Lars, the foreign medical student and weed buyer.

"What do you guys think? Should we go to Dave with this and start working on the new angle?"

"No bloody way!" William spurted. "We're doing great with the story we have. Our numbers are through the roof. Since you got that exclusive last night, we're pulling in a huge share. The viewers think we have the inside information."

"We do have inside information!"

"Not the kind they want," William scolded. "You know the game, Hannah. You can't change the storyline in the middle. They want us to get the next big scoop on who killed Angelica, not that Angelica might have been in the park buying weed when she was killed. Who cares, anyway? So what if a nineteen-year-old was buying weed? You want to try to tell people she was not as sweet and innocent as we've been saying? What does that get us? When you have a lead on who killed her, then maybe we run with the Old Dope Peddler angle. But until then, you're nuts if you think we want to start defaming the girl."

Hannah stayed silent. She knew Wilson was correct. Dave would never go for it—not based on the information she had, most of which was not attributable to anyone. She needed an on-air source. But who? "OK. I get it. I'll keep digging. But if we get corroboration and a decent interview on this, I want to run with it."

"I'll reserve judgement," Wilson said seriously. "If Dave gives it the green light, then fine, but I don't want any part of pitching that one."

Terry then spoke up. "What do you think it would help, Hannah? What difference would it make?"

"It might help the police catch the killer. This is information the cops don't have."

"Maybe they don't, or maybe they do. But it's not our job to catch the killer. It's to catch the story. You're good, Hannah. But let's be careful. It's my ass on the line, too."

"Alright. I'll see if I can use the information to track down this guy, Lars. Right now, he's the most wanted man in the city."

Chapter 14 — Everybody Has a Story

PAULO KNOCKED ON THE DOOR to the Estradas' apartment in a New York City Housing Authority complex on Avenue C. Like most NYCHA buildings, this one was badly in need of repairs and maintenance. It was a constant refrain from residents and activists. Paulo had written several articles about the appalling conditions and the city's cavalier responses to the complaints—pleading lack of funds and manpower. If a private landlord allowed a building to fall into disrepair, the residents could withhold rent and sue in housing court. Residents of city-owned housing had no similar recourse against the government. Unfortunately, the low-income residents got less than they paid for.

The heavy metal door opened an inch before catching at the end of a security chain. The quizzical face of a boy around thirteen peered through the slit, well below Paulo's eye level. "Who are you?" the boy spat out, clearly assuming the unfamiliar face was a threat, a salesman, or a panhandler.

"Hi. My name is Paulo Richardson. I'm a reporter with the *Lower East Side Tribune*. I'm so sorry about Javier. Your brother?" The boy did not reply. "I'd be very grateful to speak with your mother so we can make sure Javier's story gets properly told and folks hear about what a great kid he was. Is your mother at home?"

The door slammed closed. Paulo knew to wait patiently to see what would happen. If the mother wasn't home, there was no chance the boy would come back and open the door again. Latch-key kids knew not to let strangers into their homes, and not to talk to adults they didn't know, no matter how good their stories were. But if Javier's mother was home, there was at least a chance the boy would fetch her and that she would talk to him, even if through the door slit. If he knocked again the mother would perceive him as being pushy and rude. He waited.

After three minutes, Paulo heard footsteps on the hardwood floor behind the door. The handle turned and the door once again lurched open one inch. This time, the figure in the slit was a woman, still shorter than his eye level. He could see dark hair sitting high on her head, and the greenish-blue color of hospital scrubs covering her torso. "Francis said you're a reporter for the neighborhood paper. That right?"

"Yes, ma'am. I'm Paulo Richardson and I write for the *Lower East Side Tribune*. I write stories about the people and businesses here in the neighborhood. I'm so sorry about Javier. I want to make sure his real story gets told. Can I speak with you for a few moments?"

"You got some ID?" came the skeptical reply.

"Sure, Mrs. Estrada." Paulo drew out his wallet and showed Javier's mother his press card. He knew her name was Martha, but he didn't want to seem too familiar.

"How do I know this is real?"

"You can call my newspaper's office and confirm that I'm a reporter with them. I'll give you the number, or you can look it up. You can also check the paper's website, where I'm listed as a staff reporter. I'll be happy to wait." Paulo smiled and did his best to look non-threatening.

The door closed, but softly this time. A scraping sound of metal on metal told Paulo that Martha was unlatching the security chain from her door, exactly what he wanted. When the door opened wider than before, he got a full view of Javier's mother. Her eyes were puffy but clear. Her uncolored lips pressed together, indicating skepticism, which was amplified by her crossed arms. She made no motion toward inviting Paulo inside.

Beyond Martha, Paulo could see a long hallway with stained hardwood floors and doors on the left and right. At the far end, a lone window allowed filtered light into the apartment. Next to the door, a green metal rack held three large umbrellas. Two sets of sneakers and one pair of white nurse's shoes with thick cushioned soles stood sentry at its base. The smell of pasta sauce wafted to the door from an unseen kitchen.

"You writing an obituary for Javier?" Mrs. Estrada's tone continued to be skeptical, as if Paulo was trying to scam her. She knew that, despite the boy's prowess on the basketball court, printed obituaries of dead teens from NYCHA buildings simply didn't happen. Red skin around the corners of her eyes documented the tears she had already shed for her son.

"No, ma'am. Not primarily. I'm looking into the circumstances of his murder and I want our readers to understand how tragic this was. I understand that Javier was working hard, had a job, and had a chance to go to college on a basketball scholarship. I shop at Snyder's Grocery, where he works. I've spoken to him. I want everyone to know that he wasn't some gang member killed in a street fight." Paulo fibbed a bit. He had probably seen the kid working at the grocery, but never knew his name, and if he had said "hello" once or twice, that would have been the complete transcript of their interactions. But he truly did want to tell a sympathetic story about Javier, so he mentally justified the puffing.

"Javier was a good boy," she said, the bravado of her demeanor melting into sorrow. "You really going to write that?"

"I hope so. I just need to get the truth from you and your family. And maybe you can tell me who some of Javier's friends are so I can talk to them. I'm meeting with his basketball coach tomorrow." Again, Paulo was fibbing. He had called the school and left a message to make an appointment with the coach. The school had not called him back. Yet. It was possible he would interview the coach on Monday. He hoped he would.

Martha stared at him, evaluating his honesty and his threat level. "OK. C'mon in and we can talk. You can join us for dinner if you don't mind spaghetti."

Over dinner, Paulo got an earful from Javier's family. He pulled out his trusty notepad and filled ten pages. Martha's two remaining kids, Francisco and Elena, were eager to talk about their big brother, with Martha chiming in periodically to correct the record or fill in things the siblings didn't know. Paulo's story on Javier's life was shaping up to be much more interesting than the story of his death, about which he still had no information.

Martha admitted that Javier was in and out of the juvenile justice system until he turned sixteen. When Javier began his sophomore year of high school, the basketball coach heard that Javier, who had grown to a muscular six-two, was a respected street-ball player and recruited him to join the school team. Javier loved being on the team and quickly traded in his street-gang friends for his court-mates. He had to keep up good grades in order to keep playing. For the first time in his life, he had motivation to study. He was an innately intelligent boy. When he applied himself, Javier got outstanding grades. Martha was quite proud, and repeated it several times.

But there was more than basketball in Javier's life. Martha worked as a nurse's aide, assigned to the night shift. She had hoped to qualify as a registered nurse, but pregnancy and holding her family together didn't allow for additional schooling. The night shift paid extra, which the family needed, but it meant that the children had to care for themselves in the evenings. Javier stepped up and became a surrogate father to his younger siblings.

In his junior year, he also took on a job at the grocery store, which allowed him to pick up shifts at odd hours in between basketball practice and games in the winter. In the spring and summer, he worked nearly every morning to supplement the family's income. The job kept him so busy he didn't have any time to fall back in with his former friends. He stayed out of trouble and improved as a point guard, playing in the pick-up street games in lower Manhattan throughout the summers. While other players of his skill level attended camps run by professional players and coaches, Javier honed his game on the playground courts.

After his school team surprised everyone by winning the city public school championship, Javier got calls from college recruiters. Attending college had not been on his mind a few years earlier, but at age eighteen, he suddenly had a future to look forward to. Although his siblings and his mom still relied on him, they all urged Javier to go to college at the best school that offered him a full scholarship. He put in extra shifts at the grocery store and played pick-up games at the Sixth Avenue courts whenever he could, where the college scouts could see him.

It was a story of perseverance, hard work, and hope. Paulo could hardly wait to start writing. When the family had exhausted their outpouring of love and praise for Javier and Martha was clearing away the dinner dishes, He asked whether Javier had a pair of Air Jordans.

"You bet!" Francisco confirmed. "He saved up for six months for those shoes."

"I bet he took good care of them, huh?"

"Oh, man, he treated them like they were made of gold. He never even wore them except when he was playing. Hey, do you know whether the cops will give us back his Emirates bag and his shoes?"

"What kind of bag?" Paulo asked.

Martha cut in to explain. "Javy got this nice shoulder bag with the logo of Emirates Airlines on it from one of his basketball buddies. He told me the other guy found it in a garbage can in some building over near Battery Park while he was delivering a package. Javy won it from him in a one-on-one game and used it to carry his shoes and court clothes. He never went out to play without that bag. Francis can't fit into those big shoes yet, but I know he really wants his brother's bag. I told the detective who spoke to me this afternoon. Do you think we'll get it back?"

"I don't know. Are you sure he had it with him last night?"

"Oh, yes. I wasn't home, since I was working, but you can be sure Javy didn't go over to the courts without his Jordans, and he never wore them on the street. He had his Emirates bag all right."

"Well, I'm sure if the police found it, then it's evidence in the investigation. But once the case gets closed, I would expect that you'll get his property back."

Martha reached out her hand toward Paulo. It did not tremble. Working in a hospital must steel you to tragedy, Paulo thought, even your own. "The detective didn't tell me much. Do you know anything about how my Javy died?"

"I'm sorry, I don't. You probably know more than I do. But I tell you what, I'm going to try to find out."

He left feeling exhilarated about the upcoming story, and sad about the family's grief and the abject tragedy of the situation. He had no idea what circumstances resulted in Javier being shot, but he was convinced that the kid was not connected to Angelica Monroe's murder, at least not in any criminal way. He hurried home, already formulating paragraphs in his head.

Chapter 15 — Follow the Food

AT SEVEN O'CLOCK, Dru and Mariana were back at the northwest corner of the park. It had already been a long day. They were getting debriefed by the four teams of officers who had been continuing to canvas the park and the dorms, looking for more witnesses. A few things were in better focus than at the day's beginning. They now had the grainy photo of the mystery man Angelica was walking with shortly before her death, they had a photo of Javier Estrada while he was still breathing, and they had a solid suspicion that Angelica was either buying or selling weed, giving them a focus on finding her dealer, or her buyers.

Since Dru and Mariana left the park that morning, the eight officers working the NYU area had uncovered only one new witness worth the detectives' time. He was a food cart vendor named Enrique Rojas. He sold candied nuts from a position on the southwest quadrant of the plaza around the central fountain. According to the summary report from the officer who originally spoke to him, Mr. Rojas remembered seeing three men running across the plaza Friday night. As darkness descended, Dru and Mariana bought some nuts and questioned him.

Mariana took the lead, speaking Spanish and translating for Dru when Mr. Rojas had trouble expressing himself in English.

"I heard a bang. Then, later I saw an *hombre* running. He was, you know, limping," Rojas said.

"How long after hearing the bang did you see the man?"

"I don't know. I had customers, so, not right away. Maybe four or five minutes."

"Can you describe what you mean by limping?"

"He was trying to run, rocking side to side." Rojas demonstrated what he meant, moving with a stiff left leg, as if trying not to put pressure on a knee or ankle.

"Where did he go?" Mariana gently prodded.

Rojas pointed away to the north and east. "He kinda stopped and looked around by the fountain over there. Then he kept running down that path."

"Did you see anyone else around that same time?"

Rojas nodded. "*Si.* Another guy came running from the same direction. He stopped and looked around, like he was looking for someone. Then another guy came running and stopped next to the first guy. Then they both ran the same way as the limping guy, like they were chasing after him."

Mariana showed Mr. Rojas their photo of Javier Estrada, plucked from an online story about one of his basketball victories. The vendor could not say whether any of the three men he saw was Estrada. He said they all looked "dark" but the lighting was dim and the figures were fifty to seventy-five feet away.

Mariana made eye contact with Dru, who gave her a subtle head shake, indicating that he had no other questions. "Thank you, Mr. Rojas. You have been very helpful."

They walked toward the path where the three men ran, according to Rojas. As they walked, Dru said, "So, they could have been coming from the direction of the Hangman's Elm. Or, they could have come into the park from the south, then turned east around the fountain."

"Sure," Mariana said, "we can't be sure. But the timing is right, and the guy heard the shot, so I'm thinking it's a pretty good bet."

"I agree. It would be nice if somebody besides security guard Joe had called in hearing a gunshot."

Mariana let out a mirthless chuckle. "It would be nice if gunshots were unusual enough for folks to notice. It looks like most people who were here last night are staying away for now."

"Give it a few days," Dru said, "New Yorkers will forget about the two murders and go back to their normal routine."

"You're probably right. It sucks, but a few days is probably all it will take."

They followed the path away from the fountain to the northeast. It curved away to the north after fifty yards, but a dirt path between some trees made a beeline toward the site of Javier Estrada's murder.

Dru pointed down the compressed dirt lane. "It checks out. The preliminary on Estrada said he had an injured ankle. That makes him the limper."

"Yeah, that checks. We have two chasers, but no real description."

Dru waved an arm. "Let's get back to the shop. We've got a bunch of summary reports to type so the brass can tell the press how much progress we're making."

"Progress?"

"Yeah. Plenty. Besides, I need some food not wrapped in cellophane."

* * *

AT NINE O'CLOCK, the two detectives were back at their Upper West Side precinct. The lead officer on their investigation squad called in to say they had not uncovered anyone besides Mr. Rojas who would admit to seeing any running men the night before.

While eating a slice of mushroom pizza from the shop on Columbus Avenue near the precinct, Dru typed a summary for Captain Sullivan and fired it off in an email, while Mariana prepared a more detailed report on their interrogation of Enrique Rojas and Eldin Garfield. After a full day, they didn't have much. They logged twelve hours of overtime each. Sully would approve the extra pay, since the case was such a high priority for City Hall.

The communications office would not be happy. The media would not be happy. The mayor and the commissioner would also not be happy, which meant that Sully would not be happy. He and Mariana were certainly not happy.

Dru couldn't help but think that none of them were as unhappy as Angelica Monroe's parents—and Javier Estrada's mother.

* * *

THE NEWS OF ANGELICA MONROE'S murder broke too late to make the morning papers, but the print media outlets all had articles on their websites and on their social media feeds by the time most New Yorkers woke up on Saturday. New York One news devoted the first seven minutes of its repeated half-hour news show to the murder, including a clip of William Wilson's interview of Angelica's former roommate, attributed to American Cable News. By mid-day, all the broadcast news shows were leading with the story. It also topped the national cable news broadcasts.

By the evening news slots, Angelica Monroe's murder was the lead on every New York station as well as two out of the three national network news shows. All the networks scurried to line up guests to talk about the issues raised by the shooting for their Sunday morning opinion/discussion programs.

On social media platforms, comments and images about Angelica's murder were fodder for even more wide-ranging opinions. Spin-off threads blamed the Democrat-controlled city council for failing to ensure public safety, decried how national immigration policy left country's borders vulnerable to gun-runners, and blamed the tragedy on the corrupting influence of the gay and trans communities in New York. The hashtags connected to Angelica were among the top ten search terms for the day.

Fueled by the Twitter account of an NYU group devoted to fighting violence against women, several hundred students gathered at the Hangman's Elm for a prayer vigil at 9:05 p.m., rumored to be the time of Angelica's death. The vigil was covered by all the media outlets that had news crews camped out around Washington Square Park, providing images and interviews to accompany the continuing coverage of the shooting. Video clips from the vigil posted on the social media accounts of the news organizations were, on their own, among the most viewed content on the internet.

* * *

AT TWO-FIFTEEN SUNDAY MORNING, the *Lower East Side Tribune's* website carried a headline about Javier Estrada's murder. Paulo's article chronicled the boy's troubled youth and his admirable turn-around from gang member to model student and basketball star. The piece featured Javier's role as surrogate father to his younger siblings, his work at the grocery where so many community members got to know him off the court, and his now-shattered dreams of attending college.

It was a celebration of the promise that hard work and proper motivation could pull a local kid up from the projects and into a better life. It was also a eulogy about the tragedy of street crime and how one shooting would have repercussions through Javier's family and community. At Javier's funeral on Monday, it would be read in its entirety and would elicit tears from everyone present. *The Lower East Side Tribune* was the only news website to mention the murder of Javier Estrada.

Chapter 16 — Finding Pieces

Sunday

O N SUNDAY MORNING, Dru and Mariana had a new problem. When they arrived at the Washington Square Park command post to check in with the uniforms, they had to detour around a crowd of people blocking their path. At the front of the crowd, on some kind of elevated platform, a woman holding a bullhorn yelled at the assembled group.

"We will not let our city become a gang war. We will not let these thugs take over our streets and kill innocent women with guns they buy on the street corner like falafel. The mayor and his cronies refuse to do anything. We need new leadership. We need people who will protect innocent victims like Angelica Monroe from this rampant violence!"

The crowd responded with enthusiastic hoots and cheers. Dru and Mariana rounded the far corner of the spectators and reached their command post, where the uniformed officers were standing and looking in the direction of the amplified speaker.

"Would you like to go join the crowd?" Dru called out to the officers, shouting to be heard above the bullhorn. The officers quickly gave the detectives their full attention. "How long has this been going on?"

The lead officer on the morning team, Bill O'Dell, responded, "Sir, they started about a half-hour ago. The crowd keeps getting bigger."

"Did we have any intel that this was going to happen?" Dru bellowed from three feet away.

"No, Sir. Officer Edwards found some tweets online with the hashtag "Justice for Angelica" calling for a memorial and demonstration this morning. It must have gone viral."

"Great," Dru said at a normal volume, which nobody except Mariana heard. She was practically rubbing shoulders with her partner in the confined space. Dru turned to speak directly into her ear. "You think the media will notice?" The camera crews from the still-in-place news vans were, of course, already fully engaged in covering the impromptu protest.

"I assume you've called this in and asked for some crowd control?" Dru shouted at O'Dell, who nodded vigorously. "Fine, leave four of you here until they show up. The rest of you, get back on the assignment to canvas the park. We're still looking for witnesses from Friday night and anyone who can identify the man in the photo with Monroe." Mariana handed out more prints of a photo of Javier Estrada, wearing his basketball uniform from Lower East Side Preparatory High School. "And see if anybody recognizes Estrada and can place him in the park Friday night."

"Detective," O'Dell said haltingly, "why do we think there is anybody here today who wasn't here yesterday?"

"Because it's a different day," Dru shouted. "If we had something else to chase down, we'd do that, but for now, we're looking for witnesses. Now, get to it."

The officers fanned out as directed, seeking witnesses whose identity and whereabouts they did not know.

"We need something a little more likely to strike oil," Mariana said.

"I know. What are you thinking?"

"We think Angelica was buying weed, which makes her dealer a prime candidate to be either a suspect or a witness." Mariana paused, waiting for either confirmation or contradiction from her partner.

"Right. So, where do we go to find out who that guy might be and where to find him?"

"We have to find the criminals," Mariana winked.

Chapter 17 — The Hangover

THE THIRTY-TWO HOURS since the Angelica Monroe story broke had been the most exciting and exhausting of Hannah's admittedly short career as a producer. She was twenty-six, four years out of journalism school, and at the center of the biggest story in the country. Her segments had been picked up by twenty independent stations, along with the national FOX news. Hannah had used her youth and charm to get the Petra Burroughs exclusive on Friday night. William received lavish praise for his reporting. He occasionally gave Hannah credit for her research and copy—not on air, of course, but behind the scenes.

Dave Butler said he had mentioned to the network executives how happy he was with the stories and what a great job Hannah had done. At the same time, he pushed her to find the next fresh angle. How could she dig even deeper? Hannah was riding a glorious wave. She had given herself permission to increase her allotment of cigarettes from five to seven per day. It helped control her nerves.

She knew what she wanted the next story to be. In the ACN offices on 12th Avenue, after another morning of reporting in the field, Hannah constructed a summary report on Angelica's murder and the police investigation to date, but her attention was elsewhere.

While Terry and William squabbled over where to cut an answer in the video segment, Hannah watched her cell phone, perched precariously on the slightly sloping sound board. She was waiting for her intern, Megan, who was calling medical students named Lars.

The pitch Hannah had created was that Megan was an NYU student who met Lars at a party and that Angelica Monroe had provided his phone number. The network's research department had mined data from several expensive subscription services that reverse-engineered cell phone numbers based on data purchased from social media companies and online retailers. If Megan hit the jackpot, she would try to arrange a meet-up at The Scampering Squirrel. As much as Hannah wanted to make the calls herself, she needed a beard for this rendezvous who was younger and hotter—who could send Lars a selfie and get him to sit down so Hannah could ambush him.

When the editing session ended, Hannah walked to Dave Butler's office and tapped on the door frame. "Hey, Boss."

The managing editor glanced up briefly from the script on his desk and gave his usual grunt of annoyance at being interrupted. Upon recognizing Hannah, he broke into a blank stare, which was, for him, the moral equivalent of a smile. He then returned his attention to his paperwork, while saying, "You're doing some good work, Hawthorne. What's up?"

"I need to let you know I'm working on something that could be seriously hot."

Butler did not look up. "Great. You looking for money?"

"No, Dave, you already approved the research expense. I'm hoping to find the mystery man the cops have been looking for."

"What mystery man?" Butler was famous around the office for having what he considered non-essential conversations with underlings without ever looking up from his work, without any apology.

"He was seen with Angelica Monroe right before she was killed."

Dave removed his reading glasses, tucked his blue editing pencil behind his right ear, and sat back in his high-backed leather chair. "The fuck you say?"

"Yeah. Well, nobody seems to think he's the killer. The thing is, I'm pretty sure he's going to corroborate that Angelica was a dope dealer and went into the park Friday night to meet her source to make a buy. It's a powerful development in the case, and it might even lead the cops to the killer. My plan is to share the information with the police right after we break the story on air."

Dave held up an outstretched index finger, prompting Hannah to cease talking. "Hold that thought, sweetheart. How much would it hinder the police investigation if we held that bit of news back for a while?"

"Dave! What the hell? It's a big deal. They have had a dozen cops and the whole NYU security force looking for this guy. We can't sit on it. At least not for very long."

Dave leaned forward, putting both elbows on the surface of his desk. "We need to be careful with this. I don't think we want to be the network that trashes the girl's reputation. She's still dead. It's still a tragedy. I don't give a shit if she went into the park to snort coke and have sex with the Lacrosse team. We have spent the last two days telling our viewers that this girl was Goldilocks. You keep digging, but clear with me any copy that shines a negative light on our victim. We're in the audience business, Hawthorne. Remember that. You chase away the audience and you lose the game."

"If we run the story, every other network will be all over it in thirty seconds. If our viewers try to change the station, all they will see is our story on re-runs."

Dave picked up his glasses and pointed them toward the doorway. "Let's say you're right about the scoop and about Angelica Monroe. William texted me fifteen minutes ago to say that you two got some good stuff today. We're running that piece all night tonight. Enjoy it and get on to the next one, and then the next one—as long as this train is the lead story. When the train slows down, which should be about two more days, then we can pivot to whatever you want. Maybe you leak your blockbuster story to somebody else and earn a big favor, if it pans out. Or maybe you hold it for yourself for a few days. Your choice. Anything else?"

"No. Not now, Boss. I understand." Before she turned around, he was back to editing a script, blue pencil in hand.

As she walked away, Hannah's phone buzzed with an incoming text. Anticipation turned to puzzlement and then to surprise when she realized the message was from a headhunter who wanted to talk about a producer opening at CNN. She walked and re-read the text. Why would she leave ACN in the middle of the biggest story of her life? She saved the message and hurried back to the editing room.

Chapter 18 — At the Morgue

PAULO PUSHED THROUGH the swinging double doors into the basement space at the New York County medical examiner's laboratory. He had called ahead and knew that Natalie was working by herself on a Sunday morning. She had alerted the security guard in the building lobby to be expecting a friend named Paulo. It wasn't the first time the lobby security guard, Fausto, had seen Paulo. He wasn't exactly a regular, but he was familiar. Fausto lived on Avenue A and 8th Street and knew Paulo's face from the *LES Tribune* website. Paulo greeted him in Spanish and exchanged a fist-bump on his way past the desk. There were times, Paulo thought, when brown-skinned New Yorkers helped each other out. It wasn't often that he had an advantage over his White colleagues—but sometimes.

"Yo, Gorgeous!" he called out into the lab's echoing expanse. It was all tile and chrome and Formica, with nothing to absorb sound. It smelled of rubbing alcohol and chlorine. He could see Natalie's back, covered in green scrubs, working at a steel table. He couldn't see the corpse and didn't care to. He wasn't particularly squeamish, but seeing a body partially carved up by the assistant ME's scalpel was not his preference. He had nothing to prove.

"Take a seat, Paulo," Natalie called without turning around. "I'll be done here in a few minutes."

While Natalie went about her business, Paulo checked his messages and replied to comments from readers on his Facebook and Instagram pages. "The cell service sucks down here."

"Use the wi-fi. The password is bloodandguts99."

Paulo chuckled as he punched in the code to improve his internet signal. His story about Javier Estrada had touched a nerve in the community, generating dozens of comments, mostly fond memories of the basketball star. A few responders remembered him from the grocery store where he worked. A few more, hidden behind internet pseudonyms, posted their joy that another street gang member had been expunged from the world, making New York safer for law-abiding citizens. Paulo left the posts, but did not comment. There was no advantage in it. He would let his readers handle the hate.

These discussions under his articles were good for business, his managing editor Clarence told him. He understood. Engagement and clicks were the measurement of internet success. But he abhorred the process and could not help but feel dirty for fomenting the mostly anonymous vitriol and providing a forum for the haters. It wasn't his call. He was only the writer. His instructions were to interact with the positive comments and encourage them. More readers equaled more significance. It would have been nice if the value of an article were judged by its informational content and not by the number of comments and likes. Maybe they were the same. Maybe not.

Paulo's melancholy mood was broken by Natalie's voice. "Hey. You here to see me or to play on your phone?" Natalie's short brown hair fell along her cheeks, framing her soft face and dark eyes. She peeled off her blue latex gloves and tossed them into a plastic biohazard can. "I'd like to get out of here."

Stuffing his phone in a pocket, Paulo smiled and apologized. "Sorry. I guess I got caught up. Thanks for seeing me."

Natalie and Paulo had gotten along well ever since the reporter wrote a series of articles crediting her for uncovering the critical evidence leading to the conviction of a rapist and murderer who had preyed on young women on the Lower East Side. Paulo had asked Natalie out once but she shut him down quickly. They were friends and professional colleagues. Natalie was clear about her boundaries.

"No problem. I read your article about Javier Estrada. Seems like a sad case. We're off the record, right?"

"Absolutely. I will attribute your comments only to knowledgeable sources, like always."

"Thanks. I know you will, but I have to ask." She took a seat on a high stool next to a raised metal table strewn with microscopes, Petrie dishes, and other lab equipment.

"What can you tell me about Javier that I don't already know—off the record?"

Natalie put an elbow on the table. "The report will eventually be public record, so there's nothing that's really confidential, but this is advance information so make sure it won't come back to me. Maybe you can say you got a peek at the written report, OK?"

"Sure. Fine. No problem." Paulo stopped speaking and looked at Natalie expectantly.

"OK, the first thing is that the kid had no knife wounds. The cops said he was found with a knife and they thought he might have been in a fight. If he was, then he did all the cutting because his body was clean. The second thing is that he had no blood on him besides his own. So, again, if he was in a fight, he didn't do any punching. There were no cuts or bruises on his knuckles or hands to suggest offensive wounds. But there were bruises and scars on the back of his hands and on his arms, legs, and torso consistent with being beaten, probably kicked also. He also had a broken arm and his face was bloodied pretty good. So, if he was in a knife fight, he lost and didn't get cut, but did get beaten."

"Was there any gunpowder residue on his hands?" Paulo asked, unable to wait for the information he most wanted.

Natalie held up a scolding finger. "You have to wait, Mr. Reporter. I have a few other things first."

"Such as?"

"Such as he had a high ankle sprain, with some significant swelling. It's the kind of injury that happens when somebody is running and takes a bad step. If he was injured before he got to the park, he would have been limping and in plenty of pain. I know the kid was a basketball player, so it could have happened during a game. But it explains how he didn't outrun whoever was after him. He was handicapped big time."

"That's significant," Paulo agreed, happy to have the information. "So, we have a kid who was injured, who was beaten pretty badly, and then shot. Was it only one shot?"

"Yes. One shot, likely at pretty close range based on the penetration by the small-caliber bullet. In the chest, piercing his heart. So, he wasn't running away."

"And . . . ?"

"And there was no powder residue on his hands. He didn't shoot anyone."

Paulo lowered his head. "Poor kid."

"Yeah. It looks to me like he was beaten and then executed while he was unable to defend himself."

"Thanks, Natalie. It's what I thought, but it's great to have confirmation."

"This was a good kid, huh?"

"Yeah. He had turned his life around and was headed to college. Everybody says he was clean, helped his family, did well in school, and of course was a terrific hoops player. Everything I know about him says he was probably trying to help the girl in the park and paid the price."

"You gonna write that story?" Natalie raised an eyebrow.

"Count on it." Paulo hopped off his stool. "Thank you. I owe you one for this."

"How about the Mets game next Friday? My nephew wants to visit the press box."

"Nat. I'm not a sports reporter. I can't—"

"Can you make a few calls? Freddie is a big fan."

Paulo relented. "OK. I'll try. I can't promise anything. But if I can't get somebody to get me into the press box, I'll at least get tickets for us. Fair?"

"Fair. Now, I need to clean up and get out of here. Can you let yourself out?"

Paulo waved goodbye and exited through the swinging doors. He stopped before the elevator and pulled out his phone again, this time typing out notes about his off-the-record conversation. The information was consistent with the story he had been forming in his mind. His next report about Javier was going to generate a ton of comments.

Chapter 19 — Descent

LUIS WALKED BRISKLY from the men's bathroom in the office building on 9th Street. Behind him, a tall Black woman wearing tight-fitting jeans had an annoyed scowl. She tucked a black t-shirt into her waistband as she hurried to catch up to Luis. He was running behind schedule after having a four-minute argument with this shark, Tonnie Rae Cowell. The old boss called the distributors the sharks and the overseers the sheriffs. Luis was taught to use the code names during phone calls and conversations in case somebody overheard. The old boss was a smart man. He never even let the sheriffs know his real name. Luis was less impressed by Bull's managerial skills, but Bull had been the boss's chief enforcer. When the boss decided to take his stash of cash and retire to a warmer climate, Bull inherited the leadership role. It was not a democracy.

Tonnie Rae had balked at accompanying him into the men's room. He told her, "No inspection, no meeting with Bull." She was not persuaded, nor was she excited about stripping down in the elevator lobby, which was the only option Luis gave her. When Luis started a two-minute countdown, she finally relented.

Bull was standing at the coffee counter when Luis entered the café. "What the fuck, Luis? I'm waiting forever for your skinny ass."

"Don't give me shit, man! This bitch didn't wanna strip for me, so what was I supposed to do?"

"Don't call me a bitch!" Tonnie Rae had entered the room and stood with her left hand planted on an extended hip. "I don't need this shit."

"Sit the fuck down." Bull gestured toward the table in the back, past the thin curtain.

Tonnie Rae gave Luis a withering stare, then sauntered into Bull's private space.

Luis took a seat at the counter. Tonnie Rae was Bull's last appointment for the day. He was getting tired of the new routine with the sharks and the shit-hole café. Bull knew the owner and gave him a fat bag for his trouble. The bored teenaged barista with three gold rings in her lower lip watched the parade through the otherwise empty venue. The café wasn't technically closed, but while Bull was holding court, nobody lingered. The girl offered Luis a coffee. He requested it iced.

Stirring three sugar packets into his drink, Luis heard the crack of a slap coming from the back room, then the squeal of a wooden chair leg against the smooth floor. "Shit." He jumped from his stool, sloshing some of his iced coffee onto the bar surface.

Luis assumed the position he knew Bull expected, standing immediately outside the curtain to block the woman from dashing away without permission. With his face pressed against the thin fabric, he could see through the gap and hear what happened inside. He wasn't surprised.

Tonnie Rae was pissed off. Bull was annoyed. It was a bad combination. Tonnie Rae was one of the newest sharks and pushed Bull's buttons nearly every time they met. She was taller than Bull, a member of her college basketball team. She might have been stronger, too. Certainly quicker. She wasn't afraid of him. Tonnie Rae grew up in the inner-city area of Baltimore. Luis knew she wasn't carrying a weapon, since he had searched her. Bull knew it, too, which made him less cautious.

"You think 'cause you're a chick you get to give me attitude? Is that it? You think I won't hit back?" Bull's fist shot out in a quick jab, striking the surprised Tonnie Rae square in the nose. Her head snapped backward, but her reflex was not quite fast enough to avoid the blow. She cried out, her hands flying to her face. A trickle of blood oozed across her upper lip.

Bull grabbed a chair and threw the wooden frame against the wall. Luis heard the crunch. Tonnie Rae was on her feet, both arms now in front of her with balled fists. She turned her head toward Luis's location, naturally scouting her escape route. Luis was thin and wiry, but still presented a formidable obstacle to fleeing through the café. For a moment, Luis and Tonnie Rae made eye contact. Her eyes were frightened. His were resigned.

Bull grabbed Tonnie Rae's wrist as her head was turned and pulled her off-balance. She fell toward the wall, but Bull didn't let her hit it. Instead, he yanked her arm and plunged his left fist into her gut. She was tough and athletic, but wasn't prepared for Bull's rage. Tonnie Rae doubled over, gasping for breath.

"You gonna give me more lip now, bitch?!" Tonnie Rae made no audible answer, apparently not able to breathe, let alone speak. Bull, on the other hand, had plenty to say. "You think you're special? Huh?" He kicked Tonnie Rae in the knee, sending her crumpling to the floor. "Good thing it's not basketball season, huh? You got plenty of time to heal up. Now, you got my money? Do ya? Cause when my sharks don't bring me my money, I can get angry, and you don't want to see me angry. This here? This is just me showin' you what a bad idea it is for you to go off and slap me. You do that again and I'll rip your fuckin' arm off. Now, where's my fuckin' money?"

Tonnie Rae had regained enough breath to croak out a response. "I—I got it."

Bull stepped back. Tonnie Rae was on her hands and knees, gasping for air. Luis could see the red welt around her nose. Without standing, she dug a hand into her back pocket and pulled out a neatly clipped stack of folded bills. She held up her arm, not looking.

Bull snatched the clip and carefully counted out the hundreds. "See? That wasn't so fuckin' hard, huh? That's the kind of cooperation I expect from my sharks."

Tonnie Rae slowly got to her feet, glaring at Bull, who turned his back and walked to the corner. He extracted a gallon-sized plastic bag half-filled with weed and pre-rolled joints from a black duffle bag. He held it out to Tonnie Rae, who delicately plucked the huge baggie from Bull's fingers. Then she backed away toward the black curtain, behind which Luis still stood guard. She pulled the fabric apart and made eye contact with Luis, motioning subtly with her head for him to step aside. He did.

"I'll see you in two weeks." Bull pointed his index finger at his shark.

Tonnie Rae took a step through the archway, past Luis. Then, she turned. "Fuck you!" She hurled the baggie of weed back through the curtain toward Bull, then dashed from the café, limping slightly but leaving the two men standing flat-footed and not moving to follow.

"Nice work, Bull. You ran off another shark."

"Big fuckin' deal," Bull reached down to grab the stray bag.

"You know the system the boss set up. The sharks recruit their own replacements so, when they graduate, we have another shark to take over the territory. That's a big fuckin' part of the system. Now you got two schools—maybe three—where you got no shark. How you gonna find new ones, huh?"

"Shut the fuck up!" Bull spat, stuffing the baggie back into his duffle and zipping the top. "I got this under control."

"Do ya? Really? Cause it don't look like it to me."

"Yeah? Well, it's good that you're not running the show." Bull yanked the duffle onto his shoulder and pushed past Luis into the café's main room. He strode out the door, leaving Luis standing next to the black curtain.

Luis snatched his iced coffee from the bar, spilling more of it from its lidless cup and waving to the emotionless barista. Out on the street, Luis didn't see Bull or Tonnie Rae. He shook his head, mumbling to himself, "This shit is goin' to Hell."

Chapter 20 — One More Question

CANVASING THE PARK and the school all day Sunday did not produce any valuable witnesses. It seemed that anyone who had information about weed selling either lost their memory or decided to avoid Washington Square Park. It was not much of a surprise.

Dru and Mariana reached out to the lower Manhattan narco unit, but got only belly laughs when they inquired about weed dealers. With heroin, Fentanyl, crack, and meth creating headlines and public health emergencies, local entrepreneurs illegally selling weed, which was legal to sell if you had the right license, was an exceedingly low priority. They sent two teams of uniforms out to visit the known residences of several locals who had been arrested before legal weed undermined the hell out of their business. None of them produced any helpful leads.

A frustrated Mariana tossed her note pad into the back seat of their sedan at 5:30. "I feel like we're spinning our wheels and not getting anywhere."

"We've been through this plenty of times," Dru soothed. "We keep digging until we hit something."

"Sure, but usually there's something to follow. The money, or the people with a motive, or the forensics. Here, we got squat."

"Don't tell that to the press." Dru slid into the passenger seat.

* * *

AT SIX-FIFTEEN, timed to make it easy for the local television news programs to do a live cut-in, the NYPD scheduled a press briefing on the Angelica Monroe murder. The police commissioner, Earl Ward, provided the briefing personally, which was unusual. Normally, his communications director or a lead detective would handle a briefing, especially when there was not much to report. This case, however, was so hot and was garnering such media attention that the commissioner wanted to be in front of the cameras himself.

Ward was not the first Black commissioner, but the combination of a Black mayor and a Black police chief was a first for the city. There was nothing racial about Angelica's murder, except that an increasing number of news outlets were making the case out to be one of a White girl gunned down by a Black or Hispanic assailant and another example of the danger of liberal government allowing dangerous criminals—mostly minorities— to escape prosecution and be released from jail with little or no bail. No actual evidence suggested that Angelica's killer was not White. In fact, statistically more shootings were committed by White criminals. But the news outlets who wanted to use the case as part of a political point were happy to make the assumption that this case fell outside the statistical norm.

The commissioner had been briefed on the possible connection between Angelica's murder and Javier's. This connection, however, was not something he wanted to talk about. The media swarm was already accosting anyone connected to Angelica, making the police investigation harder. He didn't want the same to happen on the Estrada side of the investigation. The commissioner also didn't want to feed speculation. Javier had a connection to a street gang, albeit several years before. He would likely be characterized as a "former gang member," which was code for "minority thug." Javier would also likely be characterized as a suspect, which he most certainly was not. The department didn't need that.

For appearances' sake, Dru and Mariana were required to be at the press conference, standing in the background. It took valuable time away from the investigation, but the commissioner wanted it to seem like they were available to provide any key bits of information necessary to answer a question. The reality was that nobody was going to answer any questions; the investigation so far had exactly zero in the way of relevant information, even if they were inclined to share with the media. However, having the detectives there gave the appearance of control and progress.

Commissioner Ward made an initial statement about how the NYPD was following a number of leads and had dozens of officers working through the weekend tracking them down. The department would not rest until the cowardly killer was brought to justice. He hoped the networks would break away quickly, not wanting to fill their six o'clock news with boring questions and answers. He had no control over those decisions, however.

The first question was, by pre-arrangement, from Dexter Peacock, a reporter from *The New York Times*. Peacock was the dean of the local reporters who covered city hall, local politics, and crime. "Have you identified any suspects yet?"

Commissioner Ward was expecting the question. "We have a security camera image of one person of interest, who was with Angelica Monroe Friday night shortly before her murder. This person is only wanted for questioning. He is not a suspect at this time." Ward's communications director pressed the SEND button on her phone, emailing a distribution list of local press contacts with the mystery man's blurry image. "We're sending you the photo now, hoping someone will recognize the man or that he will see himself and come forward to aid our investigation. We have a number of additional leads in the case, but nothing we can disclose at this time."

Ward and his closest deputies had debated whether to release the photo. They knew that, if he were publicly identified, the press would make the man's life miserable. They hoped to get a tip or that he would come forward voluntarily. After nearly two days of futility, they decided that enlisting the public's help was the most likely way to find their mystery man.

Amid the clamor of thirty reporters shouting questions, Ward pointed to a reporter from *The New York Post*. "Have you recovered the murder weapon?"

Ward artfully parried. "I'm not at liberty to give out details about an active investigation."

Virginia Healy, the communications director who was running the press conference, announced that there would be time for only one more question. She had managed the event brilliantly and wanted her boss to get off the podium without any major gaffes. She looked around the room and pointed at the reporter least likely to cause a problem. Ward, following her suggestion, extended an arm.

"Thank you. Paulo Richardson, *Lower East Side Tribune*. The community is obviously upset about the two murders Friday night. My sources tell me that the shooting of Javier Estrada in Washington Square Park is definitely connected to Angelica Monroe. Can you tell us the status of the investigation into Javier's murder?"

A murmur washed across the assembled members of the press at this new bit of information. Ward glanced down and to his right, where Virginia stood, her face a lump of confusion. She held up a thumb and forefinger close together, indicating that a short answer would end the session.

Ward gave Paulo a warm smile and looked directly into the three cameras lined up in the back of the room. "We are all heartbroken over the loss of young Mr. Estrada. His death is tragic and another example of a shooting in our city that we cannot tolerate. Our legislators in New York have tried to give us tools to combat the flow of guns onto our streets, but the national gun lobby and the Republicans in congress refuse to take the action needed to curb this scourge. Since this is also an ongoing investigation, I cannot comment on any possible connection to other active cases."

"And that's all the time we have today, ladies and gentleman. Thank you all so much for coming." Virginia was standing at the podium by the time she finished and waved to the sea of raised hands from the disappointed reporters who never got their turn to ask a question. As Ward climbed down the two steps from the platform, the reporters shouted, but he waved a dismissive hand before disappearing through the exit door.

* * *

AFTER THE PRESS CONFERENCE, the local TV crews hurried to set up positions for live shots back to their studios, while the print reporters funneled out of the cramped space. Paulo stuffed his notebook into a worn leather briefcase. A loud throat-clearing "Ahem" caused him to raise his gaze and see the familiar bearded face of Dexter Peacock.

"May I inquire about why you think there is a connection between the Angelica Monroe murder and your neighborhood boy, Mr. . . . . Estrada?" Peacock had to consult his own notepad to remember the name. The always dapper Peacock wore his signature brown tweed jacket. Absent was his ubiquitous bowler hat, which his manners would not permit him to wear indoors.

Paulo barely suppressed a smirk, which quickly morphed into a sneer of reproach. Peacock had won every award available for a print reporter. He had never before given Paulo a second glance, despite meeting him at many local press events, including one where he presented Paulo an award. Paulo was sure Peacock would not have spoken to him except that he now had information the older reporter wanted to appropriate.

"Let's just say that Javier Estrada's story is worth telling and you can read about it tomorrow morning under my byline. I'm certain there is a connection to the Monroe case. I'm currently working several angles to prove it. If you learn of something that might help me, you give me a call and we'll see if an exchange of information might be mutually beneficial." Paulo pushed past Peacock and marched toward the door.

Chapter 21 — The Ringmaster

LUIS STRETCHED OUT on the brick steps leading down from the courtyard door of his apartment building. The scrubby tufts of grass in the quad between three twenty-story block towers barely outnumbered the islands of cracked, dry dirt. In the diminishing twilight, two teams of bedraggled pre-teens kicked a soccer ball back and forth, shooting toward goals drawn with chalk on the brick walls on either end. Pungent weed smoke wafted from the stoop, where three well-muscled young men sat or stood around Luis. Enrique, a broad-shouldered Black man wearing a San Diego Chargers jersey, passed a bottle of Michelob from a soft-sided cooler to Wilmer, a skinny, brown-skinned scarecrow in a plain white t-shirt covered by a red hoodie. Everyone had either a joint, a butt, or a bottle.

Luis, in blue jeans, a tight-fitting black t-shirt with a faded silver Nike logo, and a backward-facing Yankees cap, sucked on the last of his roach, then held in the smoke. When he finally exhaled and tossed away the spent paper, he pointed a bony finger toward Enrique. "You ain't afraid of Bull, are you, Q?"

"That's not the point," came the deep bass reply. In another life, Enrique could have been on stage in an R&B group, fighting off groupies after a smooth, soulful set. "Bull ain't coming for me 'cause he ain't got no reason. I'm not picking a fight with him."

"Well, you should think about it. You all should," Luis gestured around the misshapen circle of comrades. "Bull is out of fucking control. He's got a fine setup going, not that he built it. It was the boss who had enough brains to get it going. Bull just fell into it when the boss bailed."

"We're all doin' fine," Wilmer said, without much enthusiasm.

"Yeah. Sure," Luis glared at the smaller man. "You're fine as long as Bull holds it all together. Now, he's going crazy on us. I was there when he shot that girl. How does he do that? He's taking out his own sharks. When is one of you going to be next, huh? When will you fuck up enough for him to blow a fuse and put a knife in your back or a slug in your head?"

"Chill out, man," Oscar scolded. Oscar had run with Bull almost as long as Luis. His skin was so pale his childhood friends called him Casper. When he filled out and developed muscles and a mean streak, the ghost jokes disappeared. "If he goes down, then he goes down. We ain't got to help it happen. Long as he's there, he takes the heat. I'm good with that."

"You're good?" Luis jumped to his feet, looking down at his seated companions. "You're all fucking good until Bull gets busted and we all go down with him for murder."

"We ain't killed nobody," Enrique boomed.

"No. We ain't. But anybody with him when he takes out somebody is an accomplice. You don't think Bull will try to pin it on one of us to save his ass? You don't think he'd make a deal and sell us out?" Nobody spoke. "That's what I thought. You know he would. I'm not goin' down for him."

"Yeah? So, what're you thinking?" Wilmer took a long swig from his beer.

Luis went quiet, both thinking and making sure he had everyone's attention—and waiting for Wilmer to swallow. "If Bull goes away, we all keep the business going. We get a bigger cut and we don't go around fucking killing people."

"I'm not ratting out Bull," Oscar piped up. "You do what you want, but I ain't doin' it."

"It ain't right, man," Enrique's deep voice filled the courtyard. Everyone respected Q, because he had done a stint in prison already in his short life. "None of us gonna rat out anybody. We got a problem, we take care of it ourselves."

Luis looked around at a group of faces that all seemed to be agreeing with Enrique. "You're right. We need to do it ourselves. I think it's time we tell Bull we're voting him out of office."

"It's not a fucking democracy," Oscar pointed out.

"You got some plan?" Wilmer asked.

"Yeah." Luis looked around the group. "I need to know I'll have support, which it looks like I do. What we gotta understand is that Bull needs us more than we need him." Luis looked around the group, making eye contact with each companion. He was confident they had his back. They were his boys. He had recruited each of them to join the gang when the old boss was still in charge.

Wilmer said. "He ain't gonna walk away without a fight."

"If he wants a fight, I'll give him one," Luis puffed out his chest. He was fifty pounds lighter than Bull. Taking him on solo was not likely to end well for Luis. "But you have to have my back. If he knows we're all together, what can he do?"

"He can round up his guys," Enrique said. "He's got Ramone and Diego. He brought them in. They're his boys. What're we gonna do about that? We gonna have a war, four on three?"

"That ain't gonna end well." Wilmer tossed his empty bottle into a nearby garbage can with a clang.

"I'll work it out." Luis jumped up to the top step. "We gotta stick together and we'll make this happen. You got me?"

The three others all voiced their support.

Then, Enrique said, "As long as you got a damn good plan."

Chapter 22 — Hoops Time

AFTER THE PRESS CONFERENCE, while another demonstration got underway in Washington Square Park, Dru and Mariana watched a basketball game on the street courts at Sixth Avenue and 3rd Street.

"These guys are better than the Knicks," Dru observed.

"That's not saying much," Mariana quipped back.

"Hey, that was true a few years ago, but now my Knicks are damned good! We clinched the playoffs."

A group of young men sitting on the first row of the courtside bleachers overheard Dru's defense of the Knicks and shouted encouragement. Each had an athletic bag nearby and two held basketballs. It didn't take Sherlock Holmes to identify them as a team ready to take the court next.

At a nod from Dru, Mariana strolled over and stood next to the group. She pulled out a photo of Javier Estrada in his high school basketball uniform. During a lull in the game, she tapped the nearest player on the shoulder.

"I know you?" The boy was thin and all arms and legs, wearing a Knicks jersey and white Jordans. He didn't appear hostile, just confused at the appearance of a lady much older than the average street-ball fan. Mariana wasn't quite old enough to be the mother of any of the players, but her professional clothing was as out of place as her age.

"No. I'm a detective. NYPD. I'm investigating a murder. You know this guy?" She held out the photo of Javier.

The player glanced at the photo, then held it close to his face and took a long look. "Did you say murder?"

"I did." Mariana said nothing else, waiting for the boy to tell her what his face was already clearly showing her.

"Oh, man. Somebody killed Javy?"

"I'm afraid so. You play with him?"

"I played against him. He was smooth, man. That's fucked up."

"I agree. You play against him on Friday night?"

"Last Friday?" The boy hesitated, looking up at the lights beating down on the court. Mariana could tell he was counting backward, thinking about when he had last played with Javier. "Yeah. Yeah, we did. He was here for a few games with his crew."

"Anybody from Javier's team here tonight?"

The boy looked around, then shook his head. "Nah. Those dudes are here mostly on Fridays."

"You remember when Javier left on Friday?"

"Naw. I dunno."

Mariana was not convinced. "Were you on the court with him on Friday?"

"Yeah. We were."

"Did you win or lose?"

"We lost. It was a close game, though. We coulda beat 'em."

"So, after you lost, did Javier's team stay and take the next game?"

"Yeah, I think so."

"Did you stay and watch?" The live game had resumed, causing Mariana to move away from the court's edge and sit on the first row of bleachers, turning to face her witness.

"Yeah. We did. We had next after that so we stayed."

"Did Javier's team win the next game?"

"They did, but they didn't stay to play us again."

"That sucks," Mariana tried to sympathize with the plight of the players who didn't get a rematch. "Did you stay and play the next game?"

"Yeah, we did, but it wasn't good. Bunch of pick-ups. We smoked 'em."

"Was that your last game of the night?"

"I think so. After that we bailed."

"You remember what time it was when you left?"

"I don't know, man."

Mariana was not ready to give up. "Where'd you go afterward?"

"Nowhere. We went to get a slice, I think, over on Fourth."

"Great. Nice reward after a night of ball. When you got there, was the Knicks game still on the TV?"

"Nah. It was over, but the highlights show was on, so we watched that."

"Great. So, how long do you think your game took, with the pick-up guys you smoked? A half-hour?"

"Longer. Games run four ten-minute quarters, so about an hour with time outs and shit."

"OK, so the game before yours, the one where Javier played, that one was probably over by eight-thirty or so then. Does that sound about right?"

"I don't know, man. I wasn't watching the clock."

"OK. Thanks. You've been very helpful."

"That's cool. Man, it's too bad about Javy. He was fucking good."

Mariana sauntered back around the court, careful not to interfere with the play around her. When she got back to Dru, he said, "You had a nice long chat with that guy. I assume he got your number?"

"Screw you." Mariana worked hard, but unsuccessfully, at maintaining a straight face. "He confirmed that Javier was here Friday night and left somewhere around eight-thirty. That would give him the right amount of time to change out of his sweaty clothes and shoes and head home, cutting through Washington Square Park at the time Angelica Monroe was murdered."

"OK. The story makes sense. The kid was there. The ME says he had no powder residue on his hands, so he wasn't the shooter. So, what? A bystander caught in the wrong place at the wrong time?"

Mariana watched a player on the court execute a 360-degree dunk. "Looks that way. Let's go to the park."

* * *

DRU AND MARIANA WALKED back down 3rd Street toward the park. The sidewalk bustled with activity. The April temperatures were still running warm, encouraging the pedestrians to stroll rather than rush to their next destination. They passed the NYU security guard shack, turned north, then walked through a gate into the park. Following the paved path, which wound through bushes and trees, they arrived at the large plaza around the central fountain.

"Why does the kid stop and end up dropping his bag over by the clearing next to the elm tree?" Dru turned and retraced their steps along the path, Mariana on his heels.

Halfway back to the park exit, Mariana stopped. "Here."

"What?"

Mariana pointed to the north, through a small hole between segments of the bushes that formed a hedge next to the path. "The

Hangman's Elm is that way, through this gap." She pushed past the bushes onto a thin dirt path snaking through the trees. Dru followed, brushing away leaves from the surrounding underbrush. After forty paces, Mariana emerged past a row of forsythia bushes into a clearing. Fifty feet to the north, a pile of flower bouquets, stuffed toys, and candles surrounded the Hangman's Elm, spreading out in a circle.

Dru looked down. A yellow flag on a three-inch wire protruded from the ground, its corner partially chewed by a park rodent. "This is where the officers found the Emirates Airlines bag."

"So, Javier came through this way and dropped his bag. What happened next?"

"A better question," Dru turned around to examine the narrow path they had traversed, "is what happened before. What made him veer off the paved path on his way home? Why push through the bushes toward the tree? It's way off his course. He's in a hurry. Why stop?"

"He heard a shot?"

"That might do it. He hears the shot. But what's he thinking? A shot in a dark park isn't generally a reason to run toward the sound."

"What if he heard the girl scream?"

"After that shot to the head? I doubt she made a sound."

"No, Dru—before the shot. What if she screamed first? Maybe he would run toward the scream to see if somebody needed help."

"OK. I'll buy that. He runs through the bushes, sees . . . something happening by the Elm. The girl is already dead on the ground. Why does he drop his bag?"

"He needs his arms free. The bag is in the way. We found a knife with his prints on it near his body. He was in a knife fight. He'd want to ditch the bag during a fight."

Dru walked around the perimeter of the clearing. A group of four young women entered from the north, carrying bundles of flowers. Seeing the two detectives, they hustled to the pool of memorial items, deposited their offerings, then scurried away. Dru scanned the ground, imagining the fight. "Does he injure his ankle in the fight?"

"Could be. He's hurt, then he tries to run away. Two men chase him. They catch him on the other side of the park, beat him up, then shoot him."

"It makes sense, except for the different guns."

"Two men, two guns." Dru walked toward the fountain, retracing the possible route of Javier and his unknown assailants. "They're chasing him because he's a witness to Angelica Monroe's murder."

"That plays." The two detectives arrived back at the fountain plaza.

"Stay here." Mariana marched away. She approached the nut vendor. "Hola, Senor Rojas." She purchased a bag of candied cashews and asked him in Spanish, "You told us yesterday how you saw a man run limping across the plaza, then two other men ran after him. When you saw them, did they come into the plaza where Detective Cook is standing?" She pointed to Dru, who waved meekly.

"Si," the vendor confirmed. "That spot, for sure."

Mariana thanked Mr. Rojas, then returned to Dru, offering him the bag of nuts. She knew they were his favorite. "He says the men he saw were in the same spot where you're standing."

"Great." Dru popped a cashew. "We have a theory of what happened. Now the only question is, who were the two guys chasing Javier?"

"We still think maybe Angelica's dealer?"

"Sure," Dru agreed. "But it still doesn't quite figure why a weed dealer would execute a customer."

"Sex. Jealousy. Greed. Mistaken identity."

"I don't buy mistaken identity, but I'll give you the other three." Dru laughed and offered Mariana the cashew bag.

* * *

BY SUNDAY NIGHT, the memorial to Angelica Monroe extended forty feet out from the base of the Hangman's Elm. An NYU maintenance crew was dispatched to tidy up the area, stack the flowers, and make sure the candles were enclosed in containers that would not start a fire when they burned down. On the sidewalk outside the park, three vendors sold items for the students, area residents, and tourists to lay on the memorial pile. Pink teddy bears with a white cursive inscription reading "Angel" were the most popular. Pre-printed models inscribed with "Angelica" were not available.

The Facebook memorial page for Angelica had passed 500,000 likes and had more than twenty thousand comments and photos. The GoFundMe raising reward money for information about Angelica's killer had received $10,546 in donations.

Angelica's murder was the front page story on all the New York newspapers. It was still the lead story on all the local news broadcasts, but the amount of time devoted to those segments shrunk to under a minute. There was little new information to report, but all the local outlets still had reporters on the scene at Washington Square Park and went to live remotes for all their broadcasts. The national cable outlets did the same. Once the resources were in place, they had to be used to justify the expense.

On the internet, the social media hits on Angelica's murder were down on Sunday. There were fewer videos and new images to share. The chatter about the social and political issues swirling around the case also slowed down after the most vocal posters had said their piece and moved on to other topics. Search results for the keywords and hashtags associated with Angelica were still in the top one hundred.

In Washington Square Park, Sunday's vigil had a decidedly more religious bent, with preachers from a dozen denominations and religious groups present to say prayers and make their points about brotherhood, peace, and the need to protect citizens from violence in our cities. Several local politicians showed up, but toned down the overtly political rhetoric in deference to the priests, rabbis, and imams. The assembled news crews around the park dutifully covered the events at the services, but the videos and interviews got limited play, except on the cable outlets like ACN that had overnight news programming to fill. Behind the scenes, all the networks began discussing how much longer to staff the on-site teams at the park without any important developments in the case.

Chapter 23 — Reaction

Monday

ON MONDAY, NYU cancelled classes. Six grief counselors were dispatched to various points around campus, including the lobby of Angelica Monroe's dorm building, to help students deal with the tragedy. The university president sent an email to the parents of all students, expressing his grief and assuring them that this was a random incident and not an indication of any increase in the crime rate in the NYU area. The note rattled off statistics about how violent crime in the neighborhood was down for three consecutive years and pledged an increase in campus security.

The chairwoman of the university alumni association sent out a similar email, assuring the university's most loyal donors, former students, and future parents that the campus was as safe as ever and promising to work with university administration and security to review safety protocols.

At the Lower East Side Preparatory High School, the morning announcements included a ten-second moment of silence for Javier Estrada. Students were invited to attend the funeral service that afternoon at five o'clock at the local church the Estrada family attended. The principle gave instructions to add Javier's name to the memorial plaque sitting inside a plexiglass case near the front entrance. The case included the trophy from the NYC Public Schools basketball championship and several other awards. In the center, the memorial reminded everyone of the two students who had died during that school year. Now there would be three names on the plaque. It was April, so the principal hoped they could get through the year and stay under the annual average.

The boys' basketball coach had all his physical education classes watch the last twenty minutes of the NYC Public Schools championship game from the prior December. Javier led the team to an unexpected victory. He then had them all observe five minutes of silence in memory of their murdered classmate.

The New York Post and the *Daily News* both ran small stories in the sports sections about the promising high school basketball star who was killed over the weekend. The reports did not mention any connection between Javier and the Angelica Monroe story, which was still on the front page of the papers and at the top of the local television broadcasts.

Chapter 24 — Background Check

DRU AND MARIANA GOT the full juvenile file on Javier Monday morning. They also read Paulo Richardson's story in the *Lower East Side Tribune*, detailing information provided by the family and school contacts. The information painted a compelling picture of Javier as a kid who had turned his life around.

"Success story," Dru said while biting into a breakfast sandwich.

"Yeah," Mariana said, "now he's a dead winner."

A phone call to the property crimes division yielded a lengthy background summary from a detective named Howard Patterson, who was from the neighborhood. According to Patterson, Javier Estrada was connected to a street gang called the Antipático, which meant "bad ass" in Spanish. The gang had a constantly changing membership that ranged from fifteen to forty teens, mixed with a few older boys who never outgrew the racket and got a real life.

"We'd like to track down some of the gang members who were around when Estrada was active in the gang and see if they can give us any leads," Dru said.

Patterson rattled off the names of several known leaders, along with the places around the Lower East Side where groups of members tended to congregate.

Dru and Mariana quickly realized they needed more help if they were going to gather meaningful information. They started making calls.

"There certainly is a connection between the two murders," Dru explained to the third departmental official in the past half hour. "Right now, it's our best chance to find a lead on the Monroe murder."

"We don't want to pull any resources off the Monroe investigation," Deputy Commissioner Albert Knowles responded.

"Fine!" Dru reined himself in from shouting even louder. "Leave those officers in place searching for witnesses in the Park and interviewing students, but give me four more uniforms to question the . . . contacts who might be able to help us find the killer. Guys from the Lower East Side, maybe from the Bowery precinct."

"Give me a minute," Knowles said before muting his phone.

Dru pushed his own mute button and shook his head softly toward Mariana. "They don't get it."

"Good decision not to use the words 'gang members' for the dudes we want to question."

"Thanks. I was sure as soon as we said it was connected to the Monroe investigation, we'd get whatever we wanted."

"It's probably my fault," Mariana leaned against the squad car guarding the command post.

"Why's that?"

"Knowles figures it's me pushing for more resources on the Estrada case and he wants to deny it just to mess with me."

Dru's angry eyes softened. "Don't give yourself too much credit. Not everyone in headquarters hates you that much."

Mariana couldn't suppress a quick smile. "Thanks for the vote of confidence. Lately, I feel like I have a target on my back."

"You do. It's just not quite as big as you think."

Knowles's voice welled up from Dru's muted phone. "Cook?"

"Yeah," Dru said, then remembered to unmute himself. "Yeah?"

"I'm sending you two units for the rest of the day shift. That's it. No overtime."

"Thanks." Dru shot Mariana a satisfied glance. "We'll wait for them here at the park." He clicked off his phone, not wanting to hear any additional restrictions from the deputy commissioner.

* * *

AT FOUR O'CLOCK, the four officers assigned to the Estrada background detail gathered back at the NYPD command post. Each pair of uniforms reported on their interviews with the Lower East Side youth. Virtually all the local boys knew Javier because of his hoops prowess. The kid was a neighborhood legend. Several bragged about Javier having been an Antipático member. To a man, they swore Javier had not hung with the group for at least two years, which was consistent with the intel they already had. There was, however, one interesting bit of intelligence that made the two detectives perk up.

Officers Amed Rachman and Jenny McDonald had spent a half-hour with five older boys, who denied that they were gang members. Two of them confirmed that Javier was tight with a boy several years older named Luis Torres.

"One dude was a ball player and said he played with Javier sometimes," McDonald reported. "He was pissed off enough about the kid getting shot that he was willing to talk. He said he didn't know who killed Estrada, but he would tell me if he knew. What he did say was that this guy, Torres, sold weed."

Mariana and Dru exchanged a look. Mariana asked, "Did the kid know how to find Torres?"

"Nah. He said he didn't know. He also said Torres was in with a guy named Bull."

"Bull what?" Dru looked puzzled.

"No idea. Said he didn't know the dude's real name. Just Bull. But he was freaking scared of him. He was all brave and ready to talk about Torres and about Javier, but as soon as Bull came up, he clammed up. Said he had nothing to say about Bull."

"Did Javier have any connection to Bull?"

"Not that anyone would say," McDonald looked at her partner for confirmation and got a grunt and a nod.

"OK. Good work, Officers. You're off duty. Go reward yourselves." By the time Dru had dismissed the uniforms, Mariana was on her phone calling the precinct to gather some information about Luis Torres. After several minutes, she punched her speaker button so Dru could hear the desk sergeant's report.

"Torres has a rap sheet, but nothing serious. He's listed as a known associate of a real low-life named Reggie Millen, who is known on the street as Bull. Millen has arrests for drug possession with intent, aggravated assault, and attempted murder. No convictions. The attempted murder was a knife fight."

"Knife, eh? And drugs?" Dru turned to Mariana with a raised eyebrow. "They found a knife with Estrada."

"Yeah, but it had only the kid's prints on it."

"But there was some blood, too, right?"

"I think so."

Dru shouted toward the phone's speaker, "Do you know if we ran a DNA match on that blood sample?"

"I'll give you ten-to-one on a sawbuck that nobody ordered a DNA spread on Javier Estrada's knife," Mariana whispered to Dru.

"You're right." Dru waved a dismissive hand.

Mariana ended the call. "This scumbag, Bull, is maybe a drug dealer and has a history of violence. We think the Monroe girl was distributing."

"She was shot, though. Not a blade," Dru pointed out.

Mariana lowered her chin, looking at Dru with the tops of her eyes. "C'mon. A street thug like this guy is gonna have a gun, too."

"Her shirt was ripped. Maybe we're looking at this the wrong way. Maybe it was an attempted rape. The autopsy didn't show any sexual assault, but maybe the girl fought back and then the Bull shot her."

"OK," Mariana relaxed into a normal posture. "Let's say that's a viable scenario. Javier's on his way home, hears the girl scream, walks down the path through the bushes, finds her there being assaulted, drops his bag, tries to intervene. There are two guys with the girl. They chase Javier, who is either already injured from his basketball game or sprains his ankle during the fight. They chase him across the park, where Mr. Rojas, the nut vendor, sees them. They get to the other side of the park and one of the two guys shoots him with the little .22, which may have been taken from Monroe. How's that for a viable theory?"

Dru kicked the ground. "It feels like it could be close. But we're a long way from putting this guy Reggie at the scene, or proving he pulled the trigger."

Chapter 25 — When the Well Runs Dry

AFTER THREE DAYS, the Angelica Monroe story had been gnawed to the bone by dozens of reporters from every major network and local news outlet. There was nothing left to say about the tragic victim. After the live reports for the Monday morning news shows, the crews packed up and, one by one, retracted their satellite dishes and drove their news vans back to their garages for some much-needed cleaning. The sea of flowers and stuffed animals around the tree had reached a saturation point and wasn't growing larger.

The media outlets were eager to pivot from Angelica's backstory to the apprehension of her killer. Any nugget of information about the progress of the investigation or the identity of potential suspects would have been manna from heaven. The police, unfortunately, were locked down like a Papal convention.

That afternoon at 4:45—a time calculated to avoid live coverage since the police had nothing significant to report—Virginia Healy spent ten minutes saying nothing to the assembled reporters, who all knew there was no big break to report on but who were obligated to attend, just in case.

After the presser ended, while Terry was breaking down the ACN camera equipment, Hannah slid next to Paulo, who was chatting with some other print reporters.

Paulo waved his arms as he made a point. "I'm telling you; Javier Estrada is the key to unraveling the Angelica Monroe murder." He looked at each of his three fellow journalists and saw only skeptical faces.

"Your boy, Estrada, is also a crying shame," Dexter Peacock, from *The New York Times* replied with a condescending tone. "But he has a record of gang membership."

"That was years ago!" Hannah watched the muscles around Paulo's jaw clench.

"Maybe, Sport, but nobody is going to get excited about a dead gang member." Peacock turned and walked toward the exit door, followed by the other two reporters.

"Except you," Hannah said quietly enough that only Paulo heard.

"What about you, Hawthorne? Do you give a shit?"

Hannah relaxed her tense shoulders, rolling them backward. "I care about the story. That's my job. I get a great story and I move up. That's how it works. If Estrada is connected and we figure it out and that gets me a scoop, then I'm happy. If that helps Estrada's posthumous reputation, then great. If the story turns out to be that Estrada pulled the trigger, then it's fine with me."

"We?" Paulo interrupted with a raised eyebrow.

"What?"

"You said *we*. If *we* figure it out."

"Yeah, well, aren't we working together on this?" Hannah looked up at the taller man with her best doe-eyes. "Besides, I think you're right about Estrada. I haven't figured out why yet. But I tell you what, I'm about to get something really big. So, if you have anything that will connect the dots, maybe we can work out an exchange of assets."

Paulo put a hand on Hannah's shoulder and guided her toward the front of the room. He leaned down, putting his dark eyes even with the side of her face. "You figure my reporting isn't really your competition, is that it?"

Hannah smoothed her hair and tucked a stray strand behind her ear. "I suppose that's right, but I also respect you as a journalist and believe that if you think there's a connection, then your information is worth listening to."

"Thanks. You're not bad yourself—for a TV shill." He tapped her arm as he cracked a smile. "We could both use a break. I suppose you want me to go first?"

"We can't talk at the same time. Besides, my reporter is gone, so there's nothing I can do with any information for a few hours."

Paulo motioned to a folding chair, where a stenographer had been sitting during the press conference. As Hannah sat, Paulo took a knee at her side. "I don't have confirmation of this yet, so you can't broadcast it. If you get corroboration you have to tell me immediately, on the record. Agreed?"

"I don't know what it is yet. How about if I say yes, but only if I agree that the information is worth it."

"Fine. Good enough for me. This is between us. I've been told that the cops found a shoulder bag belonging to Javier at the scene of Angelica Monroe's murder. According to his little brother, Javier carried the bag when he went to play ball over on the west side. He had his Air Jordans in it, which he would never leave lying around. The cops didn't know who it belonged to at first, but now they do. Javier was murdered on the other side of the park, but he was near the Hangman's Elm, with his bag, sometime shortly before."

"Do they think Javier killed her?"

"No!" Paulo said louder than he intended. They both glanced around the room, which had cleared out. Only a few techs in the back futzing with their equipment still lingered. None seemed to pay any attention. He lowered his voice again. "I think Javier saw the murder and whoever killed Angelica also killed him."

"OK, so, how does that help the cops—or us—figure out who the killer is?"

"I don't know, but establishing a definite connection is big— and it might get some of these fools to pay some attention to Javier's murder."

"Why didn't you just give the information to Dexter Stuck-Up-Cock so he can put it in *The Times*?" It was a rhetorical question, so Hannah was not surprised by Paulo's blank stare. "Seriously, how do you stand that guy?"

"I don't. But he has connections and resources, so I have to pretend."

"Sorry about that. I agree the information is significant, but it still leaves a lot of holes in the story. I guess mine is similar."

"Spill, girl. I want to hear yours now."

Hannah glanced toward Terry in the back of the room. He was done packing up and was staring at her with raised eyebrows. "I'm working out a meeting with the mystery man who was seen on a security camera Friday night with Angelica a few minutes before she was killed. I found him. I don't know what he's going to tell me, but it's going to be exclusive information."

Paulo was silent, then tilted his head until his left ear nearly touched his shoulder. "Could be huge, or could be nothing. But very interesting. How'd you find him?"

"Nuh-uh, I'm not giving up *all* my secrets." Hannah sat back in her chair and crossed her arms, causing her breasts to push upward.

"Okay, okay, fine. You just climbed a notch higher on my respect meter. When are you talking to the guy?"

"Not sure. Maybe today. Maybe tomorrow. We're working on it."

"OK." Paulo stood up, stretching his back. "I tell you what, I'll give you first look at anything I get on Javier and you give me whatever you get on the mystery man, provided each of us gets to publish our own scoop first. That work for you?"

Hannah made eye contact again with Terry, who pointed to his watch. "I'm in. You tell anyone I'm sharing with you and I'll get fired."

"If my fellow print journalists find out I'm collaborating with a cable slug, they'll hang me by my balls. So, mutually assured destruction, eh?"

"Yeah, sure, but my job is more important to me than your balls." Hannah stood and held out her right hand with her pinky finger extended. Paulo hooked her finger with his own. "I'll call you." She hurried to the back of the room, picked up a black equipment case, and followed Terry out the door.

* * *

WHEN HANNAH CHECKED IN with the studio, her intern, Megan, reported that she had made contact with Lars. She was engaged in a delicate dance, attempting to entice the reluctant foreign med student to meet. Megan sent him a provocative selfie after texting him with the pitch that she had met him at a party and that she was a friend of Angelica Monroe. For two hours, Megan had exchanged sporadic messages, without reeling in her fish.

At six o'clock, Hannah's phone rang. It was Megan. "He's meeting me tonight."

"Lars?"

"No, Spider-man. Who do you think?"

"Sorry. Wonderful job, Megan. Where and when?"

"He agreed to meet at The Scampering Squirrel. He seemed to know the place. Eight o'clock tonight. But I tell you what, Hannah, I'm a little worried. What if this guy is the murderer?

What if he thinks me saying I know Angelica makes me a loose end? He might want to kill *me*."

"You've been watching too many murder mysteries on television," Hannah chided her young colleague. "But, you're right that meeting a guy who might be connected to the murder could have some risk. We'll need to get some security to be there, just in case."

"You think William Wilson would want to help?" The tone of Megan's voice suggested that she, like many other younger women working in the New York bureau, would swoon in the presence of the handsome talking head.

"Believe me, if it's security you need, William Wilson is *not* your man. I've worked with him often enough to know he's not who you want to defend you in a dark alley."

"We can ask Dave to hire security for us, or get some from the network, can't we?" Megan's voice had a hint of desperation.

"We haven't told Dave we're doing this. If it doesn't pan out, I don't want to be hung out to dry. We need someone we can trust."

"You know anyone?"

"I have an idea." Hannah ended the call and searched her contacts.

* * *

PAULO WAS HALFWAY through drafting a new article when his phone vibrated. It was a call from Hannah. "Paulo Richardson," he answered in his usual professional reporter voice. Even when he knew who was calling, he never took chances.

"Paulo, the possible break in the Angelica Monroe story I told you about is happening. We have a meeting set up for this evening and we need somebody to provide some, um, support for us. Are you interested?"

"Tell me more."

Chapter 26 — Mutiny

LUIS WAITED, BUT NOT PATIENTLY, on the edge of the Washington Square Park fountain. This dance with the sharks to send them to Bull's new meet-up location had gotten old after the first day. He tried to reconstruct how Bull had taken over the operation, and plotted about how he was going to run it. Soon.

Luis knew Bull's violent nature and inherent stupidity made him a liability. Now, Luis was waiting for another college kid he had recruited. In a few months, this shark would graduate. If he didn't bring in a replacement, Luis would have to find another kid who was desperate enough to take the bait. Mining the underclassmen at the local bars and clubs was time-consuming. Bull wasn't good at recruiting. Luis was. He knew how to set the hook. He was smarter than Bull. He should be running the operation. It was a business and Bull was putting them all at risk.

When Eddie Harper tapped Luis on the shoulder, he jumped. "Don't fucking do that, you moron."

"Sorry, man. This change of location is making me nervous. We can't meet at the big elm because of the cops, right?"

"Yeah, whatever. Things change. Deal with 'em."

"I can't keep doing this, man. Did you kill that girl? I saw her once—when I was coming to get my delivery. I recognized her. Man, this is fucked up. I have a future to protect."

"Relax, Eddie. The girl was short on her payment. You know what happens if you spend our money and don't have the cash. Bad things happen. You bring the dough an' you got nothing to worry about."

"I have your money. Here." Eddie held out a brown paper bag, folded over into a flat rectangle. Luis snatched the package and tucked it under his sweatshirt.

"OK. Good boy. You telling me you don't want your supply?"

"No, man. I want it, but this may be my last buy. I'm graduating in two months. I'm about done."

Luis scowled and stared at Eddie. "You have any plan for your successor?"

"Maybe," Eddie turned away, not making eye contact. "I don't know if I'm comfortable bringing somebody in. What if it all blows up? What if they rat me out? What if—"

"What if I cap you right here and solve the problem?" Luis's voice was soft and even, like he was suggesting which drink to order at a bar. The question had its intended effect.

"Hey, man, I'm cool."

"Are you?" Luis stepped forward, pressing his chest against the now terrified student. "Nothing's gonna blow up, unless you blow it up. Should I be worried? You open your fucking mouth and that precious future you're dreaming about will never happen. You got that?"

Eddie took a step back to get some space between him and the drug dealer. "Fuck this, man!" He hurried away and disappeared down one of the many winding paths leading away from the fountain, leaving his money behind.

"Shit!" Luis mumbled, pulling out his phone. "Bull. Yeah. Problem. . . . the kid from Pace just bailed . . . He was all freaked out about the girl . . . Yeah, I think so. Now we need to recruit *three* new sharks . . . Yeah, sure. I'll make sure to get on that. How 'bout you meet me and Enrique behind the café in ten and we'll talk about it?" Luis punched the END button on his burner phone, then called Enrique. After explaining what happened, he said, "We gotta do something now or we'll have nothing left. You in? . . . Good. Bring Wilmer and Oscar, like we talked about. Behind the café. We need to do this now."

* * *

THIRTY MINUTES LATER, Luis and Enrique leaned casually against the brick wall across the narrow alley from the back door of the 9th Street café where Bull had been meeting with their sharks. The air smelled of fetid garbage. Wilmer and Oscar stood twenty feet away, behind the dumpster that served the food service establishments on the block.

Enrique spoke in a hushed voice. "This is your show, Luis. We'll back you up, but you gotta make the deal or take him down."

"I know." Luis knew the ritual. It was the same in the Antipático. If it came to a fight, everyone else stood back and watched. Once one of the two combatants was hurt badly enough, the followers would move in to finish the job, to show support for the winner. Whether it was the old boss or the new, they would prove their value and demonstrate loyalty. They would take no sides until it was clear who would finish on top. The plan was to force Bull out without a fight, but Luis hoped his backup would jump in quickly if necessary.

The metal door creaked open, causing Luis and Enrique to straighten up and move away from the wall. Bull ambled into the alley with his usual swagger, pulling out a joint and a lighter. "How bad is it?"

"It's bad, Bull. Things are falling apart since you capped that girl. If the cops track you down or start arresting our sharks, or our sheriffs, this whole operation is going to shit. But I have a solution."

"Yeah?" Bull lit his joint and took a long drag, holding in the smoke.

"We got to have a change in leadership." As Luis finished his sentence, he sprang forward with his left foot and planted a right-hand punch into Bull's gut.

The surprised Bull exhaled his smoke and reached for Luis's head, trying to engage Luis while he caught his breath. Luis stepped back, throwing an upper-cut into Bull's chin which snapped the dazed man's head back and sent him sprawling.

"You fucked up, Bull. Game's over."

Bull was on his butt, sucking in short breaths. A trickle of blood oozed from his lip, dribbling down his chin before dripping thickly to the pavement. Luis pulled a knife from his front pocket and extended the shining blade as he sprang forward. Cocking his arm for a thrust, Luis felt a stabbing pain in his right knee as Bull kicked out a sneaker, making contact with the stiff leg. It produced a cracking sound that mingled with Luis's cry of anguish. Luis fell, grabbing his injured leg as Bull struggled to his feet, still trying to get air into his lungs.

Bull's blade was in his hand when Luis looked up and rolled quickly to his left to avoid the attack. He staggered to a standing position, putting all his weight on his good leg and extending his own knife. The enraged boss bellowed, "You ungrateful bastard!" and lunged forward.

Bull was still wobbly from the earlier punches. Luis reached and grabbed the onrushing man's knife hand at the wrist, pulling Bull off balance and whipping his body into the brick wall behind them. Enrique, who had been leaning against the same wall, moved away, making room and keeping a close eye on the struggle. Still holding Bull by the wrist, Luis slashed his blade across Bull's right forearm. Blood spurted from the wound as Bull's knife clattered to the ground.

Now even more enraged, Bull swung wildly with his left arm, scoring only a glancing blow against the side of Luis's face. Ignoring his throbbing knee amidst a fight for his life, Luis plunged his blade into Bull's exposed side, below his ribs. He pulled back, then stabbed again into the same area. Bull spun away, falling to his left along the wall and wrenching his wrist away from Luis's grip. The move shielded his bleeding side from further thrusts.

Wilmer and Oscar had left their station by the stinking dumpster and gathered with Enrique a few feet behind Luis, ready to step in and help, but only if necessary.

Bull grunted, then fell to his knees, leaning his right shoulder against the wall. "You motherfucker!" He twisted his head to glare at Luis with bared teeth, rage in his eyes. The side of Bull's t-shirt and the waistband of his pants carried an expanding crimson stain. He was seriously injured, but still had some fight left.

Luis balanced on his left leg, panting. His knife, dangling at his side, was sheathed in Bull's blood.

"C'mon, man. Finish the job and let's get out of here," Enrique urged.

Luis took a halting half-step forward, grimacing as pain shot down his right leg from his injured knee to his toes. He was attempting to shift his weight for another jab when the metal door behind them slammed open, ramming against the alley wall with the sound of a gong. Everyone but Bull turned to see a large Black man in a dirty apron in the doorway, holding aloft a twelve-inch meat cleaver. Luis recognized the man as the cook from the café.

Before he could speak, Luis's attention was diverted to the far end of the alley by the loud pop of a police siren. An NYPD patrol car blocked the alley entrance, its red and blue lights flashing.

"Shit!" Enrique called out as he immediately sprinted toward the opposite end of the narrow alley. Wilmer and Oscar were close on Enrique's heels.

Luis looked at the cook and lowered his knife. "He had it coming. It was him or me." He then limped away, following his posse.

Behind him, he heard a voice shout "Stop!" but he ignored the order that he presumed came from a policeman and rounded the corner onto 9th Street.

As he ran, his knee started to feel better. Nothing broken, apparently. Realizing he was still carrying his knife, he retracted the gory blade and shoved it into his pocket. Ahead, Enrique waved him into a doorway. The four men walked through the building lobby and out the side door onto 8th Street, then continued casually toward the park.

Chapter 27 — Escape Artist

THE OFFICERS ON THE SCENE in the alley followed protocol and stopped to render aid to the injured man, who had been attacked. They called for an ambulance. One officer tried to stem the bleeding from two wounds, while the other spoke to the cook, who said he came upon the scene just as the four other men ran away. All he saw were their backs. He claimed not to recognize Bull or any of the attackers.

When the EMT unit arrived, they spent ten minutes administering first aid in the alley, getting a pressure bandage on the puncture wounds on Bull's side and the gash on his forearm. Even in a state of semi-shock, Bull knew enough not to say anything about what happened or who stabbed him. Anything he told the paramedics would get relayed to the cops.

Eventually, they put Bull on a gurney and wheeled him to a waiting ambulance. He heard one of the officers ask where they were heading. The EMT said St. Mary's hospital.

"OK, we'll meet you there," the officer said as one EMT closed the back door, leaving Bull alone with the other. He was a medium-height White guy who looked to be in his early twenties. He fussed with putting an IV line into Bull's arm as the vehicle pulled away, siren blaring.

"You're gonna be alright," he soothed, looking sympathetically into Bull's eyes and checking for signs of dilated pupils.

The ambulance made two turns, then slowed to a crawl, stuck in Manhattan traffic despite the flashing lights and siren. Bull knew there would be cops all over him at the hospital. He also figured they would give him a sedative and that he would need stitches, or maybe even surgery. If they took his clothes, they would find his weed and his phone in the pockets of his cargo pants. They would also find the gun he kept in the zippered pocket on his left thigh. He was happy that neither the cops nor the paramedics had searched him while giving him first aid. He was the victim, so there was no need to treat him like a criminal. That was working in his favor.

While the ambulance was crawling forward, he decided to take his chances without the hospital. When the EMT turned his back, Bull sat up, wincing at the pain in his side. The startled EMT immediately said, "You need to lie back—" but didn't finish the sentence when he saw the gun in Bull's left hand.

"Thanks for the help, man, but I think I'll be on my own from here," Bull pulled the IV line from his arm. The EMT reached for the gun. Bull pulled the trigger, creating an explosion of sound akin to a bomb in the enclosed space. The EMT spun away, the bullet having entered and passed through the triceps muscle of his right arm, then embedded itself in the wall.

"You crazy bastard!" the injured EMT shouted, falling to the floor and taking cover.

Bull struggled to scoot himself to the end of the gurney. He pushed down the door handle. It popped open, revealing the shocked face of a blonde woman driving a Chevy Suburban directly behind the ambulance. The Suburban stopped short. Bull, his gun waving in the air, jumped down from the ambulance and immediately fell to one knee, absorbing the pain from his fresh wounds. He hobbled toward the curb, then disappeared into the mass of New York pedestrians. By the time the injured EMT pulled out his phone and called his partner, who was driving, Bull was out of sight.

After administering first aid to his partner's gunshot wound, the driver thought to wrap up the remnants of Bull's stay in the ambulance in a plastic bag, including the IV bag, needle, and some gauze that had fallen off the gurney. When they arrived at the hospital, the officers who had been in the alley with Bull took the bag and returned to their precinct to file a report.

Chapter 28 — What Happened?

DRU COOK FINISHED WRITING a note in his spiral notebook, then sat back in an uncomfortable wooden chair and exhaled loudly. Across a small table, two NYPD officers with sheepish expressions quietly waited for the next question. Mariana stood in the corner of the tiny conference room at the Canal Street precinct, watching. Dru and Mariana had been called after a report of an attack with a knife close to Washington Square Park. It was a long shot, but they were running out of leads and wanted to follow up on anything that seemed similar to the Angelica Monroe murder or the likely connected shooting of Javier Estrada. A knife was found in the alley, without any blood on it. They speculated the other guy's knife, with the victim's blood, was long gone. Dru wanted an ID on the guy who shot his way out of the ambulance.

"Why didn't you secure the weapon before you turned the guy over to the EMTs?" Dru asked in a tone indicating he was not going to be happy with any possible answer.

"Well, Sir," Officer Cody Bramson began haltingly, "he had been assaulted and stabbed. We saw four guys run away from the scene. We didn't have any reason to think the victim was dangerous or needed to be patted down. We were trying to save his life."

"Hmmph," Dru knew both officers were already sick over getting the EMT shot with the gun they should have noticed. "And you didn't get any ID?"

The other officer, Heather Rutherford, who looked to Dru like she was still in junior high school, held a hand up like she was asking a question in class. After Dru nodded his permission, the kid said, "I did get a picture."

"Of the victim?"

"Yeah. I took a bunch of pictures of the crime scene while the EMTs were working on the guy. He was lying there, so I'm sure I got his face."

"OK. Now we're getting somewhere." Dru's smile toward Mariana caused both officers to relax a bit. "Let's get those photos into the facial recognition database and see if we can get a match."

* * *

TWO HOURS LATER, back in their own precinct building, Dru sat in the side chair next to Mariana's desk in the bullpen. On her computer screen, a file on Reggie "Bull" Millen recounted the man's criminal history. The facial recognition database had spit out his name quickly, since Reggie had been booked multiple times. He had two arrests for drug possession with intent to distribute and two for assault stemming from bar fights. Amazingly, he had never done any prison time, but he was well acquainted with the system.

Dru was on his cell, calling a contact in the narcotics unit. After a few minutes, he hung up. "Mike Jung in narco knows this guy, Bull. Says he is likely a player in a large-scale marijuana distribution operation in lower Manhattan. It's a low priority, since it doesn't involve harder drugs."

"The priority just went up," Mariana said, getting up and walking toward Captain Sullivan's office before Dru suggested it.

Sully was not thrilled with the prospect of linking the Angelica Monroe murder to a drug ring. "You have a burning desire to commit career suicide?"

"Reggie Millen is connected to Javier Estrada, Cap," Dru pointed out. "We think Estrada is somehow connected to Monroe, but we still don't know exactly how."

"Fine." Their boss glanced at the photo of himself standing with the mayor. "Let's limit this to the Estrada investigation. Don't say anything to anybody about this being connected to the other one unless and until you have hard evidence and you've cleared it with me first. Got that?"

"Sure, Sully." Dru stood, thinking the meeting was about over. "We'll coordinate with the narco boys, right?"

"If you have to," Sullivan growled. "And only about Estrada."

"Um, Captain," Mariana interrupted cautiously, "we have a blood specimen from this guy, Bull. We'd like to send it to the lab to see if it's a DNA match for the blood that was on Javier Estrada's knife at the scene of his murder and the blood we bagged near Monroe's body."

"DNA match?" Dru and Mariana knew how much Sully hated spending money on a DNA comparison. "Is it the same blood type?"

"We don't know," Dru admitted.

"Well check that first!" Sully bellowed. "If it's a type match, then fine, send it to the lab. What are you thinking if it's this guy's blood?"

Dru had one hand on the office door, but turned to make eye contact. "If Javier Estrada had a knife fight with this Reggie Millen a few minutes after he left his athletic bag at the scene of the Monroe murder, we think maybe Estrada was a witness."

"OK, that would explain why this Reggie guy would want to shoot him. But why use two different guns and in two different places?"

"We're speculating here, but Estrada might have tried to run, but he injured his ankle, according to the autopsy. Millen chased him, maybe along with another guy. They caught him, beat him up, then shot him."

"Fine. If this Millen character was that guy—or one of those guys—then he might have also shot the Monroe girl. Is that it?"

"Yeah, that's it," Mariana said.

"So, what's the motive for killing the girl?"

"We're working on it, Cap. We'll let you know." Dru opened the door and ushered Mariana out as quickly as he could manage.

Chapter 29 — At The Scampering Squirrel

THE FINAL CHORUS of "Sweet Home Alabama" blasted from the vintage juke box at The Scampering Squirrel, but Megan was not watching the few couples gyrating on the tiny dance floor. From her vantage on a hard wooden bench in a booth opposite the entrance, she was focused on the door. A Coors Light sat untouched on the scarred table in front of her, condensation forming a moist ring at the base of the tall glass.

Megan was dressed to attract attention in a red top with spaghetti straps and a neckline low enough to expose the lace fringe of her Victoria's Secret push-up bra. Her hazel eyes darted from the doorway to the corner of the bar, where Hannah nursed a rum and coke and pretended not to be watching Megan's booth. The two women made eye contact momentarily.

Hannah saw Megan's head lift and her eyes lock on the door. Hannah turned and saw the tall, blond man standing inside the threshold, scanning the room. A demure wave of Megan's slender hand, tipped with polish matching her red top, got Lars to make eye contact and move in her direction. Hannah slid fifteen dollars in cash under her mostly empty high-ball glass and watched the tall man cross to Megan's booth. She saw a jaunty smile spread across his face as he approached and got a good look at Megan.

The fact that her in-person appearance matched the sultry selfie she texted him undoubtedly prompted his reaction.

Hannah waited until the harried waitress had taken Lars's drink order before making her move toward the booth. As she slipped past the edge of the dance floor, she nodded at Paulo, sitting at attention in a straight-backed chair next to a spindly table. Paulo returned the nod. Hannah quickly slid onto the bench next to Megan, who scooted to her left, pulling her beer glass with her.

Lars looked immediately confused at the unexpected appearance of a second woman. "Hello? Who are you?" he asked in a decidedly Scandinavian accent. Hannah guessed Norwegian.

"I'm so sorry to intrude, Lars. I'm a friend of Angelica Monroe and a producer for the American Cable News Network, and I need to get some information from you." Hannah rushed through the introduction, wanting to get to her questions before the man could catch his balance. "We know you were with Angelica on Friday night, shortly before she was murdered. You were seen on a security camera walking down 3rd Street with her."

Lars turned his body and extended his left leg out of the booth, preparing to stand. "I don't know who you are, lady, and I don't know what you're talking about. I am leaving."

"You can leave, Lars, but if you do, I'm going to have to tell the cops who you are and they aren't going to let you walk away without answering their questions. Since you're not a US citizen, you probably don't want to be listed as a fugitive. I'm a journalist, so I can protect your identity if you talk to me. I'm not interested in whatever you were doing. I just want information about Angelica. It's your choice."

Lars paused mid knee-bend, then slowly lowered back to his bench. "I don't know anything."

"You'd be surprised what you might know without realizing it. For example, it might be important to know that you and Angelica were here in this bar before you walked out onto the street. That's right, isn't it?"

Lars stared across the table, his square jaw clenching beneath deep blue eyes. His sandy hair was clipped short, emphasizing his high forehead. He stared at the two women with a mix of puzzlement and murderous anger. Hannah could see the wheels turning in his obviously impressive brain. He was a foreign med student at an English-speaking school, marking him as brilliant. That made him difficult to out-think. Hannah knew she had the element of surprise. She also had the leverage of potentially disclosing his identity to the police, which she guessed he wouldn't want. Based on his behavior in the booth, she assumed she was right. She didn't know how long her advantage would last.

Lars lowered his voice. "Yes, Angelica met me here."

"You see, that wasn't difficult. And you were here to buy some weed from Angelica, weren't you?"

A flash of panic momentarily replaced Lars's malevolent glare. "I don't know what you are talking about."

"C'mon now, Lars. If you don't tell the truth, we're going to have to let someone else do the questioning. We know Angelica was selling, what we need to know is who she was getting her pot from. You tell us that and you can walk away. I'll use all the legal power of my network to protect your identity."

"I don't know. I swear." Lars glanced toward the bar and the dance floor, as if checking for someone listening in. "Look, I was not hurting anyone. Med students need to relax sometimes. To help with sleep. But we cannot be associated with taking drugs, not even legal ones. It is not a big deal. Angelica had good stuff, but I do not know where she got it. She told me she had a problem with her supplier. She needed money. She asked me for a loan, but I could not help her. That was it."

Now, it was Hannah's turn to rethink her expected line of questions. "Wait, Angelica asked you for money?"

"Yes."

"Did she say why?"

"Only that she needed to get her supply and did not have enough cash. She said I would not get mine unless she got more money. I did not have any to loan her. Only what I brought to pay for my bag."

"So, Angelica was your supplier?" Hannah put her palms on the table and leaned forward.

"Yes."

"And you were reselling to other med students?"

"Yes."

"But you don't know who she got it from?"

"Correct."

Megan spoke for the first time since Hannah's arrival. "Was Angelica going to meet her supplier Friday night, after you two left here?" Hannah shot her intern a withering glance for interrupting the interview.

"I think so. She said I was her last hope. I walked with her to the park and then went to my apartment. I do not know what happened to her after that. If I knew anything that would help the police, I would tell you. I do not. I cannot be connected to this. You promise you will keep my name confidential?"

"Yes," Hannah readily agreed. "Just one more question. How long had you been buying weed from Angelica?"

"Since September."

"How did she hook up with you?"

"That is two questions." Lars did not show any indication he was joking.

"I still want to know."

He paused, then shrugged, as if the information was not harmful. "She did not. I was contacted by another student who graduated last year. He connected me with Angelica."

"Can you tell me the name of that student?" Hannah cocked her head, as if listening intently.

"No. You don't need to know that. I am not messing up anyone else's life."

"OK. Thank you. I'm not trying to ruin anyone's life. I promise I will keep your identity secret. But, if you do know where Angelica was getting her weed and don't tell me or the police, you will be obstructing justice and will be in more trouble than for just selling pot to classmates. You understand?"

"Yes. I understand. I will leave now." He rose and Hannah jumped up with him.

"Here." She held out a business card, pushing it into his reluctant hand. "If you decide there is anything else, you give me a call. And if you talk to anybody else in the media, then my deal to keep your identity secret is off. Got it?"

Lars did not respond, but stuffed the card into his jeans pocket and quickly walked away.

Thirty seconds later, Paulo slid onto the bench across from Hannah and Megan, bringing his beer glass. "Looked like he was talking."

"Yeah." Hannah, who had returned to her seat, nodded. She reached for Megan's beer glass and took a healthy sip. "It was tense, but quite enlightening. Did you get photos?"

"Yeah. Pretty good ones," Paulo held up his mobile phone and waved it like a baton.

"You're not going to use those pictures, are you?" Megan asked. She had not been clued in on the plan to have Paulo get some images of Lars, just in case.

"No," Hannah scolded, "of course not. They're for corroboration in case we need to document that we really did meet with the source. You recorded the conversation, right?"

Megan patted her purse, on the bench next to her.

After Hannah briefed Paulo on what Lars told them, he asked, "What's next?"

"Honestly, I don't know."

* * *

WHEN HANNAH CALLED Dave Butler and briefed him about the conversation with Lars, whose name she never used, she was not surprised by the outcome. Dave already told her that he wasn't excited about running the story. Now that her interview subject had confirmed what she already knew—that Angelica was dealing weed and was likely meeting with her supplier in the park the night she was killed—Dave's attitude had not changed. He said he was concerned about relying on a source who would not appear on camera. Hannah suspected it was more about not wanting to tell their viewers something they didn't want to hear.

The only question was whether Hannah should let somebody else break the story, or sit on it for a day or two. Since Lars had not provided any information specifically relevant to the murder investigation and could not identify the person Angelica was meeting with in the park Friday night, they would not be obstructing justice by withholding the information. At least, that was what Dave concluded. Hannah was in no position to argue.

"You want to break the story?" Hannah asked Paulo on the phone. "I can't run with it, but our deal is that you get the print rights after I've had an opportunity to get it on-air. My boss just passed, so it's your option."

"I'm not sure." Paulo sounded disappointed. "I need a way to link the information to Javier Estrada's murder. That's still missing."

"So, what? We both sit on this?"

"Yeah. For now, I think so. I feel like we're sitting on a keg of dynamite and holding a lit match."

"I know what you mean," Hannah agreed. "Let's be careful."

"That doesn't sound like you."

"I know. Maybe I'm learning."

Chapter 30 — Exit Plan

LUIS AND ENRIQUE HUDDLED around the television in the apartment where Enrique lived with his mother and sister. They watched the ten o'clock news on WPIX-11, which was the earliest local news broadcast in New York. They didn't have cable, but Wilmer had texted, saying he saw a story on New York One about a guy who shot his way out of the back of an ambulance.

The channel 11 news didn't have any pictures of the man who shot an EMT, but there was an artist's sketch of his face. Between that and the timing, Luis and Enrique were convinced the injured gunman was Bull. Luis knew Bull was too smart to go to a hospital for medical attention. He knew about doctors who would stitch up people without reporting it to the cops. Luis had been to a few, but didn't have any way of knowing where Bull would go.

"He's not coming after anybody for a while. He's hurt pretty bad." Enrique was trying to be encouraging, but his voice leaked anxiety.

"Yeah. He'd be dead if that stupid cook hadn't shown up." Luis paced around the room, his hands on his head. "We gotta do something. We sit around, trying to run the business, and Bull will heal up and then come after us. I don't wanna spend the next year wondering when he's gonna cap me."

"I feel you, man." Enrique picked up a long-necked bottle of Budweiser from an end table and threw it back for a long slug.

When he came up for air and smacked his lips, he looked serious, like he was ready to jump off a cliff. "We gotta get him first."

"Where's his crib?"

Enrique shook his head. "No clue, man."

Luis looked around the dreary room. A throw rug partially covered up dark stains on the formerly blonde hardwood, and faded drapes surrounded streaked windows overlooking the building's courtyard. "We need some help."

* * *

ON MONDAY EVENING, eleven hundred people, mostly college students from NYU and many other universities around New York, gathered for a candlelight vigil and prayer group in Washington Square Park. The area immediately around the memorial at the Hangman's Elm wasn't large enough to handle the numbers, so University security herded the group to the central plaza.

A reverend from Riverside Church delivered a rousing sermon about the value of all human life and the promise of youth. A group carrying signs calling for gun control legislation gathered in the back, nearest to the camera crews. It was a peaceful gathering that provided a backdrop of candlelight and hymn singing for the reporters taping their news programs. When the vigil was officially over, the food vendors around the park sold out their carts. The bars on 3rd Street did an overflow business.

The New York tabloids still had the Angelica Monroe murder on the front pages, calling for action by the NYPD and plugging the reward available for citizen assistance in finding Angelica's killer. The mystery man's photo ran in every paper and was posted on every media website in the city.

The broadcast news shows that night carried stories in the first segment, but not as the lead. The cable news networks were split. Some pumped the story as an adjunct to political commentary and brought in experts and activists to expound on how to use this moment to achieve change. Others rallied viewers to solidify second amendment rights, arguing that if Angelica Monroe had a gun, she could have defended herself. The one point every media outlet agreed on was that the murderer was a reprehensible animal who needed to be caught and brought to justice. It was a unifying theme.

Chapter 31 — All the News That Fits the Print

Tuesday

PAULO FILED HIS STORY electronically Tuesday morning, then waited for the usually minimal comments and edits from Clarence Wotherspoon, the editor in chief of the *Lower East Side Tribune*. Clarence was not a great writer, but he was a good copy editor, a decent administrator, and a great advertising salesman. Clarence rarely attempted to substantively edit Paulo's work. Sometimes he asked for verification about quotes or sources, but that was ass-covering, not questioning Paulo's reporting skills. It was extraordinarily rare for Clarence to want a phone call or video conference to discuss an article. It was unheard of for Clarence to insist on an in-person meeting.

The paper's "office" was a storefront on Avenue C that was formerly a deli and still had the salty smell of cured meat. Clarence had a tiny back-room office, where he met with potential advertisers and occasionally a politician who wanted to vent about the paper's coverage or angle for a favor. Paulo had attended a few of those meetings when his reporting was the source of the controversy, but he had never been called in alone to discuss an unpublished piece.

At a quarter-to-eleven, Paulo waved at the teenaged girl sitting behind the army-surplus metal desk in the front of the office. She made minimum wage to be the paper's receptionist, Clarence's secretary, and his lone customer service agent. She was on the ancient black desk phone, speaking in Spanish to someone who was unhappy with an advertisement that didn't fulfill their expectations as Paulo breezed past on his way to the back office.

"Sit down, Paulo." Clarence motioned toward the two wood-and-fabric chairs sitting opposite a maple desk strewn with a potpourri of loose paper, magnetic toys, and heavy leather-bound books. A huge video monitor hummed on a counter against the wall in front of an ergonomic keyboard. On the screen, a spreadsheet filled with financial numbers patiently awaited attention. After Paulo settled into the stiff seat, the boss swiveled his chair with a loud squeak and sat forward, his elbows resting on a stack of papers. "We need to talk about the Javier Estrada story you sent in."

"It's the truth," Paulo shot back defiantly. He suspected this was the point of the meeting. His article included the scoop that Javier's athletic bag was found near the scene of Angelica Monroe's murder and his conclusion that Javier was likely a witness, prompting the killer to chase the basketball star to the opposite side of the park before shooting him.

The article cited unnamed sources in the medical examiner's office and the police department, reporting that Javier had an injured ankle and that a knife was found at the scene with Javier's fingerprints and blood, likely from the killer. Javier's body also had wounds consistent with being beaten prior to being shot, including a broken arm and bruises on his face and torso. But the bombshell was the suggestion—not reported as a fact, but based on speculation from police sources—that Angelica may have been in the park to meet with a drug dealer.

"You want to make Estrada out to be a hero." Clarence reached with his left hand to remove his reading glasses without moving his elbow from its anchor position on the desktop. "I'm all for that. He's a local kid. Our readers want to think of him as a hero and not the former gang member. That's great stuff. You should run with that. You've talked to his mom. Go talk to his basketball coach and his friends from school."

"I already did," Paulo responded coldly.

"Great. Wonderful. Plenty for you to write about. Why do you need to trash the Monroe girl? She's a freaking saint. You're throwing mud on the Madonna."

"She's no saint." Paulo rose and walked to a bookcase against the wall opposite the desk. A photo of a much younger Clarence with Mayor Ed Koch sat in a silver frame atop the collection of dusty books. "She was involved with drug trafficking at NYU. She was there to meet her supplier—to get weed she was peddling to her fellow students. I think she was trash. I think Javier was the tragic hero in this story, not Angelica Monroe."

"Paulo, knowing you, you're probably right." Clarence sat back with a sigh. "You remember the He-Lo Industries article? Of course you do. It was one of your best investigative pieces. That girl died and you exposed the safety violations in the facility."

"It was a sweatshop!" Paulo barked.

"Right. Fine. You exposed it. It was the right thing to do. You were protecting other members of the community from suffering in those conditions. I backed you on that, even though He-Lo was a big advertiser. The principle was more important than the money. I backed you even though the reporting put He-Lo out of business and the neighborhood lost all those jobs, which the scumbag moved to Vietnam so he could keep right on producing his blood skirts. Doing the right thing was more important than the consequences."

"It's the same here." Paulo softened his tone. He knew where Clarence was going and he was formulating a response.

"It's not, though, Paulo. This is different. What's to be gained? Who is being protected? Have you seen the rallies and vigils for this girl? Have you followed the coverage? You throw shade on the virgin Angelica and the backlash will be a shit-storm like you've never seen. Twitter and Facebook will explode. We'll get a million bad reviews. Our advertisers—the few we still have—will dump us like we're the *KKK Tribune* advocating a national holiday for Hitler's birthday. You want to drop a bomb on this office and put us all out of business. For what?"

"It's the truth."

"Damn the truth!" Clarence popped up from his chair with remarkable speed for someone of his girth, throwing his hands toward the foamboard ceiling. "It's great journalism. I give you that. I don't know how you got your sources to talk, but it's fucking brilliant. If you were writing this for *The Times*, you might win a Pulitzer for it. But we're not *The Times*. Even if you had her on video handing a bag to a buyer, nobody wants to know about it. People want to believe what they want to believe and they have formed a collective opinion that Angelica Monroe is an innocent victim of urban crime. You are telling them the emperor is naked, but nobody wants to see his bare ass."

"I'm reporting the facts, Clarence, that's what I do."

"And I appreciate what you do, son." Clarence was twenty years older than Paulo, but looked more like forty. When he wanted to make a point and assert his authority, he took a fatherly attitude. "But I've got a paper to keep afloat. The truth is that if we go out of business, then I'll be responsible for the other six people who work for me, and I'm not willing to sacrifice their jobs and my paper in order for you to satisfy your need to tell the truth. You can get another job. I can't. And neither can Jesse or Florence or Emma Jean or Robert. I'm not going to let that happen to them. So, if you want this to run, you re-write it and leave out the parts about Angelica Monroe being a drug dealer. You got that?"

"Or you're not going to let it run at all?" Paulo stood and glared at his boss. "I'll sell it to somebody else as a freelance piece."

"The hell you will! You're still an employee of this paper and your article is the intellectual property of the *Lower East Side Tribune*. You need my permission to take it elsewhere and I won't give it to you."

Paulo tipped back his head and stared at the ceiling. He knew Hannah Hawthorne had met the same resistance from her network. He didn't expect it from *LES Trib*. "Fine. I'll rewrite the story without the facts. You can have that on your conscience."

"I won't lose any sleep," Clarence plopped back down, picked up the printout of Paulo's story, and handed it across the desk. "Get it edited and back to me in time to make it on the website before six."

Paulo snatched the pages of his draft article and stormed away without a glance backward.

* * *

PAULO WAS HALFWAY HOME when his cell buzzed. After briefly considering letting it roll to voicemail, he dragged the battered unit from his pocket. The screen read "UNKNOWN NUMBER".

"Hello?"

"Is this Paulo Richardson, the reporter?" The voice had an accent that could have been from the Lower East Side. Paulo was pretty sure he had never heard it before. It was not one of his usual sources, so he proceeded with caution. But a reporter always has to be open to the possibility that a stranger calling him might have useful information.

"This is Paulo Richardson." Paulo automatically fell into his professional journalist voice, the one he adopted for interviews with White politicians to make himself seem less threateningly ethnic.

"Good. Um, you want to know about Javier—the basketball player who got shot—right?"

"I have been writing a series of articles about Javier Estrada, yes. Do you have information about his murder?"

The line went silent. Paulo stopped walking, ducked into a doorway where the sidewalk noise was slightly diminished, and listened intently. It was common for new sources to be hesitant, even after they reached out to him. After twenty seconds, Paulo heard background noise, indicating that the person on the other end had unmuted his phone. "Yeah, I do. I know who did it, but I don't wanna say on the phone. Can you meet me?"

"Where?" Paulo was on guard to any suggestion that might be a set-up.

"How 'bout the alley off of Fifth Avenue between 8th and 9th, out behind the Parkside café?"

Without ever having been in that alley, Paulo instantly knew it was not someplace he wanted to meet a stranger who might bring friends. "How about we meet in Washington Square Park, at the fountain. Lots of people around, but we can still talk privately. It's just you, right?"

Another silence. Then the caller said, "Yeah. Just me. The park is good. I know what you look like, so you find a place around the fountain and I'll find you."

"When?"

"Ten minutes."

Paulo calculated how far away he was. "Make it fifteen." The line clicked and went silent.

Paulo tapped out a text to Clarence. The message said he was on his way to Washington Square Park to meet with an anonymous source claiming to have information about Javier Estrada's murder. If he never came back from the meeting, at least the cops would know where to start looking.

Fourteen minutes later, Paulo took a seat on the concrete rim of the huge central fountain in the park. He had picked a spot where there were no other people currently using the space. Across the fountain, a group of small children splashed in the water, laughing and chasing each other. It was too cold in Paulo's opinion to be getting wet, but it was a pleasant late April day in the high 60s and the sun baking the stone surface made it feel warmer.

He set his bag down on the fountain edge to his left and scanned the area, looking for his new contact, but also taking note of the vendor carts. Food carts represented safety, because the vendors were always there and often had defensive weapons. Plus, there were usually patrons buying food. Safety in numbers. There were plenty of vendors. He saw no cops.

A minute later, a tall, lanky Latino boy wearing baggy shorts, a black t-shirt, and a white baseball cap turned backward ambled in his direction, making eye contact. Luis Torres sat down to Paulo's right. "Hey, Paulo."

"That's right. And who are you?"

Luis's eyes darted around the area. "That don't matter for now. I called you because I need somebody to talk to the cops for me. I know you're from the 'hood, like me, and folks say I can trust you. I got information, but I'm gonna need immunization. You know? I figure you can be the go-between, and you get the story, right? That works, don't it?"

"You mean immunity. You want to trade your information for immunity from prosecution so you don't get arrested. Is that it?" Paulo studied his new informant's face. There was no sign of fear. The kid seemed to know what he wanted, even if he didn't know the right word.

"Yeah. Like that."

"So, you were involved?"

"Hey, man, let's just say I know what happened."

"Over at the Hangman's Elm?"

"Yeah—I mean, no, it wasn't there. It was over on the east side," Luis jerked his head back and to the right, toward the site of Javier's murder.

"You need a lawyer, kid, not a reporter."

"I don't need no lawyer!" Luis raised his voice, then lowered it again, remembering that they were trying to keep the discussion private. "A lawyer can't do what I need done and besides, I don't wanna pay no lawyer."

"So, you didn't kill Javier?"

"Naw, man. I ain't killed nobody."

"But you know who did."

"Yeah."

Paulo leaned forward, putting his elbows on his knees and stretching out his back. He turned his head to look at the face of his new informant, who claimed to have the hot scoop. "So, this other guy shot Javier and you can say so for sure?"

"Yeah."

"And Angelica Monroe, too?"

"Yeah." Luis responded without hesitation.

Paulo blew out a soft whistle. "So, why not go directly to the cops yourself?"

"Because I got some other shit goin' on and I don't wanna get arrested. I ain't stupid."

"I can tell." Paulo sat back up and spoke in a soothing voice, the one he used with mothers who were reluctant to talk about their children after their deaths or arrests. "Are you willing to testify in court—to help the DA get a conviction? Because without that you're not going to be able to make any deal."

"I know. I don't want to, but I will if I gotta. Bull is out of his mind, man. I'm scared. And I got some other guys—guys who need the protection, too. Not just me. We don't wanna go to jail, and we don't want Bull to kill us next. So, we're, like desperate."

"These other guys—they can also testify against the shooter?"

"Yeah. I guess."

"Alright. But you have to tell me something I can give to the cops that will make them believe you. They don't give out immunity deals to people they haven't met. There needs to be a specific exchange of information, and you have to be fully cooperative, and you have to disclose any crimes that you want immunity for. You willing to do that?"

Paulo was winging it now. He had never negotiated an immunity from prosecution deal. He had never actually seen one. But he had enough general knowledge of how these things worked that he was pretty sure he was at least close to the truth.

"Yeah. I get it." Luis paused, thinking. Paulo remained quiet. This was the moment when his source would either deliver the goods or prove himself to be a fraud. "Do the cops know about the gun?"

"What gun?"

"The little gun Bull took from the shark bitch and shot Javier with."

Paulo shook his head, wondering if he had heard correctly. "Wait. What shark bitch?"

"The girl, man. She pulled that pansy-ass little gun on Bull before he capped her. Then he took it and shot the basketball guy."

"Javier Estrada?"

"Yeah."

"You're saying that you saw this dude shoot Angelica Monroe, then use Angelica's gun to shoot Javier Estrada?"

"Yeah, man. That's what happened."

"What kind of gun did this Bull guy use to kill the girl?"

"Bull's got a big-ass forty-five, like Dirty Harry."

Paulo was certain these facts had not been leaked by the police. If they were true, then his boy was for real. Where did Angelica Monroe get a gun? And why would she pull it on a guy in the park, who was presumably her drug dealer? These questions flew across Paulo's mind in a nanosecond, but he knew that now was not the time to ask about them. "OK. That's pretty specific information. I can talk to the cops and they can talk to the DA. If they're willing to make a deal, how do I contact you?"

"You don't. I'll call you. I got a burner phone, so nobody can trace it."

"What's your name?" Paulo figured he wouldn't get an answer, but had to ask.

"Man, you said you thought I was smart. And I *am* smart. Smart enough to know not to tell you shit about me. I'll call you."

"What about just a first name? That way I'll know it's you when you call."

After a hesitation, Paulo got a reply. "Luis."

"OK, Luis. I think you have some very valuable information."

"You can't tell nobody, right? You got to keep it a secret that I told you, 'cause you're a reporter."

It was Paulo's turn to hesitate. "Right now, I can't tell anybody anything because I don't know who you are. I'm guessing

Luis isn't even your real name. So don't worry. I can't tell anybody anything, except I can tell the cops what you told me and that you want to make a deal. That's what you want, right?"

"And you ain't gonna print that, right? You ain't gonna tell anybody I talked to you and told you about what happened, right? I'm, like, off the record."

"Luis, nothing you told me is off the record unless I agreed to it before we spoke, which I didn't. But you can rest assured I'm not going to print anything I can't verify, and I'm not going to publish anything about what you told me until after I go to the police. I know you're trying to do the right thing here, and I'm willing to help you. I *am* from the 'hood, and I know how things are. You can trust me."

"OK." Luis jumped to his feet and jogged away to the north, toward the park exit, before Paulo could ask any more questions. Paulo watched as the lean figure moved, the white soles of his sneakers flashing in the sun with each stride. He was slightly favoring his right leg.

Paulo waited until Luis had disappeared from view, then reached for his satchel. He pulled his cell phone out from the interior pocket where it was pressed up against the tiny hole in the side and stopped the video recorder. He tapped the icon for the file he had just recorded and uploaded it to his cloud storage. As important as that video might be, he didn't want to take a chance on losing it.

Chapter 32 — The Big Break

HANNAH SAT AT THE COUNTER in her apartment between the micro-kitchen and the tiny living room. The counter doubled as her dining table, with three high-boy bar stools pushed against the half-wall. A mostly eaten container of cold shrimp chow fun perched precariously on the edge of the granite countertop next to an abandoned pair of chopsticks. The one o'clock ACN broadcast broke for its first commercials, but before Hannah reached to clean up her lunch leftovers, her phone buzzed, sending shock waves across the space. Reaching for the phone, her index finger caught the edge of a chopstick; it levered sideways, sending the container toppling to the hardwood floor with a soft splat.

"Shit!" She saw Paulo's caller ID and left the clean-up for later. The mess wasn't going anywhere. "Hey."

"Hannah. You alone?"

"Yeah. I'm at home. Why?"

"You have lawyers at your network, right?"

"In corporate, sure. Why? You need one?"

"No, but we both might need one very soon. Can I come see you? I've got something hot and I think I'm going to need your help."

"What's it about?"

"It's about the guy who killed both Javier Estrada and Angelica Monroe."

"Come on over!" After giving Paulo the address, Hannah quickly cleaned up the spilled chow fun, then spent five minutes putting dirty dishes in her apartment-sized dishwasher and making her place look somewhat presentable. If a man was coming over, she didn't want her apartment to look like a frat house after a toga party.

When Paulo arrived ten minutes later, they sat on a faded leather sofa in front of the muted television while Hannah watched the video on Paulo's phone. The camera, peeking out from the peep hole in Paulo's satchel, mostly showed Paulo's side and back. But when Paulo bent forward to stretch his back, the person sitting next to him came into view briefly. The mostly profile view of Luis's face would be enough for the police to identify him if his mug shot was in their facial recognition database, and the audio was clear. Hannah was most interested in the story Luis told about the man who killed both Angelica and Javier.

"What does he mean by 'shark?'" Hannah asked.

"No idea," Paulo admitted. "I was going to ask, but we got sidetracked once he said the girl was Angelica."

"OK." Hannah took a breath, trying to slow her racing mind. "We know Angelica was selling weed to Lars, and probably to other people. She had to be getting her supply from somebody. Do you think it was this guy, Luis? And why did she have a gun?" Hannah voiced the questions Paulo had already thought of and could not answer.

"There are a lot of open questions." Paulo rose from the sofa, stuffing his phone away in a pocket. "Do you know if the cops have released information about the guns used in the two shootings?"

"No. Not that I know about. I haven't seen any ballistics reports. You know they usually keep that kind of information to themselves until they have a suspect arrested. I'm sure they know, but it's not public yet."

"This is pretty intense, Hannah." Paulo plopped down in the only chair in the room. "I need to get some legal advice and our paper doesn't have any lawyers on staff, or on retainer. I need to know what my obligations are to the police here. Can I even bring this kind of deal to them on behalf of Luis? Would they lock me up if I don't show them the video?"

"You don't have to tell them there's a video," Hannah said confidently. "They might ask, but you can say that your journalistic notes and all audio and video taken as part of your reporting are privileged. I'm sure about that. It's happened to me a few times."

"This is why I need you. Can you reach out to your corporate lawyers so we can talk to them?"

On the muted television screen, the network sports reporter was running highlights of the Knicks game. Julius Randall had scored some ridiculous amount of points, but the Knicks had lost in overtime. Hannah thought about Javier Estrada and how he would never play in such a game.

"Paulo, I appreciate you coming to me about this, but it's your story, not mine. My network's lawyers can only advise me about *my* stories. Unless . . ." She leaned forward, stretching her arms out and grabbing the edge of a glass coffee table separating the sofa from the chair where Paulo sat.

"Unless we were working on the story together," Paulo finished the thought. He had already been considering how he was going to get cooperation from a big network without sharing the story. If he worked with Hannah, they could arrange for Paulo to break the news. A big outfit like ACN would not care that a small, local, online paper had it first, or about giving him credit, as long as they could scoop all the other broadcast media. "I'm willing to collaborate here. As long as I get to break the story, you can have non-exclusive rights."

Hannah blew out a breath. "Paulo, if this is as big as we think it will be, I'll make sure you get full credit and first publication as long as I get to break it on air after you publish—and I get the interview with Luis."

"I doubt the guy will want to go on camera."

"Leave that to me. We need to meet with him. I need to get something on video. We can blur his face and alter his voice. I can't go out with your crap-cam video on this. Besides, we need to get more information before we can go to the lawyers—and to the cops."

"What information?"

Hannah stood and paced the room while she rattled off her thoughts, which were coming faster than she could speak. "We need the killer's name. We need to know the motive. We need to know where he is or how to find him. We can't go to the cops with just your hearsay, or even your video."

"Isn't the information about the gun enough to get us there?"

"It's probably enough to get us in the door. I guess we need to talk to the lawyers about that. And we need to move fast. When is Luis calling you back?"

"He didn't say."

"Did you try to dial back his number?"

"Yeah. I tried, but the number is dead. He said it was a burner phone."

Hannah nodded. "And we know who uses burner phones."

"Criminals, and especially drug dealers." Paulo shrugged. "We know Luis is a criminal, and was probably an accomplice to the murders. He's no saint. But he says he's scared of this Bull person. The fact that he's willing to come forward says a lot."

"Did he mention the reward money?"

Paulo's face froze. "No. He didn't. You think that's what this is about?"

"I don't know, but how many street thugs do you know who want to go to the cops and rat out their buddies?"

"Not many. But he said he was scared. I believe that. If his information can lead to the guy who shot Angelica and Javier, don't you think the cops and the DA would go for the immunity deal?"

"Yes. No question. They'd be heroes. We'd be even bigger heroes. Too bad journalists can't collect reward money. You think we can pull this off?"

Paulo stood. Hannah stopped pacing. "I think we have to try. Don't you?"

"Hell yeah!" Hannah called back. "I'm going to have to call my managing editor on this. I can't call in the lawyers on my own."

"OK," Paulo agreed. "Make the call. I know a police officer I can talk to confidentially and give her the information about the two guns. She can be our conduit to the detectives and the district attorney. If Luis's information is good, that should make them interested in finding out more. Then we can talk to somebody about the idea of an immunity deal." He held his phone, but didn't immediately make a call. Instead, he looked back at Hannah, who was already in mid-dial. "Wait."

"What?" She dropped her arm.

"Are we in over our heads here?"

Hannah looked Paulo squarely in the eyes. "Probably. Let's talk to the lawyers first, before we do anything else."

* * *

NOT SURPRISINGLY, DAVE BUTLER was eager to make the call to Jay Goldstein, the general counsel of ACN, who was in the middle of a continuing legal education seminar at the time. A half-hour after that, Hannah, Butler, Goldstein, and Craig Wasserman, a lawyer from the law firm of Ropes, Patterson, and Tremaine, were on a conference call.

Butler wanted to exclude Paulo, since he was not an ACN employee, but the lawyers intervened. As a collaborator on the story, Paulo would have the same privilege protection as Hannah. They concluded that the network's legal right to protect the confidentiality of a source should provide cover for Hannah, Paulo, and Luis as long as Hannah could truthfully say she had promised to keep the identity confidential.

"To get an immunity deal," Wasserman explained, "Luis and all his companions are going to have to come forward and present themselves to the police and the DA. Or, we could get all the details and present them as the basis for a tentative deal they can agree to, provided the information pans out. We'll need the names of all the people who need immunity and a list of the crimes they want included. I doubt the DA will give them a blanket immunity without knowing what's involved. They could be killers, for all we know. And we're going to need an affidavit from Luis, or a better video of him spelling out all the facts he knows so the DA can evaluate whether the information is good enough to make the deal."

"I could meet with him," Hannah offered, "and promise him confidentiality. I could get him on video so we could have back-up for that. He can put all his information on tape for the DA. Would that work?"

The lawyers agreed it would work, if Hannah and Paulo could convince Luis to give at least a short interview.

"He's not going to want the police to know his identity until he has a deal," Paulo spoke for Luis.

"But we can blur his face and alter his voice," Hannah continued. "That way the cops will have all the information, but won't know who he is until they're ready to deal."

"Let's not get ahead of ourselves," Wasserman said. "We're assuming this guy, Luis, is the real deal and has good information. Before we approach the police or the district attorney, we should get some corroboration of his story, whatever it is."

"I have a friend at the NYPD," Paulo said. "I can give her Luis's information about the guns. If it's good, she can hook us up with somebody high enough in the department to start talking about a deal."

"Do it," Goldstein said. "Dave, can we run a story in the meantime, based on this source's statements?"

"No," Dave said firmly. "All we have now is an uncorroborated anonymous source. We don't have a name or even a description of the alleged killer, nor do we know for sure who this source is or what his real motives are. If we run this and it blows up in our faces, I'm not taking the heat for it."

After some discussion, they all agreed that there was nothing to run—yet. They were all clearly excited about the prospect of breaking such huge news about the highest-profile case of the year. Any thoughts about being tired or hungry vanished as they continued to plan strategy for meeting with the DA and the police. Hannah was already sketching out questions for an interview with Luis and how they would disguise his identity.

After the outside lawyer and the general counsel left the call, Dave told Hannah to take her phone off speaker. "This is great work, Hawthorne. It could be big. But remember, the story is about the killer and Angelica Monroe is the victim. There's nothing here shining any negative light on Monroe, right?"

"I don't know, Dave. We think Angelica was in the park to meet with her drug dealer, and that this Bull guy may be both her dealer and her killer. Everything we learned from Luis is consistent with that."

"Let's be careful," Dave said loudly enough for Paulo to hear without a speaker. "We expose the guy who shot and killed that innocent girl, along with the Hispanic boy, and we've got the motherlode. That's enough. There's no need to sully the girl's reputation along the way if we don't have to."

"What if we have to?" Hannah's question dripped with contempt.

"We don't. Figure it out." Dave hung up before Hannah could say anything more.

"Where do we go from here?" Paulo walked to the lone window in the room and gazed out at the last crimson stain of twilight above the Manhattan buildings that blocked any chance of seeing the horizon.

"We need to get together with Luis. I need to speak to him so I can promise him confidentiality. We need to get more details from him and tell him that we're working on the DA. I need him on camera. Then we can try to make the deal that Luis wants. If we get it for him, we'll have the story of the year."

"OK, I'm going to contact my friend on the force and ask about the gun used to kill Javier. If it checks out, then we'll know for sure that Luis has real information."

"Fine. But from all I see on your hidden camera video, he seems legit. Are you sure you trust him?"

"Yes. He reached out to me because he trusts me and he's from the neighborhood. He's scared. He's risking a lot by coming forward. It's just not enough to publish—yet." Paulo grabbed his satchel and walked to the door.

Hannah unlocked the deadbolt. "Thank you for coming to me, Paulo. I think we make a good team."

"I agree. You're pretty smart for a White girl."

Hannah jabbed her left fist into Paulo's chest, not hard enough to hurt him. "That's a racist thing to say."

"I know. I love to take advantage of your White liberal guilt." They shared a soft chuckle.

"Hey. I owe you one for this."

Paulo looked slightly downward into Hannah's light brown eyes. "We'll get through all this and then I'll let you buy me dinner."

"It's a date." She smiled, opening the door. She watched him descend the interior stairs until he was out of sight.

Chapter 33 — Prime Suspect

DRU DROPPED AN EMAIL PRINTOUT on Mariana's desk.

"I'm assuming this isn't a love letter," she said, picking it up and holding it at reading distance from her eyes. Dropping the page, she looked at her partner. "So, Reggie Millen's blood type is a match for the knife found at the scene of Javier Estrada's murder and the blood we found by the Hangman's Elm."

"Yep." Dru reached out to retrieve the paper. "That puts Javier in the park having a knife fight with Reggie in both places. I mean, we can't be one hundred percent sure without a DNA match, but I'm willing to run with it. Javier apparently cut him. I'm guessing that Reggie then shot Javier."

"Makes sense, unless somebody else was there to pull the trigger. Remember that Mr. Rojas saw two men chasing Javier."

"Yeah. I remember. Listen, I know we have a theory, but we aren't sure Estrada wasn't involved in the Monroe killing."

"Maybe . . ." Mariana seemed to be thinking in a different direction. "Is there any connection between Estrada and Millen? Did they both run with the Antipático?"

"The gang members all denied that Bull ran with them. Then again, they were all scared of the guy, so they might have lied."

Mariana leaned back in her desk chair. "I'm not closing off any possibilities, but there's nothing in Estrada's recent history to suggest that he was involved in drugs or anything else criminal."

"Do we have an APB out for Millen?"

"Yeah. Remember? He shot an EMT? Everybody in town is looking for him."

Dru tossed the paper back onto Mariana's desk. "OK. Maybe we'll get lucky."

* * *

THAT AFTERNOON, Mariana and Dru participated in a video call in the only conference room in the precinct with the proper tech. Captain Sullivan sat with his two detectives. On the elevated television screen, Commissioner Earl Ward, Virginia Healy, the communications director for the mayor's office, and David Zimmerman, an assistant district attorney, occupied square boxes. Ward's video background was a tropical beach, while Zimmerman's background looked like his basement, which it was.

"We've had no luck apprehending Reggie Millen," Sullivan reported to the group. "It doesn't look like he has lived at his last known address for some time. We've got uniforms canvassing his known locations, provided by the narcotics squad, but so far nobody admits to knowing where he is. We've got a bulletin out to all the local hospitals and doctors' offices, since we know he had multiple stab wounds when they put him in that ambulance. But the EMTs had given him on-scene first aid, so it's possible he could recover without further medical treatment, or with treatment from someone outside the official networks."

"Do we have any other leads?" Commissioner Ward asked.

"We're tracking down several," Sully confidently responded, "and we'll keep doing that. But I have to tell you that none of them are as promising as this one."

Zimmerman spoke up. He looked every bit the lawyer, wearing a button-down dress shirt and a conservatively patterned tie, his hair perfectly parted and combed. "It's certainly important that we can place Millen at the scene of Estrada's murder. But, remember that Millen's blood was on Estrada's knife. This would be consistent with a fight and a self-defense claim. I'm interested in all the facts, but if Millen says that Estrada attacked him and stabbed him, getting a conviction could be a problem. And, according to the police on the scene in that alley, Millen was attacked by three or four men and was stabbed multiple times. It turns out Millen had a gun on him, but unless he's an idiot, the ballistics won't match the Monroe murder. We'll test it, but any connection at this point is just speculation."

"You know how to throw cold water on an investigation," Dru mumbled.

"I don't like losing, Detective. If we prosecute, I want to make sure we have a solid case."

"We all understand that," Sully jumped back in, trying to keep everyone on track. "The ballistics on the gun that killed Estrada shows it as a .22-caliber. Monroe was shot with a .45. That suggests two shooters. One of them could be Millen, and it's not out of the question that one could have been Estrada."

"Cap, the autopsy on Estrada concluded that there was no powder residue on his hands. He did not fire a gun the night he died," Mariana cut in.

Sully gave her an unhappy scowl. He didn't like being interrupted. "We know the girl owned a .22, so it's possible it was her gun, used by one of her assailants. We don't have any other suspects at this point."

"Did we get anything from her phone?" Ward asked.

Dru responded after Sully shot him a scowl. "No, Sir. We got the father's consent, but Apple is still giving us a hard time."

Virginia inquired whether there was anything they could use for a press update. The mayor wanted to report that the investigation was progressing and that they were getting closer to finding the killer. "Can we at least say we have new evidence and we're getting closer to an arrest?"

The group consensus was that Virginia's suggested statement was not wrong, although it probably gave an impression that they were closer than they really were. It was still accurate enough to go with. Virginia signed off the call to draft the press release so the commissioner could deliver the message at the evening's press briefing. They wanted a positive sound bite ready for the six o'clock news.

After Ward and Zimmerman said good-bye, Sully sat with Dru and Mariana for several minutes. "You defending this dead kid?" Sully stared across the conference table at Mariana.

"I'm just pointing out the facts," she said evenly, without any apology.

Before Sully could respond, Dru's phone buzzed. "It's Mike Jung, from the narco unit." Dru ducked outside the room, leaving Sully and Mariana alone.

"Listen, Vega, it's fine to point out the facts, but don't make me look bad in front of my boss, you get it?"

"I get it," Mariana held her captain's eyes. "We have to have each other's backs. Do I get the same consideration?"

Sully sighed and looked down, breaking the eye contact. "You gotta take that up with your partner. There's nobody else in this station who could have backed you up on Floyd Merriman."

Dru returned to the conference room, set down his phone on the table, and pushed the speaker button. "Mike, I've got

Mariana and Captain Sullivan here with me and you're on speaker. Please tell them what you just told me."

The tinny-sounding voice coming through the speaker said, "I have a beat cop down here on the Lower East Side who says she had a conversation with a friend of hers, a reporter for a local rag. He got a tip that Javier Estrada was shot by a small-caliber pistol and that Angelica Monroe was shot by a .45. The reporter's source claims that the same guy shot both victims and that the little gun used to kill Estrada belonged to Monroe."

Sully whistled. "I don't suppose this reporter is willing to reveal the identity of his source?"

"No. Not a surprise. Was the information about the ballistics on the two guns leaked to the press?"

"No," Dru called out, louder than necessary. "We kept the details about the two guns confidential. It's possible that someone from the lab leaked it, but only a few people know about Monroe owning a twenty-two. Anybody who knows all that must have been there or heard it from somebody who was."

"What do we do with this?" Sully asked the group.

The voice on the phone said, "According to Officer Wresh, the informant might be willing to talk, but the reporter wanted to see if the information was good. He didn't mention the reward money, but I'm betting that has something to do with it."

"Tell him it's good and that we want to talk to his source, as soon as possible." Sully ended the call when nobody else had anything to say. "I hope I don't have to tell you two to jump on this. Go talk to Officer Wresh and track down the reporter."

Dru and Mariana left the conference room without another word.

Chapter 34 — Confirmation

MAKING CONTACT WITH THE POLICE was never a problem for Paulo. His cop friend, Jodi Wresh, was the daughter of Paulo's mother's best friend. They grew up in the same building. Five years older, Paulo served as Jodi's surrogate big brother. Since she became an officer, Paulo always knew he had a conduit for information, but he used it sparingly. He didn't want to abuse the privilege or get Jodi in trouble for leaking information to the media. Fortunately, the NYPD hardly considered the *LES Tribune* to be part of the media. He flew under the radar.

In this particular case, Paulo had no worries, since he knew the police brass would be thrilled to have any tip about the Angelica Monroe murder. Jodi wouldn't even need to protect his identity. Paulo could have called Detective Dru Cook directly, but he was still annoyed at the way the detective had brushed him off at their last meeting. He hoped Jodi would be able to make contact with somebody higher up.

When the call back came from Jodi's NYPD mobile number, Paulo answered on the second ring. It had been less than an hour since he had left Hannah's apartment. Things were moving fast. He attempted to sound casual as his pulse raced. "What's the good word, Officer Wresh?"

"It's just me, Paulo. There's nobody else listening, so you can drop the *Officer Wresh* bit."

"Great, Jodi. So, what's happening?"

"I got your information to the detectives on the case, and I think also to the big brass at City Hall. I got a call back from Detective Cook, who's the lead. He says the information your informant provided was legit. He wants to talk to you and to your witness."

"I knew the guy was telling it straight. I have someone else working with me who has some lawyers. We should be in a position to arrange a meeting soon, but we need to get some more information from the witness first. I don't know who he is, or where to find him, or how to contact him. So, there's no point interrogating me. Tell Detective Cook that I'm not talking and the lawyers tell me I wouldn't have to reveal my source even if I knew his identity. So, you need to give me a little time. I'll try to get with him and with the lawyers tomorrow and then I'll let you know if we're ready for a meeting. My guy wants an immunity deal."

Jodi whistled softly. "That's gonna be a tall order, but what the hell do I know?"

"I don't expect it to be easy, Jodi. Thanks for your assist. I met Cook on Saturday. I have his card. I'll call him directly when we're ready to talk."

"Don't wait too long, Paulo. Everybody is in a big-ass rush to break this case. If you don't get back to Cook pretty fast, somebody will probably pay you a visit in the middle of the night."

"Thanks. That'll help me sleep." He hung up and considered calling Hannah, but decided she didn't need any more pressure. The cops knew he was the link to an important witness. They didn't know Hannah was involved yet. There was no hurry to tell the cops about her. Paulo tried calling Luis's burner phone again, but got a message that the voicemail box for the number was not set up. He opened his laptop and began typing a draft for a story. He had no idea how it would end.

Chapter 35 — On Camera

PAULO SPENT THE NEXT HOUR working on his hypothetical draft for the Javier Estrada/Angelica Monroe scoop. Then he turned his attention to two small stories that had been pushed aside by the breaking news. His heart was not in them, however. The economic struggles of a small business owner and the losing battle against rat infestation at a local playground didn't seem as important as they had a week earlier.

Clarence had taken Paulo off any other stories, which freed him to work on DEADHOOPS, the code name for the reporting about Javier Estrada. Clarence insisted on using secretive pseudonyms like the big papers, as if anyone would be trying to steal scoops from the *LES Tribune*.

He was re-writing his lede paragraph for the RATPLAY story, having trouble concentrating while constantly peeking at his phone on the end table next to his combination sofa and work station. He recalled explaining the day before to a group of high school students why newspapers called the subject paragraph of a story the *lede* and not the *lead*. In the old days, the manual typesetters used hot lead to format the letters for the printing presses. So as not to confuse the two homophones, writers used the word *lede* to make sure there were no mix-ups. The convention continued in modern newsrooms, even though hot-lead printing presses became obsolete fifty years ago. Those students had been on the school paper at Lower East Side Preparatory High School—Javier Estrada's school.

Paulo's distracted writing efforts melted from his mind when his phone vibrated. The screen showed UNKNOWN NUMBER. It was Luis. Paulo explained that the cops wanted to talk. Luis wanted to know if Paulo had worked out a deal for immunity, but Paulo broke the news that he needed more information. Knowing about the guns opened the door and got the cops' attention, but for an immunity deal, he would need to provide evidence that would secure a conviction.

Paulo also explained that he needed to bring in somebody with the resources to get the job done. Luis needed to come to another meeting with Paulo and his television producer partner. Luis wasn't happy, but Paulo spent five minutes explaining the reasons, concluding that there would not be any deal without another meeting first.

Luis refused to meet at Paulo's apartment, fearing that the cops would be there. Nothing Paulo could say would change his mind. Luis insisted they meet on the softball field on the FDR Drive near 6th Street. Paulo understood. There was a large empty space all around, so it would be impossible for the cops to sneak up on him. There were also a dozen ways to get out if it was a trap.

He called Hannah. "The guy's not stupid," Paulo said after summarizing the call with Luis.

Hannah took a long, slow breath. "I hope that's good for us, and not a problem."

"Meet me here in an hour. We'll walk over together."

* * *

AT THE APPOINTED TIME, Paulo and Hannah arrived and stood in the semi-darkness at home plate with only the city's ever-present ambient light around them. The Williamsburg Bridge twinkled across the East River's calm water. The field had no lights, which Luis must have known. Hannah set up her portable tripod and mounted her phone, ready to record Luis. The balmy April temperatures of the past few days had taken a chilly turn, leaving Paulo wishing he had worn a heavier jacket.

When it was five minutes past the meeting time, Hannah pulled the hood of her ACN-logo sweatshirt over her head. "What are the chances our boy shows up with a gang and murders us both?" She laughed nervously at her own joke.

"I'm not worried about that. Remember, it was his idea to have me contact the cops for him. He needs me. He needs *us*." Paulo moved next to Hannah and put an arm around her shoulders. He wanted to comfort her and also share her body heat. Hannah leaned in, happy to have both.

"Thanks for trusting me, Paulo."

He squeezed Hannah's right shoulder. "We're both at the bottom of the totem pole. Us bottom-dwellers need to help each other."

Hannah leaned her head onto Paulo's shoulder. "We're not bottom-dwellers. We're both on the rise. We've got nowhere to go but up."

Paulo didn't need to face the question of how long to maintain his posture because two dark figures walked toward them across the grass.

"I ain't happy to be here," Luis said without any preliminary greeting.

"Who's this?" Paulo kept his voice casual.

"My boy, Enrique. You said you were bringing somebody else, so I got Q." Luis folded his arms and leaned backward on his left leg, posing like a rapper who had just completed a song.

"Alright. That's fine. As long as you don't mind Enrique hearing what you have to say."

"Q knows everything, Bro. I got no secrets."

"Fine. Come over here, by home plate." Paulo directed Luis to stand where the light from a distant street lamp cast an eerie glow across the ball field. "This is Hannah Hawthorne, with American Cable News. We met with the network's lawyers and we're clear about our rights to protect your identity and keep you confidential until you're ready to talk to the police. You want an immunity deal, so you need to tell us the information that you think is worth a grant of immunity. We'll share it with the cops, but we'll blur out your face and electronically alter your voice so they won't be able to identify you. If the district attorney agrees that your testimony is worth a grant of immunity, then we'll try to make the deal happen. You understand?"

"Yeah. I get it."

Hannah stepped forward furtively, extending her hand. "I'm Hannah." Luis made no move to shake hands, prompting Hannah to swing her arm down and step back. "I'm a producer with ACN, and I'm authorized to promise you that we will protect your identity to the maximum extent permitted by law."

"That better be total protection." Enrique spoke for the first time. His deep voice boomed across the empty field.

Hannah reflexively took another step back. "Yes. We won't expose your identity, not that we really know it, frankly. And we won't show your face or your real voice, so the cops won't be able to come get you."

"Let's get this over with," Luis said, standing in front of the phone. Hannah adjusted the tripod, then tapped the screen to begin recording and motioned to Paulo that they were live.

Over the next seven minutes, prompted by some gentle questions from Paulo, Luis explained that he was the second in command of the weed distribution operation headed up by Bull. Luis didn't know Bull's real name, but Bull had taken over the operation from the prior boss, whose name Luis also didn't know.

"How did you know Angelica Monroe?"

"Who?"

"The girl who got shot at the Hangman's Elm Friday night." Paulo struggled to avoid sounding annoyed.

"Oh, yeah. She was one of our sharks."

"What's a shark?"

"See, the sharks are the distributors. The old boss set it all up. We give the weed to the sharks and they got other dudes who they sell to. We call them the minnows. The minnows sell to the users. It's mostly college kids. They don't wanna admit they're buying weed, and even if they tried to rat us out, the minnow only knows the shark. They don't know us. So, it's like, very well organized."

"How did Angelica become a shark?"

"Who?"

Paulo made a conscious effort to not show annoyance. "The girl."

"Oh, she got recruited by the old NYU shark. That's part of the operation. When the sharks are gonna graduate, they recruit their own replacement. The boss pays 'em a finder's fee. So, the girl came from the old shark."

"OK. Fine. So, what happened on Friday night?"

"The shark bitch texted me and said she was short. She didn't have the money to pay for her next supply. She also ain't paid off her nut yet."

"What's a nut?"

"When the new sharks start up, the boss gives 'em their first supply on credit. They owe the boss the money, so they pay some back every time they come to get a new supply. They buy the new supply with the money from selling to the minnows, plus they pay back their loan. That's their nut."

Paulo wasn't interested in delving into the finances for the drug distribution operation any further. "OK, so Angelica was short. So, what happened?"

"I told Bull that the bitch was short. So, Bull decided he was gonna make sure she learned a lesson. That's the way Bull operates. So, he's there with me when the shark shows up an' she says some bullshit about how she got robbed and she lost her money an' shit. Well, Bull ain't buyin' that, so he grabs her and tells her she gotta suck his dick and beg for forgiveness or else he's gonna fuck her up."

"And where were you when that was happening?"

"I was standin' there. I ain't into that kinda shit, man. I don't wanna hurt nobody. I'm just tryin' to make a buck. I ain't gonna tell Bull how to handle a shark."

"OK, so then what happened?"

"Man, that's when the ball player showed up. He yelled from the bushes, like, 'Yo, everything cool here?' You know, like he was tryin'a stick his nose in."

"That was Javier Estrada?"

"Yeah. The big hoops star. Yeah. That's him."

"Then what happened?"

"So, Bull has the bitch down on her knees after he roughed her up some, but he tells Javier to mind his own damn business. The kid, like, tells Bull to leave the girl alone, like he's some kind of boy scout. Then, Bull pulls a knife and the kid pulls a knife and they start goin' at it. But then, the shark bitch yells at Bull. I pretty much forgot she was there while Bull and the other dude were fighting so when I look at her, she's holding this little gun. She tells Bull to leave him alone."

"Did she shoot at Bull?"

"No, man. She could barely hold up the gun she was so scared. Bull stops fighting with the kid and dives onto the ground toward the girl. He comes up with some dirt in his hand and throws it into the bitch's face, then knocks the gun away."

"What were you doing while this was happening?"

"Nothin', man. I was watching. So, Bull grabs the girl by the hair and tells her she shouldn't point guns at people. Then he pulls out his own piece and blasts her right between the eyes."

Paulo and Hannah both flinched involuntarily. Enrique, who had no doubt heard the story before, stood passively.

"What happened to Javier?"

"He ran."

"Did you run after him?"

"Bull ran after him, then I followed Bull. Then the kid took a bad step and fell down. When he got back up, he was, like, limping. So, we—well, Bull—caught up to him and tackled him and Bull started beating on him. Bull's a big guy. Then he was kicking the dude. Then Bull shot him with the little girl's little gun."

"Where were you while this was happening?"

"Man, I was watching."

"To be clear, you did not try to prevent Bull from shooting Javier Estrada?"

"No, man. I wasn't gonna get in between that. When Bull gets mad, ain't nobody gonna get in his way."

"OK. I understand. Then what did you do?"

"We got outta there, fast."

"Alright. Now, why are you telling us all this now?"

"Man, I want that immunity, so I don't get arrested, and so my boys don't get arrested because of selling weed or because we tried to handle the situation ourselves."

"What do you mean? You need to be specific," Paulo prodded.

"Me and my boys decided Bull was out of control, so we tried to take over the operation ourselves. We told Bull we were gonna cut him out. Bull didn't like that, so he jumps me in an alley and he and I get into it with our blades. I was givin' it to him good when the cops showed up. We're like, Good Samaritans an' shit on that one, you know? I'm not goin' down for trying to handle our business."

"OK. So, you want immunity from prosecution for your involvement in the Angelica Monroe and Javier Estrada murders, your involvement in the drug distribution operation, and your assault on Bull. And you want similar immunity for your gang—"

"Hey! We ain't no gang!" Enrique spoke up from beyond the camera frame.

"Sorry," Paulo said. "Immunity for your associates, including Enrique . . . and who else?"

"Oscar and Wilmer," Luis rattled off the first names.

"And you're ready to testify against Bull in court about all this?"

Luis put his head down and kicked the dirt in the batter's box. "Yeah. I guess I will, if I have to."

Paulo gave a "cut" signal to Hannah, who ended the recording and packed up her phone and tripod quickly. "Alright. I think that's enough for now. We'll probably need the last names of your boys for a formal immunity agreement, but we'll handle that later. We have what we need for now. We'll try our best to get the DA to go along with it."

Enrique sprang forward with the speed of a linebacker breaking on a receiver running a crossing route. Paulo saw a black gun in the big man's extended hand a split-second before it smacked him across the side of his head. Paulo dropped to the ground. Hannah let out a muted scream, before catching herself and covering her mouth with a trembling hand.

Enrique pointed the gun at Hannah. Her hand fell away from her face as she dropped to her knees on the dusty ground. Her pulse spiked to twice its usual rate, pounding in her ears. The gun's dark shape was all she could see as she sucked in a breath, frozen in place.

"Chill, Q," Luis shouted. "Paulo here is helpin' us."

Enrique lowered the gun and turned to Paulo, still on the ground. "You and this bitch need to do better than just try." Enrique's voice was filled with menace. Hannah had no doubt that the muscular figure holding the gun wouldn't hesitate to murder them if he thought there was the slightest reason.

Luis and Enrique turned without another word and walked away, leaving Hannah and Paulo in the dirt.

Paulo crawled to Hannah, reaching out a hand and touching her ankle. "I'm so sorry, Hannah. You OK?"

Rolling onto her side and sitting up, she replied, "Yeah. Better than you." She scrambled forward while reaching into her pocket for her phone. She then grabbed her small equipment bag and extracted a tissue. By the light of her flashlight app, she dabbed blood from Paulo's head. It was a shallow wound and had already stopped actively bleeding. "This doesn't look too bad. You want to go to the hospital?"

"No!" Paulo shouted, more loudly than he intended. "I don't want to have to explain how this happened. I'm fine. He caught me off guard." He put his hand over Hannah's on his temple and took over holding the tissue against the gash. His fingers lingered on top of hers for a few extra seconds.

"Do we believe Luis's story—that he was just a bystander and it was Bull who killed both Angelica and Javier?"

"I do." Paulo got to his feet and dusted off his pants with one hand. "He came to me because he was scared of Bull. He's a drug dealer, for sure, but look at him. He's not a thug like his buddy,

Enrique. There are a hundred young men like Luis in my neighborhood. It's a fine line between collecting garbage and selling drugs. I don't fault him for getting involved with Bull's operation. Anyway, we're committed. The cops will want us to give up their identity. If we don't make a deal, both the authorities and these guys are going to want our asses on a barbeque."

Hannah laughed at the simile, unable to control herself. "I'll take my Paulo brisket slow-cooked and on a brioche bun."

Paulo smiled, despite the pain still throbbing in his head. "That's a prime cut, but I'd prefer to keep it in my pants." They both laughed at Paulo's unintended double entendre. After a minute of gathering themselves and their gear, they headed back toward Paulo's apartment. Hannah planned to upload the video to her laptop and edit the material that night, so they would be ready to show it to the cops the next day.

* * *

THE FRONT PAGES of all the New York papers Tuesday morning still blared headlines about the Angelica Monroe murder, fueled by a large rally the night before. The accompanying articles provided few new details, but reported encouraging statements from the NYPD about the progress of the investigation.

The local news shows all continued to cover the story, even after their vans departed from Washington Square Park. CNN, CNBC, MSNBC, FOX NEWS, and ACN did the same. Like their print colleagues, the broadcast outlets had nothing truly new to say. A few put on interviews with experts on murder investigations, who speculated about what might have happened and what the police were probably doing. So far, nobody had been able to identify the man in the photo the police had sent around to all the media outlets.

At nine o'clock, at the urging of several social media accounts, a crowd gathered around the Hangman's Elm. Two local stations sent crews back to the park to shoot video and ran clips on their late news broadcasts. Amateur cell phone videos generated millions of hits on dozens of internet sites. A consortium of gun-control advocacy groups organized signs and candles, and provided a microphone and sound system for speeches that few in the crowd could hear clearly. The activists shouted about the flow of illegal guns, rampant drug use and crime, and the failure of the city, state, and federal government to do something to stop them.

The number of food and souvenir vendors servicing the demonstrators had nearly doubled as entrepreneurs from other neighborhoods migrated to Washington Square Park seeking the increased business. The regular vendors, who had sold out the night before, didn't mind the competition. There was business enough for all, although the crowd was only half the size of Monday night's.

The NYU administration made a decision not to participate officially in the demonstration, although many university employees joined the students in the crowd, chanting, "Justice for Angelica!" Students from colleges around New York also joined the crowd, along with students from New Jersey and Connecticut. Small groups advocating socialism, anarchism, white supremacy, gun rights, and, oddly, LGBTQ+ rights attempted to get their own chants going, without much success. University security asked the organizers to lower the volume in accordance with noise-abatement regulations, after which the crowd slowly dispersed.

Chapter 36 — The Center Ring

Wednesday

WEDNESDAY MORNING, after an exchange of messages with Jodi, Paulo phoned Dru Cook. The detective attempted to extract information over the phone about the specifics of Paulo's witness and his information. Paulo refused to divulge anything until he was talking directly to somebody who had the authority to grant the immunity deal Luis wanted. Considering how unhelpful the detective had been when Paulo first came to him with information, Paulo was not inclined to give any ground. Plus, after being pistol-whipped the night before, he wasn't intimidated. A half-hour later, Dru invited Paulo to a meeting at the district attorney's office in Foley Square.

Hannah and Paulo had spoken with their bosses and secured permission to proceed with the plan. They also received assurances that they could keep Luis's identity secret until the cops agreed to the deal. Dave Butler promised to bail out Hannah if she got arrested for obstruction of justice—and Paulo, if it came to that. ACN's legal department had contacted an outside firm to provide a criminal defense lawyer, who would have some experience with an immunity agreement.

Butler reminded Hannah that, in order to run the story, the ACN lawyers needed to know the identity of their informant. They could keep his name off the air, but they had to be confident he was authentic. No identification, no story. Hannah said she understood, not knowing whether Luis would appreciate the journalistic ethics issue or whether he would agree to provide a driver's license.

A few hours later, a prim administrative assistant escorted Paulo and Hannah, along with Doug Motzenbecker from the firm of Ballo, Cannon, & Taylor, into a brightly lit conference room on the 12th floor of the hulking municipal building at One Hogan Place. The gray cinder-block structure housed the headquarters of the Manhattan District Attorney.

Around a polished maple table, six pairs of eyes followed their movements. Detectives Dru Cook and Mariana Vega sat next to each other. Assistant District Attorney David Zimmerman sat to Dru's left. Virginia Healy, the mayor's communications chief, Albert Knowles—the deputy police commissioner—and Edward Longfellow—an attorney from the city's corporation counsel's office—completed the city's contingent. All sat at attention with pads and pens in front of them. Everyone but Mariana had coffee cups.

Zimmerman, their host, introduced everyone around the table. After Paulo, Hannah, and Motzenbecker declined offers of coffee, the ADA got right down to business. "Mr. Richardson, I understand you have evidence relevant to the Angelica Monroe murder?"

"And the Javier Estrada murder," Paulo replied. "Javier was the hero here. He tried to protect a complete stranger, Angelica Monroe, in the park last Friday. For his bravery, he was killed. Let's make sure everybody is clear on that point." He swung his gaze around the table, making eye contact with each person, but lingering on Mariana.

"We'll get to all that," Zimmerman said, waiting for Paulo to look back at him before continuing. "Are you going to tell us the identity of your source?"

"No," Paulo replied evenly. He could feel his pulse racing. The ADA had the power to have him thrown in jail. "Not until we have an agreement on immunity for the witnesses."

"How many witnesses are there?" Mariana cut in.

"One primary witness and three secondary players who were tangentially involved, all of whom should get immunity in exchange for their cooperation."

Zimmerman, wearing a light blue suit jacket with a dark blue necktie, held out a hand to make sure he had the floor. "Hold on. We're a very long way away from granting anyone immunity. Let's take this one step at a time. First, Mr. Motzenbecker, do you represent the witness or witnesses who are requesting immunity?"

"Not yet," Motzenbecker responded confidently. "I have not had the chance to speak directly to them, but they granted Mr. Richardson and Ms. Hawthorne authority to negotiate for them, so my expectation is that I will be their authorized attorney at some point."

Zimmerman nodded noncommittally. "Do you represent Mr. Richardson and Ms. Hawthorne?"

"Yes, I do. My firm has been retained by ACN to represent these individuals, the company, and the witnesses, assuming they give their consent."

"What about the *Lower East Side Tribune*? Do you represent it also?"

Motzenbecker looked at Paulo, who shrugged. "No, Sir. I don't formally represent that publication, but I believe all our interests are aligned."

"Fine," Zimmerman said, without conceding anything. "Why don't you explain to us what evidence you think your witnesses have?"

Hannah pulled out her laptop and set it on the conference table. "We'll do better than that. We'll show it to you." This caused an audible reaction from everyone in the room, making Hannah and Paulo both stifle satisfied grins.

The group spent several minutes futzing with AV cords extending through an opening in the conference table, connected to a large television screen against the wall nearest to Hannah and Paulo. Everyone sat in silence when Hannah started the seven-minute video of Luis—his face blurred out and his voice altered—explaining what happened Friday night in Washington Square Park. Dru, Mariana, and Zimmerman furiously took notes.

When the video ended, Motzenbecker set out the terms of the anticipated deal. "The witness and his associates want immunity from prosecution for their involvement in the drug trafficking operation; for their role, if any, in the murders of Angelica Monroe and Javier Estrada; and from charges stemming from their assault on the shooter, the man he called Bull. In exchange for the immunity agreement, they will cooperate and testify."

Dru looked at Virginia Healy. "This guy, Bull—he's the one we now know as Reggie Millen. He was stabbed multiple times in an alley on Monday. He shot his way out of an ambulance and ran off." Turning back to Paulo, he asked, "Am I correct in assuming that Millen's injuries were inflicted by your witnesses during their fight?"

"Yes, I think that's right."

Dru kept his poker face in place. "Mr. Millen suffered two puncture stab wounds to the side of his chest. He was lucky they didn't pierce any major organs or he'd be dead now. That wasn't just a fight, Mr. Richardson, it was an ambush. Four male suspects ran from the scene, leaving Millen—Bull—on the ground bleeding out. The paramedics got to him barely in time to save his life. So, your witnesses are guilty of attempted murder. You expect us to give them immunity from that?"

Paulo and Hannah exchanged eye contact. The cops' version of the story seemed somewhat different from Luis's account. They had talked with their new lawyer about how to handle this question, but were not sure whether it made a difference how injured Bull was.

They both looked at Motzenbecker, who launched into his prepared answer. "Mr. Zimmerman, you have a high-profile murder case here and from what I can gather the police are a long way from even identifying a suspect."

Al Knowles was there to represent Earl Ward and to report back so the commissioner could plan a press conference to announce a huge break in the case. He knew how anxious his boss was to make an arrest. "Actually, we have already identified Mr. Millen as a prime suspect and we're working to apprehend him now."

"I'll have to take that on faith," Motzenbecker said, "but my expectation is that you will very much want some admissible evidence linking him to Angelica Monroe's murder. Right now, I'm guessing you have little or nothing. Here you have one eyewitness and several corroborating witnesses. This guy is a killer, so if my future clients and their associates got into a fight with him, I'm sure any injuries to Bull were inflicted in self-defense."

After a pause, Zimmerman continued. "So, we're to understand that this witness we saw on video is second in command of a drug ring, of which Reggie Millen is the leader?"

"Yes," Paulo responded curtly.

"OK, so your witness wants us to arrest and convict his boss and get him out of the way so the witness can take over the operation and, in the process, give him and all his accomplices immunity from prosecution for all past crimes? That's it?"

Paulo had not thought about the request in exactly those terms before. "I suppose that's one way of thinking about it. They're taking a big risk, so they want an appropriate benefit."

"So, when we put him on the witness stand, the defense attorney is going to be able to establish that he has several exceptionally good reasons to be lying. First, he's an admitted criminal who has been dealing illegal drugs and he admits being an accomplice to Angelica Monroe's murder."

"He didn't kill anybody," Paulo protested.

"Maybe, but he's still an accomplice, and has reason to lie about it. Second, he stabbed Reggie Millen in a fight, for which he could be prosecuted for attempted murder—a crime for which the witness gets immunity only if he testifies."

"That was self-defense," Paulo spoke up again, despite Motzenbecker's hand on his arm urging him to keep quiet.

"Reggie can also claim self-defense," Zimmerman said, then continued. "The police found a knife at the scene of Mr. Estrada's murder with Millen's blood on it, and Estrada's prints. It would appear that Estrada assaulted Millen."

"You heard the explanation on the video," Hannah protested.

"Yes, but that's only one possible story. In any event, there are more problems. Your witness would be asking the jury to convict his boss and send him away forever, after which the witness will become the new boss, which will give him more money and power. He gets immunity for himself and all his associates for all past crimes related to the drug ring and any other related crimes, but again, only if he testifies. And, it's a pretty good bet that if Millen is found not guilty, he's going to be coming after your witness, so the witness needs to make sure Millen goes down."

"Are you his lawyer, now?" Motzenbecker asked.

"No, but when Millen testifies that it was your witness who pulled the trigger on both murders and that he was acting in self-defense after being attacked and stabbed, our case will hang on whether the jury believes one drug dealer who's a rat rather than the other drug dealer who almost got stabbed to death. I'm not sure that's such a great case."

Motzenbecker looked like he was about to speak when Hannah beat him to it. "Our guy knows about the two guns. That proves he was really there. His associates will testify about the drug distribution operation and how Bull was the leader and Lu— our guy worked for him." Hannah cursed herself for nearly slipping and mentioning Luis's name. Of course, she wasn't sure it was a real name, but she needed to be more careful. "That gives you more than just one witness."

"Maybe," Zimmerman said slowly, "but your boy is also going to testify that Angelica Monroe was a part of the operation—that she was a drug dealer and that she was killed by her drug ring boss. That's not going to go down well with any future jurors. What other evidence do you have to back it up?" When nobody spoke, he looked to Motzenbecker. "You see the problem?"

Paulo burst from his chair, startling everyone, including Hannah. "I'm sorry, but I am sick of everyone being worried about protecting the reputation of Angelica Monroe. It's pretty clear that she was dealing weed, and that she was in the park Friday night to meet with her supplier. It's also crystal clear

Javier tried to intervene. If the evidence showed that Javier was involved in the drug ring, you would all be thrilled to leak that and smear his name to make it seem less tragic that he was killed. But for the White girl, you want to protect the lie that she was an innocent bystander and a saintly suburban princess who was caught up in street violence because that helps your political narrative. Well, it's bullshit and I'm not going to sit by and let you keep feeding that racist monster."

Paulo glared around the room. Dru had his head turned toward Mariana, who looked down at the table, not making eye contact.

"Calm down, Mr. Richardson," Zimmerman said as nonconfrontationally as possible. "Nobody is smearing anyone or protecting anyone. I'm only protecting a possible case. You came here wanting immunity for your witness. Now, you can go out and publish a story based on your reporting and your source and I'm sure you'll get a lot of hits on your website. But if you do that it will compromise your witness and, since Reggie Millen is still at large, it might put him in a ton of danger. So, let's all try to focus on what matters—arresting and convicting this killer.

"I'm not questioning the veracity of your witness. In fact, I believe what he said. But I also have to think about how it all plays out in court. If we try Millen and lose, then he walks, and we will have given immunity to everyone else who might have been involved. We all look like idiots and all the criminals get away Scot-free. I'm not a big fan of that outcome."

"Nobody would be," Motzenbecker said. Paulo and Hannah remained silent.

"Let's take a little break, shall we?" Zimmerman suggested, standing. The others left Paulo, Hannah, and their lawyer in the room.

Once alone, Hannah started to say something, but Motzenbecker held up a hand to shush her. "Don't say anything. There could be listening devices in this room, so anything you say may be on tape."

"You really think the cops would bug their own conference room?" Hannah was incredulous.

"I do." Motzenbecker's face was serious.

They sat for ten minutes in virtual silence, save for the sound effects coming from their cell phones. When the door opened again and the city officials marched back to their seats, the tension level in the room jumped as if a jury was coming back with a verdict.

Zimmerman took his seat and adopted a somber expression, his lips pressed into a straight line. "First, let me say to you three that we truly appreciate you sharing this information. I realize that your source is reluctant to come forward without an immunity deal. That's understandable, given his involvement. But it is precisely his involvement that gives me pause. This person may be more culpable than his version of the story suggests. At the very least, he's an accomplice and, under the felony murder rule, may be guilty of murder. He admits to being a high-ranking member of the drug distribution scheme. These are extraordinarily serious crimes. Granting him immunity, let alone his accomplices in the drug ring, would be an unprecedented deal. The district attorney would consider it only if there were no other way to secure a conviction. At this time, we can't know whether we will be able to apprehend and convict Reggie Millen without your client's cooperation. It's also possible that his cooperation can be secured without this particular immunity deal. I cannot in good conscience agree to it."

Motzenbecker held up a hand, seeing that both Paulo and Hannah were leaning forward, ready to speak. "Don't you want to convict the man who killed Angelica Monroe?"

"Of course we do!" The ADA tossed his pen onto the pad in front of him and sat back. "But we're not likely to have physical evidence proving that Millen pulled the trigger. He may claim that your guy did. Now it's one drug dealer's word against another."

Hannah shouted, "What's the guy supposed to do? He's come forward and offered to testify. What else do you want?"

"And he has all kinds of selfish motives," Zimmerman calmly replied. "He knows he's a criminal and is neck-deep in this shit-hole, if you excuse my language. He's not credible enough for us to put our whole case on his testimony. But I'll tell you what he can do. He can give us better evidence. He can deliver a murder weapon with Millen's prints on it, or he could give us something even better."

"What's better than a murder weapon?" Motzenbecker queried.

Zimmerman turned to look at Knowles. "He could get us a confession."

Paulo couldn't suppress a snorting laugh. "Oh, sure. Like Bull is going to—Wait. You want my source to wear a wire and get Bull to incriminate himself?"

"That would be worth making a deal," Zimmerman said.

"Sure, except that the only way Bull is going to meet with my source again is to kill him. There's no way to set up a meeting."

"Of course," Zimmerman said, "there certainly is an element of risk. I'm sure your guy could figure out a way to get Millen to show for a meeting if he wanted to."

"Yeah, I'm sure he could, but I'm also sure Millen would bring a big gun."

"Maybe the same one he used to shoot Angelica Monroe?"

Paulo stared silently at the ADA. "I have no idea. I just know my guy would never agree to it."

"So, you already thought about it and asked him?"

"No, of course not," Paulo had to admit.

"Then I suggest you ask him, because it's the only way he's going to get a deal. He wants immunity for a host of major crimes. For that, he needs to deliver something that's going to ensure a rock-solid conviction."

The silence in the room felt like the moments before a funeral service. Finally, Motzenbecker said, "May I consult with my clients privately?"

Zimmerman rose from his chair and picked up his pad and pen. "Sure, but you can do it outside. We're done here. There's no need for us to wait for you. I've told you that there's no deal based on your boy's testimony. I've told you what would get it done. If the witness wants to accept, then call me and we'll work out the details. The NYPD will provide support and protection. If you have some other idea, you can let me know, but we're done for today."

Zimmerman led the rest of the city's delegation from the room. Mariana, the last one in the line, exchanged a sympathetic glance with Paulo, then closed the door.

"Let's get out of here." Motzenbecker grabbed his briefcase.

Chapter 37 — Aftermath

PAULO AND HANNAH PUT Motzenbecker in a cab and adjourned to an Irish Pub called The Tilted Windmill on Mulberry Street to consider their options.

"Were we so focused on our story that we couldn't see how weak Luis's testimony would be?"

Paulo lifted his Dos Equis and peered through the deep amber liquid at Hannah, across the table. After a sip, he held the glass directly against his left eye. "Blinded by hubris and the pursuit of a scoop, we plunged ahead like drunken sailors, doomed from the start."

"Nice. You should be a writer."

"Oh, what I wouldn't give . . ." Paulo lowered his bubbly eyepiece.

After an exchange of chuckles and a clink of glasses, Hannah put down her Coors Light. "What are we going to tell him?"

"Luis? We tell him the truth straight up. Remember, it was *his* idea to ask for an immunity deal, not ours. It's not like we tricked him into making that video."

"But now it's our obligation to keep his identity confidential and keep that video away from the cops. His friend, Enrique, seems like the kind of guy who's not going to forgive us and walk away if we don't get the deal. Should I delete the recording?"

"If the cops try to force you to give it up and you destroyed it, knowing it was potentially evidence in a murder case, you'll go to jail for obstruction of justice. I don't think you want that."

"I know. So, what do I do?"

"If you trust your corporate lawyers, I'd say give it to them and let them hold it. They can shield it from discovery better than you, and you don't want to lose it or have it stolen."

"Thanks," Hannah slid her glass a few inches across the pock-marked black wood. "That's great advice, which I should have thought of myself. I guess I'm not used to this kind of pressure. I'm usually the one writing the copy, not facing down the barrel of a gun."

Paulo laid his right hand on top of Hannah's and patted it gently. He felt the tiny hairs on his arm stand at attention. "You're good, Hannah. Don't let anybody tell you differently." He removed his hand and pulled back his arm to grab his glass.

"You think he'll agree to cooperate with the police and wear a wire for a meeting with Bull?"

"If I were him?" Paulo tipped back his glass and drained his beer, buying a little thinking time. "I probably wouldn't trust the police. I would figure Bull will be there to kill me. If the cops are involved, they probably won't let Luis have a gun for the meet, so Luis will be at a major disadvantage, even with a dozen officers nearby. Of course, if Bull shoots Luis, he'll probably get caught, but that won't make a dead Luis feel any better."

"So, you wouldn't do it?"

"I think he *will* do it. What other choice does he have? He's already snitched on the guy. He's dead unless he kills Bull first."

"If Bull kills him, it will be our fault."

"I know, and it's making me sick. He came to me for help. He trusted me. Now he may be hung out to dry. If he agrees to wear the wire, I need to make sure the cops protect him."

"You're doing all you can," Hannah said.

"I'm not doing much for Luis. But I can still write a story. I'm going to publish the story about Angelica being a drug dealer. I've got enough for that. It's an unnamed source—two unnamed sources, counting Lars. But I have enough other reporting to do it."

"Will your editor let you publish without confirming Luis's identity?"

"I think so. I'll have to give him the information on Lars, but I think he'll understand that Luis is not in a position to provide his full name and address just yet."

"You really want to poke that hornets' nest?"

"I do. I'm so tired of playing nice. After I go live with it you can have the first broadcast scoop. Deal?"

Hannah slumped backward. "My boss isn't going to let me. It's *not part of our narrative.*" She mockingly imitated Dave Butler's voice. "I doubt many networks will go with it based on an anonymous source. But they will certainly report that you reported it. You'll get crucified."

"For telling the truth?"

"Only we know for sure it's the truth, assuming Luis is being honest. For anybody else, it seems like sour grapes from the guy who has been barking about Javier Estrada for a week. You've seen the coverage. Plenty of people will not believe you and think you're giving them fake news. Are you sure you want that heat? You need to focus on the big picture. What do you hope to accomplish?"

Paulo slid his empty glass to the edge of the table, hoping their waitress would notice and ask him if he wanted another. "I want people to know that not every White girl is innocent and not every brown boy is a gang member. I want them to mourn Javier."

"Great. Tell that story. Don't let people minimize the message because they're pissed off at you for trashing Angelica."

"Even if she deserves to be trashed?"

"How does that help Javier's family?"

"What do you mean?" Paulo caught their server's eye and motioned with two fingers for another round.

"What's better for Javier's reputation? That he tried to save a stranger's innocent life, or that because of him and Paulo Richardson, Angelica's sainted memory has been falsely besmirched?"

"It's not false!"

"In *your* mind it's not. But in the minds of all the people who have been watching television for the past week, it's absolutely false. I should know, I'm one of the people who have been telling them what to think. Believe me, no ten-second sound bite from a drug dealer is going to change people's minds. It's your voice against the voices of a hundred reporters and anchors with a million times more viewers than you have readers. Hell, even ACN will be against you."

"Not if you report the truth!" Paulo slammed his palm on the table, making the empty glasses jump and wobble.

Hannah lowered her voice and leaned across the table. "I can't. I don't report, I produce. I can write whatever copy I want but somebody else edits it before it goes on the air. My boss doesn't want to tell the true story, so I'm powerless."

"You had power to tell the *false* Angelica story."

Hannah sat back and crossed her arms. "I didn't know it was false when we started telling the story. I was getting a scoop. It wasn't like the Lower East Side Baby. My witness knew Angelica and told the truth about how sad it was that she got shot to death."

"Yeah," Paulo sighed, "but her roommate knew she was dealing drugs, too. She didn't tell you that, and you didn't ask."

"Like I was supposed to ask that?"

"No. I know. You had no reason to. But you fed the dragon and kept feeding it until now nobody wants to know the real facts."

"I did. I'll admit that. I wish I had your passion for the ultimate truth, Paulo. I really do. But sometimes you need to be practical."

"Does *practical* mean focusing on the ratings, the clicks, and the likes?"

"It *is* our job, isn't it?" Hannah leaned forward, a strand of hair falling across her right eye.

"We're not in the entertainment business." Paulo lifted his glass, forgetting it was empty. "The object isn't to get ratings, it's to provide important and accurate information."

"But if nobody watches, then they won't get any information."

"That's not our concern," Paulo broke eye contact and traced a figure-eight pattern in the condensation on the table.

"But what information is important? And who gets to decide? You? Why do you get to decide?"

Paulo shook his head slightly. "I'm not deciding, I'm reporting. I report on what's important and relevant."

"What if Javier's mother was a drug addict? would you report that?" Hannah maintained her eye contact, daring Paulo to answer.

"No. It wouldn't be relevant."

"Why not?" Hannah pressed her interview subject.

"It has nothing to do with the story about how Javier got shot and killed."

Hannah wasn't ready to give up the argument. "So, what is the story? Angelica was shot and killed. Javier tried to help her and he was killed. Bull, the drug dealer, killed both of them. That's the story. Why does it matter whether Angelica was in the park to buy from Bull, or whether she was reselling the weed? She got killed. What else is relevant?"

"It's important to distinguish Angelica from Javier. Javier was trying to do something good." Paulo spread his arms, as if the point was self-evident.

"Javier was doing something good regardless. We can report that without caring how Angelia got herself into that spot. Right?"

"I think it's relevant."

"You think it's relevant because Angelica was White and you want people to know that she was not as innocent as everyone thinks."

"That's right!" Paulo set down his glass with more force than he intended.

"So, *you* are deciding what's relevant to *you* and what information you want your readers to know because you're trying to make a point and sway their emotions and attitudes."

Paulo was silent, then said softly, "That's not what I'm doing."

"It is exactly what you're doing. I'm not telling you it's bad. It's what we do every day. But don't criticize me for it when you're doing the same thing."

Paulo did not respond, since their waitress arrived with two fresh glasses. After a somber sip, he looked away as he spoke. "I sometimes envy your ability to not care."

"It's not that I don't care. I care about my story, and my career. When getting the story right helps those things, then the truth matters. My job is to get the story that will play best on air and get us the best share and eventually get me out of ACN and into a better job. Maybe one where my boss will care more about the truth."

"The ends justify the means, eh?" Paulo turned his head away.

"It's not Machiavellian, mister journalist. Besides, *The Prince* was a parody—Machiavelli was being sarcastic, which I'm sure you know."

"I guess it's like the assistant DA said, huh? It's not about the truth, it's about getting a jury to convict. Our jury is the court of public opinion. Is that it?"

"Pretty much." Hannah relaxed back into her bench seat. "But isn't the most important thing revealing Javier's killer, and Angelica's? Getting *that* story is the goal, right?"

"There's more than one story here." Paulo twirled his beer glass, beads of condensation forming a puddle at its base on the stained table top.

"Would you feel the same way if Angelica were Black?"

"Yes," Paulo shot back quickly, then added, "what do you mean?"

"I mean, what if Angelica were a Black girl from the Lower East Side, working her way through NYU by selling weed? What if she got killed exactly the same way and there was the same outpouring of sympathy and support and the same amount of media coverage?"

"There would never be as much media coverage for a Black girl," Paulo interjected softly.

"Sure, but if there was, by some miracle, and the whole world loved Black Angelica, would you still want to report about how she was a drug dealer?"

Paulo took a long, slow sip of his second Dos Equis, then looked directly at Hannah. "No. If I'm honest with myself, it's no."

"So, why are you so fixated on trashing Angelica just because she's White?"

"It's not her, and it's not because she's White. It's because of how the public and you guys in the broadcast media have blinders on. You need to see how it really is sometimes."

"When it comes out that Bull shot her and Javier, and that he's a known drug dealer, the public will figure it out for themselves."

Paulo laughed. "Right. Because they are so perceptive? C'mon, Hannah, who do you think you're fooling?"

"So, are you going to jump off that cliff? Because if you do, I'm not promising to jump after you."

Paulo didn't respond. He pulled out his phone and called the number Luis had given him for post-meeting communication. The line rang six times, then clicked over to a message saying that no voicemail had been established for this line.

Paulo looked up. "This guy is pretty savvy. I'm guessing I'll get a call back now from a different burner." A moment later, Paulo's phone lit up and vibrated. "Hey . . . Yeah, we're done, but we don't have a deal yet . . . Maybe, but we need to talk, and not on the phone . . . Today? Yes . . . OK, we'll see you there . . . Yes, she's coming with me." Paulo's eyes darted to Hannah's. "She's got the lawyers who are going to protect your identity and make sure the cops don't get your video, so I'd be nice to her, if I were you." Paulo shot his phone an annoyed look, then stuffed it back into his pocket.

"Where are we going?"

"He wants to meet in Rockefeller Park."

"Where's that?"

"And you call yourself a New Yorker?" Paulo jabbed, raising his left eyebrow. Seeing Hannah's grumpy face, he relented. "It's on the Hudson, north of the marina. Over by Stuyvesant High School."

"When?"

"Now."

Chapter 38 — Magic Act

IMMEDIATELY AFTER THE MEETING with Paulo, Hannah, and their lawyer, the government contingent gathered on the other side of the DA's office. Zimmerman, who had been working his phone hard since they left the large conference room, fiddled with the remote control for a large television screen. It sprang to life showing four white squares containing the faces of Police Commissioner Earl Ward, Mayor Frederick Douglass, District Attorney Woodly Truitt, and Charlie Foster, Captain of the Manhattan narcotics unit.

Zimmerman summarized their meeting with the reporters and their lawyer. Ward then took the floor from his talking-head perch on the wall. "We can arrest and prosecute Reggie Millen for shooting the EMT, if we can find him. If the scumbag doesn't go for the wire, do we have enough to prosecute Millen for the Monroe murder based on the witness's testimony?"

Truitt answered quickly. "No. I'm not putting myself on the line based on the word of a drug dealer and an acknowledged accomplice of the killer. Plus, without the immunity deal, the witness probably won't testify. I don't see any way to get a conviction."

"Do we have any information on the whereabouts of Reggie Millen so we can arrest him?" Ward asked.

Dru loudly blew out a breath and held up two open hands toward the table. "We're working on that, Sir, but right now he seems to have dropped out of sight. We have every cop in the city looking for him and we're trolling all our sources. We have an FBI alert out for him in case he left town and we have him on the no-fly list. It may take some time, but we'll get him unless he's already lying dead somewhere."

"And his known accomplices?"

"Yes, Sir." Foster spoke for the first time. "The narcotics unit is working with the homicide team to track down anyone we suspect to be part of Millen's drug distribution operation. But we doubt Reggie will be turning up with them any time soon."

"What about this idea that Angelica Monroe was a drug distributor?" Mayor Douglass said. Even over the video conference, it was obvious he was looking at Virginia. "That's still just an uncorroborated accusation, correct?"

"There is evidence to support that," Mariana said. "There isn't any reason for this informant to lie, since he's admitting he was with Millen. Reggie Millen is a known drug dealer, Monroe was found with cash and weed in her purse, she had bins with cannabis residue in her dorm room. There are other witnesses who have suggested Monroe's involvement with selling drugs."

"We're putting a lid on that!" Douglass bellowed. "I don't want to see that in the press."

"We've got it contained," Virginia quickly cut in. "Those facts are confidential and important to the investigation."

"What are we saying in today's press conference?" Ward asked.

Virginia looked around the room, where she was getting no help. "We say that the investigation has uncovered some significant new facts and we are progressing toward what we hope will be a swift arrest. We can't talk about the specific facts or the suspects because it is an active investigation. How's that?"

"It works," Ward said with a firm tone suggesting that the discussion was over.

DA Truitt, however, had one more question. "How much immunity are we willing to give this informant if he's able to actually get Millen to incriminate himself?"

"Sir," Zimmerman leaned forward, as if his boss was actually in the room, "if we can get an admission that will stand up in court and you can get in front of a camera and say we have captured Angelica Monroe's killer, nobody will care how we did it or what other petty criminals got immunity in the process."

"And Javier Estrada," Mariana mumbled loud enough for Dru to hear.

"You sound like that reporter," her partner responded in a hushed voice.

"Yeah. Sometimes they're right."

"You have something to say, Detective?" Mariana's head snapped up at Zimmerman's question.

"No," Dru answered for her.

"Yes!" Mariana elbowed Dru as she sat forward in her cushioned chair. "I said there were two murders Friday night and Reggie Millen may have been the killer in both cases. We should not forget that Javier Estrada is also dead. Angelica Monroe is not the only victim. If Richardson's witness is telling the truth, or anything near to it, then Javier tried to intervene when Angelica was being assaulted. That story is entirely consistent with everything we have learned during this investigation. Because he took action to protect a stranger, he was beaten and killed. Javier Estrada was a hero."

"You are right, Detective," the deep voice of Frederick Douglass boomed through the room, causing everyone else to cease the murmuring that began after Mariana's plea. "I want you all to make sure any public statement about the arrest of Reggie

Millen includes both Ms. Monroe and Mr. Estrada and will refer to the case as a double murder."

"Mr. Mayor." Zimmerman spoke softly, while raising his hand toward the video screen. "I agree with that, of course, but we will need to see what Millen admits to. If he admits to killing Monroe, but not Estrada, we might not have enough evidence to convict for both murders."

"I don't want to hear that!" Douglass's voice was so loud it became distorted through the speaker. "We will charge him and try him. We will make sure the public hears the full story. Is that understood?"

Nobody spoke, but everyone nodded.

"OK, let's see if we can make this happen, and happen quickly." The mayor's face disappeared, along with the white outline of his square. The other three video callers rearranged into a line across the screen like a game of three-card-Monty.

"That's it," the DA said. "Make it happen, David."

* * *

AFTER ZIMMERMAN ENDED the teleconference, everyone except Deputy commissioner Knowles quickly left the room. As soon as the door closed, Knowles turned to Mariana and Dru. "Do we have a problem?"

"Not at all," Dru quickly interjected. "We have no problem."

"I'm glad to hear you say that, Detective." He fixed a stare at Mariana, almost daring her to speak.

"You heard what the mayor said." Mariana held her superior's gaze defiantly. "I'm concerned that we don't overlook the brown boy in this story."

"It's not about White versus Hispanic," Zimmerman cut in.

"It is *always* about White versus Hispanic," Mariana shot back. "Or it's White and Black. Don't kid yourself."

"That's what you said about the Floyd Merriman situation," Knowles responded. "Seems to me that you're the one who's fixated on it, not anybody else."

"Floyd who?" Zimmerman said. "Is there something here I need to know? If I'm putting these two detectives on a witness stand, I don't want any surprises."

"It's not important." Dru calmly reached for a pitcher of water on the table and poured himself a glass while he spoke. "Detective Vega and I witnessed an incident two weeks ago involving an officer who used excessive force during an arrest. A complaint was filed, it was investigated, the officer was suspended and is now on desk duty pending an arbitration hearing. It's nothing to worry about."

"Then why are we talking about it?" Zimmerman turned to Knowles.

"Because Detective Vega's report included her *opinion* that the incident was racially motivated."

Zimmerman's head swiveled back to Mariana. "Is that right?"

"Yes. That's right. But the department chose to ignore me and sweep it under the rug so they wouldn't be embarrassed."

"That's not true!" Knowles shouted. "The investigation was inconclusive about any racial motivation. We followed established protocols."

"And we all know what that means." Mariana stood and walked to the back of the room, distancing herself from the deputy commissioner.

Zimmerman turned to Dru. "Were you present for this incident, Detective?"

"I was," Dru monotoned. This was the last conversation he wanted to have. He was annoyed that Knowles had brought up the subject. But now the wound was open.

"Let's stay calm." The ADA put both hands on the table, palms down. "We're all on the same side. If this is something that could compromise Detective Vega, or you, as a witness, then I need to hear about it now."

Dru took a sip of water and looked at Mariana. "We were engaged in an investigation of a double-murder on the Upper West Side. We got a call that a potential witness had been located. Officers were dispatched to the scene and we arrived after the witness had been detained. One of the uniformed officers was restraining the guy. He was not a suspect, nor was he under arrest.

"As we approached, the witness was yelling at the officer, who had the man's arm pinned behind his back. There was a scuffle. Two other officers put the man on the ground, then the first officer, whose name is Ketcham, beat him with a baton, kicked him, then put him in handcuffs. Detective Vega and I both instructed the officers to stand down, but they did not follow our orders. It's possible they didn't realize we were the detectives on the case."

"I don't recall hearing about this incident," Zimmerman noted.

"I don't expect that you would," Knowles said. "There's no citizen video of the incident. It was handled. The man in question, Floyd Merriman, was a known associate of some criminals who were suspected of being involved in the murder. The guy did not want to press charges or make a complaint. He was happy to walk away."

"Wait," Zimmerman looked around the room. "You said there *was* a complaint."

"There was," Mariana put her left hand on the table and leaned toward the men on the other side of the room. "*I* filed the complaint."

"That's a bit unusual," Zimmerman said.

"Maybe, but I saw what I saw. Officer Ketcham beat Merriman without any need and used excessive force. The officer treated him like he was an active shooter. There was no cause for it. Ketcham was enjoying it. He pulled out his baton as soon as he thought he had provocation. Officers like that give the force a bad name. I wasn't going to let a racist thug with a badge get away with it. So, I filed the complaint."

"The investigation found no evidence of racist motivation," Knowles quickly retorted. "We confirmed the use of excessive force and the officer was suspended without pay and given a final warning. He had no prior disciplinary action or complaints. The union filed a grievance."

"He should have been fired," Mariana turned away, clenching her fists and attempting to remain calm so she didn't say anything she would regret.

"It doesn't work that way," Knowles, for the first time, had a note of sympathy in his voice.

"Do you think the officer was racially motivated, Detective Cook?" Zimmerman was acting as inquisitor since the other three people in the room seemed to know everything already.

"I do," Dru said.

Mariana spun around, staring mouth agape toward her partner.

"I confirmed the excessive force. No question about that. I believe the officer was racist and was looking for any excuse to beat the crap out of Merriman."

"You didn't say that in your report," Mariana said softly.

"Because my opinion isn't a fact. I didn't hear anybody use any racial slurs. I didn't have any objective evidence of racial motivation. I've never seen those officers handle the detention of a White witness, so I have no basis to compare their behavior. That's what I put in my report, and that's what I told Internal Affairs when they interviewed me. What the department does with the information is out of my control."

Mariana spoke directly to Dru. "Why didn't you back me up?"

"It wasn't about backing you up. I backed you up on the excessive force complaint. I told the truth. I had no evidence. You had no evidence. My opinion is irrelevant. But I'm backing you up now. I think you were right."

Dru turned to Knowles. "It's up to you and IA and the commissioner and the mayor to decide these things. My job is to solve cases. We need uniformed officers to help us do that. I'm not in the habit of leveling charges of racism at officers without any evidence. It's bad for my business." He looked at Mariana, repeating what he had told her before.

Zimmerman attempted to wrap up the discussion and calm the atmosphere. "OK, I get it. Detective Vega is perhaps more perceptive about discriminatory treatment given to minority suspects and witnesses than Detective Cook." He looked at Knowles. "Sounds to me like Detective Vega did the exact right thing. Maybe all our detectives and officers can take a lesson and be more assertive on the subject in the future. For now, let's concentrate on catching Reggie Millen, no matter what color his skin is. Deal?"

"Fine with me," Mariana said, "as long as we get him for the murder of both Angelica Monroe *and* Javier Estrada."

"Alright. Let's see if their witness is willing to go along."

Chapter 39 — A Walk in the Park

LUIS AND ENRIQUE LEANED against the thick iron railing separating a paved walking path from the inky water of the Hudson River. The metal had been smoothed and polished by a million hands caressing the surface, icy in winter and burning hot in summer. On this April evening the air was warm, the breeze off the water gentle, and the pedestrians inhabiting the park plentiful. Released from a long winter of confinement, New Yorkers streamed from their Lego-block apartments and into the fresh air.

Rockefeller park was built from the dirt and rock excavated to build the World Trade Center, expanding Manhattan Island and reclaiming usable land from the river. The open green area was part of the price extracted by the city from the developers who salivated over two hundred stories of prime office space. The rectangular park extends out from West Street toward New Jersey, then makes a ninety-degree turn south toward the marina and the Battery beyond. Paved paths crisscross grassy fields between stands of trees, planted to provide shelter, shade, and a bit of nature in the shadow of surrounding skyscrapers.

In the northwest corner, where the path turned south, the two men had a clear view of all who approached as the gentle river waves lapped against the concrete footings of the platform on which the park sat. They saw Paulo and Hannah walking toward them long before their guests recognized them. Luis made eye contact with Paulo and motioned to the south, then walked quickly away, the two journalists following.

Luis and Enrique took seats on an empty bench facing the river, leaving space between them. When Paulo and Hannah caught up, Luis extended an arm toward the open seat and invited Paulo to sit. Hannah chose to stand in front.

Behind the bench, a group of trees growing in the musky mulch shielded the riverside walk from a large field. Hannah could hear the happy laughter of uncaged New Yorkers mixed with music from multiple boom boxes. Despite hundreds of people all around them, including groups of strolling couples walking on the path behind Hannah, there was little chance of being overheard.

Paulo explained that the DA had rejected their immunity deal because Luis was not a credible enough witness, and because it would be his word against Bull's. But the DA would make the deal if Luis was willing to set up a meeting with Bull, wear a wire, and get him to confess.

"That's such bullshit!" Luis spat across Paulo's lap, drawing no attention. New Yorkers knew better than to get involved in the business of strangers. "Like I'm going to make up a story like that."

"The DA thinks you have a lot of motives to lie, including wanting to take over the operation once you've got Bull out of the way. Not to mention getting immunity from prosecution for attempted murder."

Luis leaned in close to Paulo's face, keeping his voice down through clenched teeth. "You didn't fucking tell him who I am, did you!?"

"I don't know who you are," Paulo replied calmly, "but no, I didn't even tell him your name, if that's even your real name. We blurred your face and altered your voice, like we promised. The cops have no idea who you are."

"But they know I was there, and that I work—worked—for Bull. They prob'ly know about the business, so they can find me if they try hard. I'm screwed now, ain't I? Fucking bastards!"

Enrique sat silently, but Paulo saw the big man clenching his fists. "You still have a few plays, Luis."

"Yeah? You mean wear a wire for them? Be a snitch?"

"You're already a snitch." Enrique turned his head toward Paulo and Luis. "You got us all into this, man. You gotta finish it, one way or the other."

Luis punched his left hand down into the wooden slats of the bench, leaving a bloody smear but not showing any indication of pain. "What's my other option?"

Paulo held out an upward-facing palm. "You can leave—get out of town."

"Run away, like some scared girl?"

"Might be a smart move if you think Bull is still here and looking for you." Paulo looked at Hannah, who was paying close attention to the discussion.

Luis stared past the railing that prevented park-goers from accidentally falling into the river. The afternoon sun reflected off the buildings in Weehawken. After a long pause, Luis abruptly stood, prompting Enrique to jump up behind him. His angry, dark eyes flashed at Paulo.

"Fuck it. Tell 'em I'll do it, but they gotta give us the immunity deal. I'll call you." He walked away to the south, leaving Paulo and Hannah on the bench and requiring Enrique to hustle to catch up.

After traversing the paved walkway for a hundred yards, Luis turned east along a winding path, then halted. Enrique slid up next to him, watching the surrounding field to make sure nobody was close enough to overhear. "What are you thinkin', man?"

"I'm thinkin' this ain't so bad. We gotta figure out how to get Bull to show up somewhere, but we'll have the cops on our side. Knowing Bull, he'll come loaded and pissed off. The cops will prob'ly shoot him. Or maybe I'll kill him."

"Or maybe he caps you." Enrique didn't seem upset about the prospect.

"True that, but I ain't goin' to jail, and I ain't gonna be lookin' over my shoulder all day, waitin' for Bull to find me. I gotta go at it with him eventually. With the cops there, I got a better shot at coming out still walking. Like you said, one way or the other, we're gonna finish it."

Chapter 40 — Uptown Train

PAULO WALKED HANNAH to the subway stop at Canal Street. They stood outside the turnstiles, waiting for an uptown train that would take Hannah home. With her MetroCard in hand, ready to swipe and run when the train arrived, they rehashed the day's events and planned their next moves.

Since they left Rockefeller Park, Hannah had texted Motzenbecker to confirm that Luis was in for the plan to meet with Reggie Millen and wear a wire. The lawyer texted back fifteen minutes later to confirm a meeting at the DA's office at noon on Thursday. They had no idea whether Luis would be able to coax Millen into a meeting or when it might happen. Regardless, they needed to set up the details with the cops and the DA.

Hannah's hands filled the pockets of her light jacket. "If Luis shows up for a meeting with Bull, the guy is going to immediately shoot him. There's not much chance of them having a calm conversation."

"That's on Luis. The two have been working together for a while. I bet he can make it happen, but I agree with you that Bull will likely come with murder on his mind. The guy's a killer. We're going to have to make sure the cops protect Luis."

"Don't you think we can trust the cops?"

"I've got news for you: Sometimes the cops don't tell the truth."

Hannah playfully slapped the side of Paulo's arm. "I'm not some naive Barbie doll, you know. I also know that guys like *you* don't always tell the truth. As a matter of fact, reporters probably lie more than drug dealers."

"I've known a few TV producers who were less than completely honest. But as far as I know you've been straight with me, so I'll keep giving you the benefit of the doubt until you give me a reason to think otherwise."

"Very nice of you." Hannah realized her slap had pulled her closer than she would normally stand next to Paulo. The day's activity left him sweaty from exertion and tension. He smelled like a gym at the end of a basketball game. Stepping back, she said, "It's going to kill me to not write a script for the morning news about what happened today."

"I know, but I'm going to take that pent-up energy and use it to write a new story, about how Javier tried to save Angelica from a drug dealer—based on an anonymous but reliable source."

"Are you sure?"

"I need to change the story from Javier the former gang member, and Angelica the saintly suburban victim. Luis gave us the truth, which we already suspected. It's time at least part of that story gets told. It won't affect Luis and Bull having their meet-up, if it even happens. There's a hundred ways that the true story never gets told here. Bull could get himself killed. Or he could get arrested and locked up without ever making a public statement. Everyone will believe the story you and your broadcast zombies keep telling. By then, writing a story about how Angelica was really there to buy weed and how Javier tried to save her from Bull's abuse won't be believed and nobody will care."

"I'm not a zombie!" Hannah objected.

"Maybe not, but you're not going to tell the truth, either."

"I told you, it's not my choice!" Hannah stamped her foot on the concrete floor. "I tried that angle, but my boss shot me down. It's not my fault."

A rumble from the tunnel portended the arrival of the uptown train. Travelers on the platform beyond the turnstiles began gathering up their belongings and moving toward the platform edge. Paulo stepped aside to allow Hannah easy access to her train. "Maybe not, but I get to decide what I print. I don't care if I get fired, which I won't be. Somebody has to be Javier's champion before the story fades away and you all move on to the next scandal."

"You're really going to do it?" Hannah said as she swiped her card and pushed through the barrier. The train had arrived and was nearly stopped. Looking back across the turnstile, she said, "Be careful." She dashed toward the now open doors. Once inside, she turned back to see Paulo watching her.

* * *

AT 2:53 A.M., PAULO'S INDEX FINGER hovered over his mouse, poised to click the button that would send his article out live on the *LES Tribune* website. It would also immediately go to his Twitter followers and on the paper's Facebook page.

In the background, his hulk of a television flashed images of sharks falling from the sky. He worked best when he had some background noise that distracted some portion of his brain while he concentrated on his words. Tonight, Channel 9 was showing the campy cult classic *Sharknado 2*. Paulo had seen it as a teenager when it was the hot, if stupid, feature on the Sci-Fi channel.

He caught a snippet of dialogue. "I know you're scared. I'm scared, too. Sharks are scary and nobody wants to get eaten."

He couldn't hold back a chuckle. Somehow, the moronic movie scene held some allegorical significance. He was about to set loose the hounds. He was scared. He didn't want to get eaten.

Hannah's cautionary words had repeated in his head all night. He wanted to fully expose Angelica Monroe as a drug dealer whose death, while not deserved, was not worthy of the outpouring of support and sympathy. Javier was the hero and the victim. But he also recalled Clarence's predictions about what would happen if he printed the whole truth.

In the end, his article broke the news that Angelica was in the park Friday night to buy drugs. He didn't mention what she intended to do with them and expected readers to assume they were for her personal use. Hardly damning information. Angelica was not the first college student to buy weed in the park. It didn't mean she deserved to be shot. It was a compromise. Paulo hated compromises in his reporting.

Sometimes, he thought, the hero has to dive into the mouth of the shark. But he might as well bring along a chainsaw. And a life vest. He clicked the button, closed his laptop, and went to bed. Thursday figured to be a busy day.

* * *

THE NIGHTLY ASSEMBLY at the makeshift memorial around the Hangman's Elm Wednesday night was smaller than on Tuesday. Almost everyone was from NYU and the surrounding neighborhood. The interlopers from other parts of the city and from out of town didn't make the trip. The memorial itself had ceased expanding, but still covered almost all the dirt clearing around the old tree. The candles had all burned down to their wicks. The cut flowers drooped. Yet, the overall impression was still impressive and sad.

The NYU undergrad women's a cappella group performed three numbers. After the finale, "The Sound of Silence," the group accepted subdued applause, then left the park.

No high-def cameras or reporters with microphones recorded the events. No dignitaries made speeches. Three women from an NYU sorority passed out small candles with paper shields to prevent the synthetic wax from dripping on sensitive hands. They had only ninety candles, so some in the crowd had to share.

After five minutes of near silence, the candles had burned down. Somebody in the back chanted Kaddish, the Hebrew prayer for the dead. Afterward, somebody else began reciting The Lord's Prayer, which was joined in by many others, despite variations in the words among those from different denominations. The crowd then dispersed back to their studies or evening activities. The vendors in and around the park sold less than half the merchandise they had gathered for the day's assembly.

The front pages of the New York tabloids on Wednesday had covered the arrest of an athletic trainer at Fordham University who was accused of molesting female athletes. After similar scandals elsewhere in recent years, university officials were quick to fire the trainer and launch a sweeping investigation into who else knew about the activity and failed to report it. Many heads were likely to roll. A lawsuit was already filed on behalf of all known and unknown victims of the "Treacherous Trainer," as *The Post* dubbed the accused. It was the first time in three days that the Angelica Monroe murder was nudged off the front pages.

The late local news broadcasts carried clips from the commissioner's press conference, but otherwise had nothing new to report. The story was relegated to the third segment. On channel two, Otis Livingston devoted thirty precious seconds of his sports report to clips of Javier Estrada, the basketball star who was also murdered on Friday. Livingston closed by saying, "A talented young man who will never play a college game. Our thoughts go out to his family." It was the only mention of Javier's murder on any TV news broadcast.

Chapter 41 — Backlash

Thursday

THERE WAS A TIME when a newspaper reporter was a name on a byline, but was otherwise anonymous. If you wrote a regular column, you had more name recognition. But unless the paper ran your photo next to your articles, John Q. Public would not recognize you if you were standing in the ticket-buyers' line next to them, chatting about the previous night's Mets game. If a reporter wrote a controversial story, they would get hate mail—the old-fashioned kind that came in an envelope with a stamp. In a few infamous instances, irate readers sent toxic substances along with their letters. But most of the time, the nasty letter-writers were easy to ignore. The reporter could still walk around town and few people would associate them with their published stories.

Those days ended with the advent of the internet, social media, and the absolute necessity for newspapers to be both digital and visual. The *LES Trib* was no exception. Its website featured photos of all the writers. Links for videos and podcasts featuring Paulo Richardson flashed under his articles and on the website's homepage. On the paper's Facebook page, brightly colored banners and graphics invited readers to click through for additional content, including photo montages, profiles, and more podcasts. Readers were invited to submit comments on articles and participate in chat discussions. Paulo's face and voice were well known to all his loyal readers. Anyone with an internet connection could easily find his photo.

Paulo was proud to be a member of the community about which he wrote so passionately. He lived in the neighborhood. His address was not easily obtainable, but anyone who wanted to find him knew that he usually got coffee at Big Al's Deli and that he frequented Snyder's Grocery and The Lazy River tavern. Paulo was not a hard man to locate.

When the Friday morning sun found the crack between his window shades, the glowing red numbers on the bedside clock read 9:42. He had plenty of time to get ready for the noon meeting with the ADA. The thought crossed his mind to call Hannah before anything else, but curiosity and ego forced him to boot up his laptop first, to see if there were any comments about his article.

Each time he posted a new article, he played a game with himself to guess how many comments there would be on the *LES Tribune* website the next morning. Some had zero. His top number one day after publication was sixty-three. That didn't count Facebook or Twitter comments. He clicked his headline in the upper-right position on the front page.

Murdered Girl Was Drug Buyer: Javier Estrada Shot Defending a Stranger, According to Eyewitness.

He scrolled to the bottom, where the comments began. There were 138. The article had only been live for seven hours, much of which had been sleeping time for most people.

Skimming through the reader reactions, Paulo thought about sharks falling from the sky. Some commenters expressed sympathy and support for Javier. A few congratulated Paulo on his excellent reporting. The majority, however—the vast majority—were clearly on Team Angelica and refused to believe that she was buying weed in the park the night she died.

Many commenters accused Paulo of having an agenda, of fabricating the story, of smearing Angelica's reputation, and of hating White people. Others opined that buying pot was no big deal and wondered why Paulo and his paper would care. A few included threats of bodily harm. He dismissed those as internet bluster, but his gut was clenched. He knew there would be a negative reaction, but this was faster and nastier than expected.

The comments on Twitter were even worse. "*Die in Hell you gay liberal bastard*", "*You will regret the day you besmirched the reputation of that poor girl with your lies*", "*I'm going to hurt you bad you spic hack.*"

There were plenty more. He closed his laptop and picked up his phone. He got a sinking feeling in the pit of his stomach when he saw the text message on his phone from Clarence: "Call me." Of course, he expected it, but the reality of what he had done—despite Clarence's explicit instructions to the contrary—made bile rise in his throat.

To say his boss was pissed was an understatement. Paulo listened without interjecting many statements of justification. He knew the story contained the content Clarence had quashed a day earlier. He offered to take it down, but he knew Clarence had a strict rule about never removing a story once published. He wasn't going to make an exception in this case.

"I'll tell you this, Paulo—if things get too hot and the advertisers start calling for your head, I'm going to have to fire you."

"You won't have to," Paulo spoke softly, "I'll resign. I don't want to take down the paper over this. But before that happens, there's one more amazing scoop I'm probably going to have for you very soon." He knew Clarence's curiosity would overcome his anger and waited.

"Yeah? What?"

Paulo explained about the upcoming meeting between Luis and Bull, at which Luis would be wearing a wire in an attempt to get Bull to confess to the murders. "The police will stage the sting, but I'll be there and I'll have the exclusive rights to break the story on our site."

"You're shitting me."

"Clarence, I shit you not. The cops are likely to arrest the killer at this meeting and I'll have it before anybody else. You want me to keep working for *LES Trib* on this, or should I consider myself freelance?"

"I haven't fired you yet. You still work for me. If you can, please let me know when this meeting is going down. And, Paulo, when you write the story, try to focus on the fact that the killer has been captured, justice will prevail, and Javier was truly the hero. Don't go out of your way to smear the girl this time, OK?"

"I can do that." Paulo hung up before Clarence asked about the website comments. There would be time for that later. He called Hannah next.

"You put a huge target on your back," Hannah said before any greeting.

"You think?" Paulo tried to be nonchalant about the situation. "Have any other media outlets picked it up?"

"A few that I've seen." Hannah's voice faded, like she had put down her phone. "I'm clicking around now. Looks like New York One has something on its homepage. I haven't watched their broadcast yet today. CNN also has a story, with your name and your paper's name prominently featured. Your boss will be happy about that, I'll bet."

"Maybe." Paulo wondered if he should let Clarence know. "What about ACN?"

Hannah coughed, or maybe stifled a laugh—Paulo couldn't tell over the phone. "No way. Like I said yesterday, my managing editor is absolutely opposed to the idea. We're running a fifteen-second sidebar on our daily Angelica story. According to a source inside the NYPD, the police are pursuing a lead that the same person may have killed both Angelica and Javier. We may run something later today about the backlash against your article and how everyone thinks it's a total fabrication attributed to an unnamed source, but that's the best you can hope for."

"Will they mention my name?"

"I'm sure we will, since the story is now you and not who killed Angelica Monroe."

"It's the truth. Not the whole truth, but I can live with it. Motzenbecker is meeting me at Killarney's at eleven-thirty to prep for our noon meeting with the DA. Can you be there?"

"Sure. Any word from Luis?"

"Naw. Nothing yet. I doubt he gets up this early."

"OK. Let me know if he calls you. And, Paulo . . . stay off social media today. It's getting pretty ugly."

"Yeah. I saw a bit of it. They say clicks and comments are what it's all about, right? So, this is a big story."

Hannah's voice cracked as she replied, "I—I'm just worried that the story isn't about Javier . . . that it's about people wanting to crucify *you* for blaspheming Saint Angelica. I'll see you in a couple hours."

* * *

PAULO EXITED HIS BUILDING carrying a satchel containing his laptop, notepad, and provisions for the day, in case he didn't have time to eat a proper meal. A few energy bars, a bag of mixed nuts, and two bottles of water had carried him through plenty of long reporting days.

Crossing the courtyard formed by three apartment towers, he passed under an archway and headed west. He immediately noticed three men on the far side of 7th Street. Paulo recognized most of the neighborhood regulars who hung out on the sidewalks and stoops. He knew the homeless residents and where they liked to set up shop. These three were definitely out of place. Two wore white t-shirts over their blue jeans, while the other had a leather jacket obscuring his choice of chest covering and sported a shaved head and dark sunglasses. They were all muscular.

Paulo increased his pace, watching out of his peripheral vision as the three strangers mirrored his steps on the far side of the narrow street, lined with parked cars. He didn't want them to see him looking, hoping they would incorrectly assume they had the element of surprise on their side.

Although his route required him to turn right and head north, he made a left at the corner, away from the three ominous-looking strangers. At the next intersection, he turned right to cross the street, giving him an angle to see if they were following. He caught a flash of white t-shirt. This was his neighborhood, which gave him an advantage. He hoped they had not yet figured out that he had spotted them. The biggest question was whether these three were the whole group or if they were coordinating with additional members of the Proud Boys or whatever organization they might call friends.

Paulo continued west, toward Third Avenue. The pedestrian traffic was moderate, but enough to provide plenty of witnesses who could call 9-1-1 if his followers tried to jump him. At Third Avenue, the sidewalks were even more jammed with people. Now, Paulo turned north, forming a plan. Passing Cooper Square, it took all his willpower not to turn and look for his stalkers. Maybe they had broken off? Could they have split up, intending to corner him somewhere?

Then, passing 9th Street, he saw his target. Striding to a half-wall separating the street from a courtyard belonging to a New York University building, Paulo tapped the blue "Emergency Call" button on a tall pole. A blue light, like the ones on top of police cruisers, turned and flashed. Paulo kept walking, stopped halfway up the block, then turned to look at the approaching New Yorkers. At first, he didn't see his pursuers and briefly relaxed. Then, he made eye contact with the shaved head in the leather jacket, emerging from behind a mother with a huge stroller. His two white-shirted companions were a few feet behind. Paulo waited.

The leader walked directly at Paulo, who could not see his eyes under the dark sunglasses. When he was five feet away, Paulo said, "Are you looking for me?"

"Yes!" the leather jacket said as he lunged forward, planting his left fist into Paulo's gut.

Even expecting an attack, the move caught Paulo by surprise. He exhaled all the air in his lungs and doubled over. His plan had been to yell for help as soon as he perceived any hostile act. Now he couldn't breathe, let alone speak.

The two white t-shirts rushed forward, flanking Paulo and grabbing his arms, as if trying to assist him. In actuality they clamped him and pulled him upright so Leather Jacket could punch him again. The second blow was also to the midsection, causing Paulo to cough up phlegm. He felt bile rising in his esophagus, but still could not inhale. His eyes watered as pain radiated through his torso.

"You got some nerve, you spic bastard! This is what happens when you go after a girl who can't defend herself!" Paulo saw his own face reflected in the man's mirrored lenses.

The two men holding his arms lifted again, forcing Paulo to straighten his back. Oddly, this movement caused some air to suck into his mouth and to his oxygen-starved lungs. He was helpless to fend off the attack. As he tried to twist sideways, his two vice-clamps held firm. Leather Jacket's fist found Paulo's jaw, snapping his head to the side. He tasted his own blood on his tongue.

"Hey!" someone shouted nearby, seeing the assault.

At that moment, a loud pop and the whine of a police siren shattered the morning air. An amplified voice broke through speakers on the top of the NYPD patrol car, now parked at the curb less than ten feet away. "Freeze right there!" shouted the officer through the speaker.

The two white t-shirts released Paulo, leaving him to tumble to the sidewalk as they sprinted away to the north. Leather Jacket was right behind them. The cop raced around his squad car, pulling out his service pistol. It was a one-man patrol, so there was no partner to chase the assailants. The officer pulled a walkie-talkie receiver mounted on his shoulder to his mouth and called in the incident, alerting other units to look for the three men who had assaulted Paulo. Then he hustled to Paulo's prone form on the sidewalk to give assistance and see whether he would need to call for an ambulance.

A crowd of pedestrians quickly formed around the scene. The officer waved them back as Paulo struggled to a sitting position, breathing in shallow gasps. "Did you pull the call button?"

Paulo nodded and croaked out, "Yes. Thanks for coming so fast."

"Good move. Do you know who those guys are?"

Paulo shook his head. "No," he groaned, feeling his lungs start to refill a little more with each inhalation. He felt the side of his mouth with his hand and moved his lower jaw from side to side, testing to see if anything was broken. "I have no idea who they are."

"Do you want an ambulance?"

"No," Paulo said, now speaking more clearly. He rolled on his side, then struggled to a standing position. "I'm alright. They jumped me, but only got in a few punches before you showed up."

"I'm gonna need to file a report," the officer said, holding Paulo's arm to make sure he wouldn't fall back to the ground.

"Sure," Paulo said, looking around at the concerned faces in the crowd, which was dispersing now that the show was over.

He spent five minutes answering questions while Officer Sean McLaughlin took notes on a small spiral pad. Paulo said he had no idea why the thugs attacked him. He considered giving the officer the full story, including the motive for the beating, but he wasn't sure the cop would be sympathetic. It wasn't going to help the police find the three attackers.

If there were some security cameras in the area, the men might be identifiable on video, but Paulo doubted the NYPD would consider the case serious enough to start checking. It seemed like a run-of-the-mill mugging—not good, but not something that was worth much investigation time unless the victim was famous or rich. Paulo gave his name and contact information and the officer said someone from the violent crimes unit would call him.

When the cop left, Paulo continued his trek toward the meeting with Motzenbecker and Hannah. He was breathing normally now, and although he expected to have a bruised mouth and jaw, he had experienced worse. As he walked, he wondered whether his own beating would be the most violence he would see on that brilliant April day. Like the character in the silly movie said, "Nobody wants to get eaten."

Chapter 42 — Out of the Shadows

HANNAH ARRIVED at the meeting with Motzenbecker before Paulo. The little coffee shop had six small tables crowded in a horseshoe around the narrow counter, all squeezed into the smallest possible storefront. They ordered coffee and pulled an empty chair to their table for Paulo.

When Hannah explained how Paulo's article had revealed Angelica to be a drug-buyer, Motzenbecker was not happy. "He might scare Millen away."

"Paulo's article didn't mention any names. It doesn't say who the dealer was, and the same information could have been leaked by the cops as much as by Luis. Plus, I doubt Bull reads the *Lower East Side Tribune*. The story has not been widely reported, so he may not even have heard about it."

"Let's hope," the lawyer grumbled.

"Hope what?" Paulo hurried to his chair, unstrapping his satchel, which dropped to the linoleum floor.

"What happened to you?" Hannah reached out and gently stroked the red welt on the side of Paulo's jaw.

"Is that coffee?" Paulo pointed at Hannah's cup.

"Yeah?"

Paulo grabbed the tall cup and took a long draught.

"Help yourself." Hannah accepted back her cup from Paulo's hand.

"Sorry. I needed that. I had a little run-in with three literary critics."

After Paulo gave a brief summary of his encounter, Hannah said, "That's awful, but I can't say I'm shocked. People's emotions are running hot when it comes to Angelica Monroe. It's lucky the cop showed up."

"Speaking of cops, what's our strategy for this meeting? We need the cops to protect Luis if he's going to put his neck on the line here. How do we make sure that happens?"

Motzenbecker sketched out his plan, which included having the DA agree to the immunity deal as a condition of Luis's participation, regardless of whether Bull made an incriminating statement. "He's risking death when he gets within twenty feet of the guy. Bull may pull a gun and shoot before they have any chance to have a chat. I expect they will give him body armor for the meeting, but that's not always effective."

"They'd better," Paulo huffed.

"If Millen shoots at him, the cops will have Bull for another attempted murder even if Luis survives. They will also have enough to try him for the Monroe murder, with Luis's testimony and the fact that Bull tried to kill him. That's worth the immunity. If they don't agree, then there's no deal. We can't put our client in peril without a guaranteed deal."

"He's not your client," Hannah reminded the lawyer. "I'm your client. The company is paying you to consult with me on this situation." Hannah and Paulo looked at each other. Hannah's brown eyes were determined.

Paulo's expression was softer. "No matter who your client is, protecting Luis is imperative. He's risking his life."

"But we also care about being there," Hannah piped up. "We're bringing them their witness, so we get our scoops."

"I'm not sure the cops are going to go for it," Motzenbecker said.

Hannah turned to the lawyer. "Remember what I said. You work for ACN, which means you work for me. Our interest is in getting live video of the meeting, along with live audio. That's our only goal."

"The cops are not going to let you tap into their wire." Motzenbecker crushed his empty coffee cup and stretched behind his chair to reach a trash bin.

"We don't need their wire. We'll have our own audio."

"It won't be very good."

Hannah waved a dismissive hand. "It won't matter. We'll have the cops' transcript of the wire after the fact. And our microphones are pretty damned sensitive. We'll be fine. I'm happy to have our guys at a safe distance. We might be able to use remote units or even drones, depending on the venue, but we need to have access."

"That's not generally part of a set-up like this."

"So, we'll do something unique. That's the deal for us. We're not going to cooperate without access."

Paulo rubbed his throbbing jaw and nodded his agreement.

"OK, then. Let's go have a chat with the assistant district attorney."

* * *

THE MEETING WITH ZIMMERMAN and the other members of the city's team took two hours. The ADA pointed out that they didn't even know if the meeting would happen, or where. If Luis were in custody, that might be different, but there was no chance he was going to surrender himself without the deal in place. Motzenbecker conceded that if Millen didn't show up for the meeting, or if the meeting never happened, or if the cops decided to arrest Millen before the meeting, then the whole deal would be off.

Zimmerman at first refused to even entertain the idea that the network would be allowed to have a camera crew at the meeting, or that Hannah and Paulo would be allowed to attend. Motzenbecker, however, was a solid wall on the subject. He assured the ADA that there would be no meeting, and no wire, without access for the network and Paulo.

In the end, after taking a break to consult with their bosses, Zimmerman and the police representatives agreed. Paulo had to identify Luis and name the other members of the gang who would get immunity if the deal was fulfilled. DA Truitt agreed to grant it to Luis based on his participation. They would grant immunity to his associates only if they obtained an admission from Reggie Millen. They insisted on an iron-clad liability waiver for any injuries to the media people present. If there was gunfire and a stray shot killed a cameraman, the city was not going to pay damages. Motzenbecker agreed. They all waited another forty-five minutes while the lawyers hammered out a written agreement, which they all signed.

While they waited for photocopies, Paulo caught the attention of Mariana, motioning her to a window looking down on Foley Square. "I just want to say how much I appreciate what you said yesterday—about making sure everyone remembers that Javier Estrada was also murdered."

"Thanks. I read your article this morning. You're doing a nice job profiling Javier. I hope it gets widely read. And I hope it doesn't cause you too much trouble."

"Off the record, have you learned anything in your investigation to suggest that Javier was involved other than as a Good Samaritan?"

"Off the record?" Mariana got a confirming nod. "No. So far as we know, your articles have it exactly right."

Chapter 43 — Into the Light

LUIS CALLED THE LAST BURNER NUMBER he had for Bull. It had been only three days since their last meeting—when Luis tried to kill his boss. The call bounced to voicemail, which was no surprise. Bull never answered; he only called, usually from a different burner. The old boss had taught him to be careful. They never communicated via text messages, even though that would be easier. Texts left a record, which was bad for staying out of prison. Right now, Luis didn't care, but Bull would care, and he would be suspicious of a text.

When his phone buzzed and the display flashed UNKNOWN NUMBER, Luis exchanged a confirming glance with Enrique, then answered. "Yo, Bull."

Bull's voice dripped with venom, but was slow and controlled, which made it that much more ominous. "Some motherfucker's got a lot a nerve callin' me."

"What're we gonna do, Bull? We're both still here. I'm with Enrique now. You wanna walk away? I'm ready to take over the business."

"You're takin' nothing! I got stitched up. I still got the keys and I'm still driving. You're gonna hafta find yourself a new ride."

Luis knew Bull would not surrender the business without a fight. The old boss had connected Bull with the main supplier in Colombia, so Luis was not going to be able to swoop in and claim to be the boss without Bull's consent—unless Bull was dead.

"Maybe we need to settle things between us man to man, just you and me."

"Last time you showed up with your whole posse. I ain't playin' that game again."

"Yeah, Bull, I know. But it was just you and me goin' at it. How about I let you decide where and when this time? I'll be there without Q or any of my guys. You still got the other sheriffs runnin' with you, right? We can get them to hang with Q so they're all together somewhere else. Maybe we can work something out, you and me. Maybe not. But one way or another we gotta get settled."

The line was quiet. When Bull spoke again, his tone of voice had changed, as if he was suddenly conciliatory. "Sure. You're right. One way or the other. Maybe we make a deal, huh? We'll see. I'll get back to you about when and where." The line disconnected. Luis cocked his head and rose from his couch.

"What's the plan?" Enrique asked.

"Not sure yet. Seems like Bull may agree to a meet. We'll see. I gotta go talk to my boy Paulo and see how much help we're gonna get from the cops."

* * *

LUIS AND ENRIQUE JOINED their compatriots who had been present for the knife fight with Bull in the alley. They were all relatively happy about the immunity deal Luis had promised them. Nobody was happy about being snitches, but Luis assured them that nobody on the street would ever know. He told them about the plan to have a meet-up of all the sheriffs to hang out while he and Bull settled things. If one of them came back alive, then he would run the business. If they worked out an arrangement and Bull decided to forget about their little tussle, then everything would go back to the way it was before.

"I'll take that bet." Oscar raised a bony hand. "A hundred to one against Bull forgiving and forgetting." Nobody took the odds.

When Luis's burner phone rang again, it was Paulo. Luis rejected the call and pulled out a second burner. "Yo, Paulo."

Luis listened for a long time, punctuating the conversation with several "uh-huhs" and "OKs" and, finally, a smile. "That's good. Bull's gonna call me back to set the meeting." Luis had no idea where or when it would be but he was confident that there would be a meeting. They wanted Bull in prison or dead. It was the only way they could keep things going and keep the money rolling in. They liked the idea of immunity from the cops for any past crimes. If Bull was the one who came out alive, anybody who had sided with Luis would be out of the operation—or worse. It was a pretty easy decision.

* * *

WHEN BULL CALLED BACK at four o'clock, Luis was surprised it was so fast. He was in his room in the apartment he shared with Enrique and Wilmer. He was listening to the Mets game on the radio, imagining the ivy-covered outfield walls at Wrigley field. He only got to watch the games when they were on free TV. Buying cable was a way the cops could trace you. He had been napping to Howie Rose calling the afternoon game. When he saw the UNKNOWN NUMBER on his phone's screen, he sat up and was immediately fully awake. "What's up, Bull?"

"You said you wanted to work things out. So, let's do it and get back to business. First off, you tell Enrique and the rest of your posse to meet up with the other sheriffs at the end of the Pier 45 park. Right at the river. Got that?"

"Sure. What about us?"

"Meet me on the soccer field at 6th Street and the FDR. Inside the running track. You know the place?"

"Yeah. I know it."

"Good. Midnight tonight. Tell Enrique and your boys to meet the other sheriffs at eleven-thirty."

Luis held the phone away from his ear, shock obvious on his face. "Tonight?"

"Damn right. Tonight."

"OK. I'll be there." Luis yelled out to the living room of their shared space, which looked like a college dorm with one common room and three tiny bedrooms around its circumference. "Yo! Q! We got a plan."

Chapter 44 — Hasty Preparations

WHEN DRU AND MARIANA explained the hastily arranged operation to capture Reggie Millen to Captain Sullivan, his reaction didn't surprise them.

"For the love of Aunt Millie, Cook! This has shit-show written all over it! They're letting the criminals control the venue and we're setting up a sting on a half-hour's notice?"

"I know, Cap. But it's our one shot. His accomplice is flipping on him and will be wearing a wire, so we have a good chance of getting enough of a confession to button it down."

"This accomplice will be wearing a suit of armor, I hope?"

"Yeah. We know. We'll outfit him with a vest and tell him to keep his distance."

Sully picked up a squishy hand-massage ball he kept on his desk. It was a sure sign of nerves—or anger. "Make sure the DA makes all the strategic decisions. If this goes down the tubes, I want you two to have deniability." He clenched his hand around the black rubber until his knuckles were white. "And, please, for the love of God, try not to get any civilians killed."

Dru and Mariana left Sully's office as quickly as they could manage without looking like frightened pigeons. They had not even mentioned the overtime that would be involved. In this case, the commissioner would not give their captain any trouble over the cost.

* * *

AT NINE P.M., DRU AND MARIANA gathered their support team of nine NYPD uniformed officers and one Sergeant at the Bowery precinct. Sergeant David Bibb, a twenty-year veteran, immediately pointed out all the problems, as if Dru and Mariana didn't already know. In his thick Brooklyn accent, Bibb gestured toward an image of the soccer field Mariana had clipped from Google Maps and projected on a screen in the precinct's briefing room.

"You're telling us we have to stay out of sight when this Reggie approaches the meeting point, which is the middle of the frickin' soccer field. You got four or five different approaches he could take, so we don't know where to expect him. But, as soon as he's inside, we gotta cover the whole field and all the escape routes, still without letting the perp notice that we're there. Right?"

"That's the assignment, Sergeant." Dru did not want to admit that the prospect was daunting. The commissioner had authorized the squad of officers for the operation, along with the two detectives. Dru had never seen so many officers assigned to a single-suspect stake-out.

"We'll have communication with all the units. Once the suspect is on the field, we can move in to points around the perimeter on the northeast, northwest, southeast, and southwest corners." Dru pointed to the screen as he explained his thinking. "The mobile command center will roll into place along the pedestrian path behind the restroom building, without lights. We'll have drone coverage overhead, so we'll have eyes on him if the suspect gets past us somehow. That should cover all possibilities."

"It's still an awful site," Sgt. Bibb said dismissively. "If he bolts toward one of the corners, we'll have only two officers to take him down. We won't be able to shoot him unless he's armed and presents a direct threat, so that means our officers gotta take him down with batons and fists. It's times like this I wish we could have our stun guns back."

"I know what you mean," Dru agreed, "but we have what we have. Deal with it. Two NYPD officers with the element of surprise should be able to detain a single suspect long enough for the back-up to arrive. Don't you think?" Dru scanned his eyes around the room of blue uniforms. Seven were men, who were all nodding and mumbling supportive expletives. The two women, who were strong and fit, responded even more enthusiastically.

"Hell yeah!" a young Black officer shouted. "I'll gladly be the one to take this sucker down."

"That's the attitude I like." Dru snuck a quick glance toward Mariana, who gave him a pumped fist. "The harder part is going to be avoiding any civilian casualties, or shooting any fellow officers if Millen shows up with a gun, which is likely. We're also going to have media hanging around the fringes, so let's try not to take any of them out. They have a tendency to file negative reports about the NYPD when one of their ranks gets shot by an officer."

The faces around the room all looked like they had done a double tequila shot without a lime to put in their mouths afterward. Bibb said, "Why don't we have the drone drop a net on the guy?"

"You got a net handy? And a drone large enough?" Dru shot back, clearly unhappy with the sergeant's cheek. Bibb scowled, but didn't reply. "The object is for our guy with the wire to get

Millen to confess. As soon as we have what we need on tape, we can move in."

"This is the worst-planned operation in history," the sergeant mumbled.

Dru held out his open palms. "Look, we all know this is a last-minute operation put together with crazy glue. All we can ask from you all is to stay alert, don't blow the operation by spooking the suspect, and do the best you can when the shit hits the fan. You'll all have body armor and we've got twelve of us and only one of him."

"What about the other guy at the meeting?" A young, fresh-faced officer asked. "What if he runs?"

"Good question. Our informant, Luis, is to be treated like he's a cop. We'll give him body armor also. Do not engage with him. If he runs, let him go. As long as he doesn't do anything to interfere with the bust, ignore him." He scanned the room, noting that every cop there was focused and paying attention. "Any other questions?"

"I got just one more." Bibb stood up. "Why won't anybody tell us what this suspect did—is accused of doing?"

"We told you, he's a prime suspect in a double murder."

"He murder anyone in particular?"

"Why, Sergeant? Would you and your team treat the assignment any differently depending on who he killed?"

"No, 'course not. I'm just curious."

"Stay curious. I'm sure you'll find out after we catch the son of a bitch."

Chapter 45 — Hiding in Plain Sight

HANNAH ASKED THE MANAGER of the lawyer's league softball team, "What's the hardest thing about leading a group of lawyers?"

The field was two blocks south of the 6th Street soccer pitch and track. As soon as the ACN van arrived, the players and spectators became excited. The pre-game warm-up drills got more serious and the equipment was arranged neatly for the expected cameras. The midnight meeting was four hours away, but Hannah wanted to be entrenched long in advance. She instructed Terry to shoot some video. Team captain Harry Packman was happy to give Hannah an interview, between batters. When the game ended at 9:30, the players vacated, hoping to see themselves on that night's news broadcast. The van remained in place.

Hannah coordinated two techs who ventured north with backpacks containing remote-controlled hidden camera units. These had been hastily obtained from the investigative reporting team at ACN. Usually, they were planted in factories suspected of unsafe working conditions, or in briefcases taken to clandestine meetings with corrupt politicians. The tech team was reluctant to give up their favorite toys and warned Hannah that they were fragile and super-expensive. Heads would roll if they got lost or damaged.

Hannah wasn't concerned. Dave Butler had given carte blanche to use any resources necessary to secure the scoop. It rankled Dave that Hannah refused to tell him the name of the suspect, but she said the police insisted on confidentiality until after the bust.

Hannah and Dave discussed the option of using live camera operators and microphone jockeys, but there were no secure shooting locations where the cameras wouldn't be seen and the operators wouldn't be in danger. So, they opted for the hidden cameras. The only exception was one long-range parabolic microphone, which was manually operated. They needed to record the conversation in the middle of the soccer field. The cops would have a microphone hidden on Luis, but ACN would not likely get that audio.

The problem was where to put Terry, who would be operating the satellite dish-like contraption. He needed to be safe, but to have a clear line of sight for the powerful mic. After scoping out the field, they decided to station Terry on the roof of the bathroom building next to the field. The police authorized it only if Terry agreed to lie down flat until both meeting participants were on the field. Hannah thought it was a reasonable request. Terry, as always, was game for anything.

Once the cameras were in place, the techs adjourned to their own van, parked a block to the west. Hannah watched the soccer game in progress through the two cameras as soon as they came online. The picture was sharp and the microphones picked up the crowd noise as well as grunts and shouts from the players. As Hannah and Paulo watched, the cameras panned side to side and zoomed in to make sure they had a good view of the field. After a goal, both cameras were able to get clear shots of the black and white pentagons on the ball as it sat on the center circle, waiting for the kickoff. Hannah was confident they would get solid video if Bull showed for the meeting.

Next to Hannah in the van, Connor Osborne played with a hand-held video game. He was twenty-three and dressed in cargo shorts and a Pokémon t-shirt. He was her drone operator. The drone was perched atop the van, waiting to be deployed above the soccer field with a high-definition camera controlled through a VR headset. It had a microphone, but it wasn't sensitive enough to get any meaningful audio of the conversation on the field from the height at which it would be flying.

"I still can't believe you got permission to fly the drone in Manhattan." Paulo inclined his head toward Connor, who did not give any indication of hearing over the game sounds in his headphones.

"I think it was mostly because we had it available on short notice. They're letting us have cameras, so why not give us the drone? We did have to agree to all their terms."

In giving ACN a waiver of the local law prohibiting drones in Manhattan, the police insisted it not dip below 200 feet so as not to attract any attention, not that its plastic propellers and low-power motors would be heard even at fifty feet. They also reserved the right to direct the drone if Bull bolted from the soccer field so they could use it to track him. Connor seemed unconcerned about the upcoming assignment, even with all the restrictions.

Trying to get to know her new team member, Hannah got Connor's attention and asked, "What are you playing?"

"Zelda," Connor replied, immediately returning his attention to the small console in his hands.

"Is that a Game Boy?"

Connor glanced up with an annoyed look. "Switch."

Hannah shrugged. Abandoning idle banter with Connor, she leaned in close to Paulo. "I sure hope Bull shows for the meeting after we went to so much trouble."

Paulo nodded. "I'm more concerned about whether Luis will show. We need to get him outfitted. The officer in charge of his prep is outside waiting."

"He still wants the immunity deal," Hannah said with conviction. "He'll be here."

Chapter 46 — The Main Event

THE NYPD MOBILE COMMAND CENTER is a sixty-foot mobile home outfitted with every piece of tech, communications, and surveillance gear available, along with weaponry, body armor, and riot control supplies. On any significant field operation, the command center serves as base camp for the highest-ranking officers making the real-time decisions. Normally, the behemoth is emblazoned with huge blue letters reading "NYPD" and "POLICE", but on this Friday night it was in camouflage mode, with black magnetic vinyl sheets covering the normal trappings. The Command Center was parked on a pedestrian walkway a half-mile south of the soccer field.

Mariana and Dru attempted to appear calm and in control, sitting in two semi-comfortable cushioned seats against the side wall of the CC. Sergeant Bibb lounged in a captain's chair behind the driver's seat, facing forward. He seemed unconcerned about the upcoming operation. Blue-gray smoke curled away from the cigarette between his fingers.

Dru stalked to the front of the vehicle and stood over him, looking down. "Sergeant!"

"Yeah?"

"Can I bum one? I've been trying to quit, but tonight doesn't seem to be the night."

"Sure." Bibb dug out his pack and offered it to Dru, who took one Marlboro and walked back to where Mariana waited.

He put the filter in his mouth and patted his jacket pockets. "I don't suppose you have a light?"

"You told me to never give you one. You made me promise. You said your girlfriend told you it was a dealbreaker."

Dru removed the cigarette and shrugged. "I did, didn't I? Fine. I'll suck in the second-hand smoke."

One of their officers, a communications specialist named Patricia Suggs, operated a console of dials and switches against the other wall. She was coordinating the radio chatter among all the teams of officers. With so many units, it was nearly impossible to maintain order and get the correct information to Dru, who was the operation's designated leader. Patty, somehow, listened to all the incoming lines and decided which to connect into the main channel that Dru, Mariana, and Bibb heard in their headphones. Patty also was responsible for the three television monitors mounted near the ceiling. Since the ACN crew had planted cameras, the cops insisted on getting a video feed. The center monitor was dark, but was reserved for the feed from the ACN drone.

It was a few minutes past eleven. The soccer game had ended a half-hour earlier and all the spectators and players had cleared out, heading for the pubs on the other side of the FDR Drive for an after-match drink, or home to their families. A few half-empty water bottles and other debris from the game dotted the grass around the field. The lights were still on, brightly illuminating the playing surface and casting ambient light on the surrounding red running track made of rubberized asphalt.

Two slender, long-legged figures rounded the turn at the northeast corner and headed down the home stretch toward the finish line, a thick white stripe painted across the track at the midpoint of the straight-away. Team four, stationed near the northwest corner, reported that the pair had been running together for six laps. They speculated that the runners would likely be finished before midnight.

"If they're not off the track by eleven forty-five, we'll need somebody in plain clothes to nudge them away without attracting attention," Dru replied into his microphone.

Meanwhile, a few late-night runners and dog-walkers padded down the walking path between the field and the FDR Drive. It was a typical spring evening. The pedestrians had no idea there was a police operation underway. Two pairs of traffic enforcement officers, in their ubiquitous brown uniforms, had been reassigned to crowd control for the event. Once the meeting between Luis and Bull started, the Brownies would quietly redirect any pedestrians and close off the walkway.

On the opposite side of the field, a low wall separated the running track from a pedestrian plaza abutting the East River. An arrangement of tables with umbrellas speckled the wide spot in the East River Promenade. It was another place pedestrians and runners frequented. The second pair of Brownies on that side would similarly turn back any bystanders. A line of police tape and a few orange traffic cones would also convey the proper message to anyone who came upon the obstructions. All the officers had instructions to stay out of sight until their target entered the meeting area.

"This setup is a recipe for civilian casualties if it turns into a shoot-out," Dru lamented.

"Is there a scenario where it doesn't end with Millen shooting Luis?" Mariana raised both eyebrows.

"Sure. The scenario where Millen doesn't show up."

Mariana did not reply. The CC was quiet. There was no chatter on the open radio channel. The entire team waited for the arrival of Reggie "Bull" Millen.

* * *

TEN MINUTES LATER, team four reported that the two runners had left the track and were heading toward the path leading to the FDR overpass.

"Keep watching," Dru called back. "Make sure they leave. We'll keep the walking path open until our target clears onto the field. We want everything to look normal until then." Dru dialed Hannah. He still was unhappy that the DA had agreed to the media presence. "We're set here and receiving your feeds. I'll let you know when you can launch your drone. If something happens and we need the drone, I'll call on this line to give instructions. Copy?"

Hannah confirmed the arrangement. She had fought against letting the police direct their drone, but relented on the theory that if Bull was running and the cops needed to follow him from the air, she was going to want the footage.

Next, Dru dialed Paulo, who was outside the ACN van along with Luis and the last of their uniformed officers, Alexander Teut. Luis had arrived at 10:30, which was closer to the meeting than Dru and Mariana wanted. But they had no control over Luis.

Officer Teut had outfitted Luis with a tiny microphone hidden in the waistband of his black sweat pants. He also gave Luis a Kevlar vest, tucking it under his t-shirt and brown hoodie. The vest would absorb any bullet to his torso. If fired from more than fifteen feet, the vest would hold. A shot from a .45—if that was Bull's gun of choice—would still knock Luis down and hurt like hell, but the vest would keep him alive. Officer Teut instructed Luis to keep his distance and try to avoid taking a slug in the head.

"I make it eleven forty-five," Mariana said into her headset. Patty confirmed the time check to all the units into all the channels at once.

"All units, be alert for our target. He should arrive soon." Mariana muted her microphone so she could speak to Dru. "How long do we wait if Millen doesn't show?"

"Don't be so negative. He'll be here. We wait as long as it takes."

Five minutes later, the live channel squawked. "Unit one. I have one Black male approximately six-two, wearing blue sweatpants and a baggy gray sweatshirt, walking north along the walkway into the target area."

Dru replied, "Could be our mark. Unit one, keep under surveillance but do not engage."

"Ten-four. Target turning east toward the field."

"Confirmed." Dru turned to Mariana and gave her a thumbs-up sign. "Unit two, do you have eyes on target?"

"Negative," came a quick response.

"Never mind," Patty said. "We have video." She pointed upward to the far left monitor, where a dark figure walked across a strip of concrete and onto the red track surface, then continued onto the field's green grass.

"Unit two—confirmed visual on target."

"Unit three—confirmed visual."

"All teams," Dru said, "maintain surveillance. Units two and three, tell your Brownies to close down the walkway and the pedestrian plaza. Nobody goes in now except our man." He then punched a button on his phone to call Paulo, who was waiting with Luis and the officer who had been assigned to babysit their snitch. "OK, mister reporter. It's show time. Your guy Reggie just showed up. Send Luis in."

"I'm sending Luis. Make sure you protect him."

"We know our job!"

Paulo hung up and turned to Luis. "Be careful, and remember your instructions. The cops will move in as soon as Bull says what we hope he's going to say. If Bull has a gun, they'll move in as soon as there is any danger to you. Keep your distance, and keep him talking."

"I got it." Luis stood.

Officer Teut stood also. "Hold out your arms," he barked.

Luis slumped his shoulders, turned his back on the officer, and held out his arms while Teut patted him down. "Yo, you stripped me and wired me already. You think I pulled a piece outta my ass since then and stashed it in my pants?"

Teut did not respond. The detectives had insisted that Luis be checked for weapons before he went to the meeting, even after the officer had put on his bullet-proof vest. They didn't trust him to be unarmed. When the officer was satisfied that Luis was clean, he nodded. "Remember your instructions."

"Yeah. I got 'em," Luis jerked away from the pat-down and walked north, toward the soccer field.

Two of the three monitors in the CC now showed the dark figure of Reggie Millen from different angles. He walked calmly to midfield, paused, then kept moving in the direction of the East River. Reggie crossed the red running surface and peered down a gentle embankment leading to the concrete wall separating the Promenade plaza from the athletic field. When he completed his examination, he returned to the track and walked north, following the curve around, swinging his head from side to side, and examining the surrounding landscape.

"All units, target confirmed. He's making a perimeter sweep. Stay out of sight."

Bull completed his circuit around the running track and stopped where he started, at the midpoint of the back straightaway opposite the finish line. He sat down cross-legged on the turf at the edge of the track. The night air had cooled significantly after the warm day. Bull wore a bulky sweatshirt over his blue sweatpants. He looked like a heavyweight boxer getting ready for a training session. It was 11:59.

"Unit one, confirming that Eagle has entered target area."

Dru held up his right hand toward Mariana, with his fingers crossed. "Confirmed, unit one. Seal the target area. All units, be sharp."

The officer assigned to drive the Command Center slowly eased the awkwardly large vehicle up the paved pathway toward the soccer field, without any lights on. With the black camouflage in place and the trees separating the field from the walkway, they were nearly invisible to anyone standing on the pitch.

Dru then called Hannah in the ACN van. Without any small talk, he said, "You are clear to launch your drone. Make sure you keep it above 200 feet and out of our hair." After disconnecting, he turned to Patty. "How's our wire?"

"It was solid a few minutes ago, Detective. Right now, he's not saying anything, but we're good." They watched while Luis, wearing his dark sweat pants and brown hoodie, dropped to one knee next to a tree on the edge of the paved area around the bathroom building. He tied his sneaker, then continued toward the field.

Mariana pointed at the center monitor. "Look, we got the drone video up."

Dru and Mariana watched the overhead view from the drone, moving slowly across the soccer field. Luis stopped at the edge of the grass, inside the oval running track. Bull was standing on the far side. One camera showed Reggie Millen's face with a zoom close enough to confirm it was a match for his mug shot. The other monitor was focused on Luis's back. Both men walked slowly toward the center of the field.

When they were twenty-five feet apart, Bull called out, "How you doin', Luis?"

"Better than you, I think. I heard you didn't want to go to the hospital."

"I hate hospitals, man. The doctors always ask a lot of questions, and the cops show up sometimes."

Luis moved to his left, around the white center circle painted on the field. Bull mirrored the movement, maintaining the radius of the circle between them. "You fucked things up, Bull. We had a good thing going. You had to shoot the girl. Now we're all fucked."

"I had it under control, you stupid motherfucker!" Bull punched his left arm into the air toward Luis, then grimaced.

"You hurt'n, Bull? Huh? I'm sorry about that. You know, sometimes you gotta do what's best for the business."

Bull broke the pattern of their little dance by stepping inside the center circle, closer to Luis, who stopped where he was. "I know, man. Sometimes you gotta make hard-ass choices." Bull took another step toward the center.

"You didn't have to kill that bitch. Slap her around like you did, sure, but see what happened? You got the cops all up on us."

"She pulled a gun on me, remember?"

Luis let out a belly laugh loud enough for the officers in their hiding places around the field to hear. The perimeter teams were on their communications channels, but could not hear the feed from Luis's wire.

"Oh, shit, man. That little thing? You knocked it outta the little girl's hand so easy. That was a nice move, by the way, throwin' dirt in her face like a ninja."

"I got lots of moves, Luis. You know that. So do you. That was some move jumpin' me in the alley, you and your boys."

"Hey, my boys were just watching. The rest was just you and me, like now."

"Is that right? Just you an' me?"

"Yeah? What moves you gonna throw at me tonight?" Luis stepped toward Bull, now only ten feet away.

"What's he doing?" Dru mumbled. "He's supposed to keep his distance."

The drone camera zoomed in, showing the overhead view of the center circle and the two men now both inside. A knife blade flashed in the bright stadium lights.

"Luis has a knife!" Mariana called out.

"Damn! How'd he get a knife?" Dru mumbled, more to himself than to anyone in the CC.

"When he knelt down—next to the tree to tie his shoe." Mariana slammed an open palm against the side of the CC. "Damn! He must have planted it there before we got here and picked it up right under our nose."

On the field, Luis went into a fighting stance—knees bent, arms extended for balance, ready to move in any direction.

Bull stood still. "I ain't gonna have another knife fight with you, Luis. You got the advantage, seein' how you ain't got no stitches in you." Bull reached behind his back with both arms, lifted his sweatshirt with his left hand, and emerged with a gun in his right. It had a fat middle and a long muzzle. Luis froze in place.

"Gun!" Mariana called into her microphone.

"Hold!" Dru yelled a half-second later. "Hold your ground, all units!"

Mariana tore off her headset, sending strands of hair flying wildly. Covering her microphone with a clenched hand, she looked incredulously at Dru. "We have to move in."

"We don't have a confession yet." Dru's reply was broadcast to all the units. "Luis pulled a knife. He's on his own. No shots fired yet, so we hold!"

Chapter 47 — Quick Decisions

INSIDE THE ACN VAN, Paulo and Hannah watched the camera feeds. Terry had emerged from his prone position when Hannah spoke into his earphone that Bull was on the field. From his perch atop the bathroom building, he directed his parabolic microphone, the size and shape of a small satellite dish. He pointed the dish at the center of the field to pick up the conversation. It wasn't perfect, but most of the conversation was piped back to the van.

"Luis has a knife!" Hannah cried out.

"And Bull has a gun!" Paulo shouted. "Luis needs to keep his distance, or his vest won't protect him. What's he doing?"

They watched as Luis moved toward Bull. Hannah put a hand on Paulo's shoulder. "Don't worry, the cops will move in, now that they see Bull's gun."

They waited, watching the overhead drone feed and expecting to see officers moving from the corners of the field toward the two men in the middle. There was no movement.

Paulo shouted to Officer Teut, who was still with them in the van, "What's happening? Why aren't they moving in?"

Teut responded, "They're holding."

"That's bullshit!" Paulo slammed his palm against the side of the vehicle. "They're supposed to protect Luis. They're gonna let

Bull shoot him." Paulo opened the van door and leapt to the ground.

"Stop!" Teut yelled. He moved to follow, but tripped over Hannah's leg, landing on his face on the metal floor.

Paulo sprinted to the north, toward the soccer field. Teut sprang to his feet and followed Paulo into the darkness.

Chapter 48 — The Flying Trapeze

LUIS MAINTAINED HIS STANCE, too far away from Bull to lunge with his knife before a bullet found his body.

"I thought we was gonna talk, Luis. Didn't you say you wanted to make a deal? Make peace and shit. You think we can? You think you can go back to bein' my sheriff like you never jumped me and tried to put me down?"

Luis moved to his left, again circling and keeping his distance. Bull did the same, his gun held casually in his right hand. "That's up to you, Bull. You can walk away, or you can stick around and be one of my boys."

"Ha!" Bull's laugh echoed around the field. "Like I'm gonna work for you, you piece of shit."

"So, you gonna shoot me now, Bull? Huh?"

"You really didn't bring a gun, Luis? That's pretty damn stupid if you ask me. What happened to that little bitty pistol our shark had, huh? You was smart to pick it up after I put her down. Made it hard on the cops, shootin' basketball boy with it. I bet you still got it, don't ya? You're gonna whip it out any minute now. Am I right?"

"I don't need no gun, Bull. You toss that one away and we'll settle this without any metal."

Dru and Mariana watched the image from the drone zoom in even farther. Bull's head got bigger and bigger, filling the screen. Then, they saw Bull look up, directly at the drone's camera.

Bull raised his right arm. An explosion ruptured the quiet soccer field when Bull fired his gun, reverberating off the cinder-block bathroom building. Terry flinched as his earphones amplified the sound.

"What the fuck!?" Dru yelled.

"Shots fired. All units move in!" Mariana called into her microphone, which she was now holding in her hand. She hurriedly snapped her set back onto her head while watching the video monitors. Muting her microphone, she said, "Did Reggie just say Luis shot Estrada?"

Chapter 49 — Man Down

PAULO RUSHED TOWARD the soccer field. He didn't have a specific plan. He only knew that the cops had double-crossed Luis. They were supposed to protect him. They were supposed to move in as soon as Bull pulled a gun. Luis had put himself on the line to get the immunity deal. He had trusted Paulo. He was just a weed dealer, not a killer. Bull was the bad guy.

They needed to arrest Bull now, before he shot Luis. Even with the Kevlar vest, Bull's big gun could do damage—and Bull knew how to shoot somebody in the head, where Luis had no protection. Paulo had to force the cops' hand. If he went in, they would have to act. All he had to do was get to the scene.

* * *

HANNAH LISTENED to the feed from Terry's long-range microphone. She heard Bull say that Luis used Angelica's gun to kill Javier. "Shit!" She rushed to the front of the van, jumped into the driver's seat, and turned the key.

"What are you doing?" Connor yelled. He could not see anything through the VR goggles he used to pilot the drone, but he heard the sound and felt the engine starting.

"Paulo ran in to protect Luis, but Luis lied to us. We have to stop him." Hannah disengaged the parking break. "Hang on!"

The white van sprang forward, skidding on the dewy grass as Hannah maneuvered around the metal bleachers, then onto the paved walking path. She gunned the engine, driving north toward the field and scanning to her right for Paulo and Officer Teut. She didn't see either.

Within seconds, the van's headlights illuminated a line of bright yellow police crime scene tape strung across the narrow asphalt path. Three orange traffic cones signaled to anyone approaching that the walkway was closed. A traffic enforcement officer in a brown uniform dashed from the shadows onto the pavement, holding out a white-gloved hand to signal Hannah to stop. Instead, she swerved around the Brownie, crushing a traffic cone and snapping the crime scene tape, then barreled across the grass toward the bathroom building.

Hannah's heart pounded in her ears. A tree appeared in her headlights. She swerved. The van's tires caught their grip on the concrete plaza surrounding the cinder-block building. She stomped on the brakes, drawing in a panicked breath. The van skidded and twisted, then rammed into the corner. Hannah—who had not taken the time to fasten her seatbelt—lurched forward, banging her side and shoulder into the steering wheel.

The drone image shook on the screen inside the van and inside the CC. Connor was thrown off his chair when the vehicle banged into the bathroom. Even at a relatively slow speed, the impact was jarring, causing him to momentarily lose control of the drone. He sat up on the van floor, controller in hand, and quickly brought the plastic craft back to level.

Connor let out a whistle. "Man, that was bad-ass."

* * *

AS PAULO APPROACHED the southwest corner of the soccer field, he saw the backs of the two officers assigned to that position. They were standing with weapons drawn behind two trees ten feet off the running track. Their eyes were fixed on the soccer field.

Paulo ran past them, onto the track.

"Stop!" one officer called out in a loud whisper. The police were still under instructions to not let Reggie Millen know they had him surrounded.

Paulo ignored the command. He took a stride onto the grass. Out of the corner of his eye, he saw a flash of white and the glare of a headlight. The ACN logo emblazoned on the side of the van left no doubt about its origin.

He slipped on the damp turf, coming to a stop and breathing heavily after sprinting from the softball field. He looked forward and heard the explosion of a gunshot coming from in front of him.

Chapter 50 — Double Barrel

WHEN BULL HEARD THE WHINE of plastic rotors, he looked up and saw the ACN drone, which was dive-bombing his head. He instinctively turned and fired at the approaching menace.

Luis instantly saw his opportunity and sprang forward, knife extended. He slashed at Bull's right arm but missed the elbow, instead cutting into Bull's sweatshirt under the armpit. The knife was sharp and drew blood; Bull grunted and pulled the gun down. The drone was retreating to a higher altitude.

Luis grabbed a fist full of Bull's sweatshirt as his momentum carried him past his target, pulling both men down to the grass. Bull groaned. Luis locked his hand around Bull's right wrist, under the gun.

"Units two and three, move in!" Dru shouted into his microphone. "One and four, maintain a perimeter."

"This is unit one, we have a runner on the field."

"What the fuck?" Dru yelled into his microphone. He exchanged puzzled looks with Mariana, then heard a crash outside the Command Center. They had no windows and the cameras were still focused on the field. At the edge of the drone camera image, Dru saw the white ACN van pressed against the bathroom building.

Dru steadied himself. "Hold your position, unit one. We don't want you in the cross-fire. Do you have an ID on your runner?"

"Negative," came the reply. "Male, six feet, thin, wearing a dark t-shirt and jeans."

"Base, this is Teut," a new voice came through Dru's and Mariana's headphones. "The runner is the reporter, Richardson."

Dru motioned to Patty with an open hand. "All units, the runner is a reporter. Try not to shoot him."

Units two and three moved onto the field the moment Dru gave the order after the gunshot. Unit three approached from the northeast corner, unit two from the southeast. In their pre-event prep, Dru had cautioned the officers that two advancing units would be less likely to shoot each other than if all eight officers encircled their target. They had not figured on Paulo being in the cross-fire.

When Paulo sprinted in from the southwest, Officer Teut stopped at the edge of the track. The unit one officers signaled to him that they were supposed to hold their ground. The drone had regained altitude and broadcast a wide-angle view of the approaching officers. The four dark uniforms maintained a defensive posture, guns extended. There was an active shooter in front of them, forcing them to proceed with caution.

Paulo, however, was exercising no such care. He saw Luis and Bull fighting in close quarters and sprinted forward.

* * *

HANNAH TRIED TO OPEN the driver's-side door, but it banged against the building. Under the bright lights, she saw Paulo running across the field. There was no way she was going to stop him from charging into the fight between Luis and Bull. He was too far away. She thrust her hand into the center of the steering wheel and leaned on the horn.

* * *

WITH THE COPS STILL seventy feet away, Luis and Bull rolled toward the midfield stripe. Luis twisted his knife blade and nipped Bull's exposed wrist, causing Bull to loosen his grip on Luis's right arm. Bellowing in pain, Bull thrust his upper body forward, slamming his forehead into Luis's. The headbutt stunned Luis momentarily and allowed Bull to free his gun hand.

The scene played out on the video monitors in the Command Center. Bull's gun discharged again. The blast was deafening inside Dru's headphones. He and Mariana both cringed, closed their eyes, and snatched the headsets off their ears.

Luis fell away onto his right side, his knife spilling to the grass from a limp hand. Bull looked up, his breath coming in short gasps. Blood from the knife wound in his armpit seeped into the fabric of his sweatshirt. Blood from Luis's neck covered his gun and dripped down his clenched hand.

He saw a figure running toward him, shouting, "Luis! Luis!"

Paulo skidded to a halt, twenty feet from the two figures on the ground. Bull rose to a knee and pointed his .45 at the defenseless reporter.

A car horn split the relative silence of the midnight air. Paulo turned toward the sound, seeing the white ACN van jammed against the bathroom.

Bull jerked his head in the direction of the loud horn, just as he pulled the trigger.

Paulo cried out in pain, collapsing to the ground.

Bull spun on his knee, then saw a police officer closing toward him, a gun extended at the end of her arm.

"Drop the gun!" the cop yelled.

Bull stood and extended his gun arm toward the officer. Shots riddled the field, booming simultaneously like the finale of a fireworks show.

Four officers moved in as Bull's head hit the turf. They surrounded the center circle, all holding their service weapons with extended arms, kneeling or crouching and ready to fire again if needed. The overhead drone captured the image of three men lying on the green grass while four officers fanned out to secure each one. Five more officers stormed forward from their positions around the field.

Bull lay motionless, his gun having tumbled onto the brightly lit turf. The acrid stench of gunpowder filled the air.

Dru, still holding a hand over his ear said, "Patty, call for ambulances."

* * *

INSIDE THE ACN VAN, Hannah screamed as she watched the events unfold on the soccer field. The gunfire rang out in the microphones embedded in the remote cameras, through Terry's parabolic dish, and through the van's partially open windows.

"Holy shit!" Hannah rolled over to the passenger seat and pushed through the door, falling onto the concrete below.

"He's moving," Connor announced.

"Who?" Hannah sprang back to her feet, putting her face back through the open van door.

"Paulo. He's on the ground, but moving around. I'll go in closer and get an image."

"You're not supposed to go below 200 feet."

"The police gig is over," Connor said matter-of-factly as the soccer field image got larger on the video screen. A few seconds later, Connor had zoomed the drone's camera in on Paulo, lying on the ground, twenty feet outside the center circle. Paulo lifted an arm toward the drone, giving a thumbs-up signal.

"He's alive. He's OK." Hannah slumped against the side of the van, wiping sweat from her forehead. She pulled out her phone and punched the icon for their tech team's van. "Did we get it?"

"Yeah. We got it," Robert, the head video editor, replied. "It's gonna need some editing."

"Get on that right now, but clip the drone footage first. That's the best overall view. Cut out the kamikaze part and just give me the high-angle view of the cops moving in. Fifteen or twenty seconds, including the shooting."

"Aren't we gonna want to blur that or something?" Robert seemed worried.

"No. The high angle and distance will take care of that for us. Get it ready!"

"Including the guy shooting your friend?"

"Everything."

Hannah spun back toward the field. A cluster of three officers knelt next to the spot where Paulo had fallen. She sprinted in that direction. When she was close enough for the officers to hear her footfalls, one jumped up and intercepted Hannah, grabbing her arm. "Paulo!" she called.

"I'm OK," Paulo's voice sang back, out of her eyesight. "He got me in the leg."

* * *

WITHIN TWO MINUTES, an ambulance arrived on the running track, lights flashing. The EMT crew rushed to Paulo's prone figure while two cops nudged Hannah away from the area. Nobody seemed concerned about Bull or Luis.

Hannah returned to the van. Terry had clambered down from the roof and was setting up camera equipment and light stands. Connor sat in the same place, his VR goggles now on his lap. He still held the drone controls in his hands, watching the high-angle view of the field on the video screen.

"You know the cops are going to question you about violating their instructions for the drone, right?"

"Whatever," Connor said, not moving his head. "That big guy pulled a gun on our guy. What was I supposed to do?"

"Our guy had body armor," Hannah replied. "We expected Bull to have a gun, but the plan was for Luis to stay far enough away that any shot to his center mass would not be lethal. We wanted to keep him out of a close-quarters fight so he could keep Bull talking. Do you remember that conversation we had an hour ago?" Hannah's raised voice seemed even louder inside the closed space.

"You've got to chill out. It was the right move."

Hannah leaned in to see the image on the 20-inch monitor. Another set of EMTs had arrived, but were standing on the perimeter of the center circle. Two uniformed officers put white flags on the grass next to the two dark figures that were not moving.

"One for Bull, and one for Luis," she whispered.

Hannah grabbed a black baseball cap emblazoned with the ACN logo from a hook on the van's wall, and dashed back outside. Then she stopped, pulled Paulo's satchel off another hook, and rushed to follow Terry. Her heart was racing from the crash, the terror of the shooting and Paulo's injury, and from the excitement of being the first journalist at the scene of the biggest story of her life.

Chapter 51 — Cue the Lights

IVE MINUTES LATER, Hannah knelt on the turf next to Paulo while an EMT finished wrapping tape around his thigh. The medics had cut the leg off his jeans at the crotch in order to access the wounds where Bull's bullet had entered and exited his muscle. When the white tape fully obscured the gauze pads below, Hannah and the EMT helped Paulo to his feet. Paulo gingerly put some weight on his injured leg and winced, gripping Hannah's shoulder.

When they arrived at the open rear doors of the nearby ambulance, Paulo asked, "You got a crutch in there?"

The EMT chuckled. "Yeah, I do, but you need to go to the hospital, dude."

"I will. Later," Paulo replied. He noticed his satchel dangling from Hannah's shoulder. "Thanks for bringing my gear. We both have some work to do."

Hannah shrugged off the bag's strap and held it by the handle. "I'll carry this for you. I have a place over by the bathroom where you can sit."

"I can't believe the cops hung Luis out to dry like that. The bastards! I mean, I guess I'm not surprised, but they promised to protect him. He trusted me, and I trusted the cops. It's partly my fault that he's dead."

Hannah interrupted Paulo's mourning. "You ran out to protect him. That was freaking brave. I know I wouldn't have done it. But it was also stupid, and unnecessary."

"What do you mean, *unnecessary*? He was a human being. A drug dealer, sure, but—"

"He murdered Javier."

"What?" Paulo's mouth hung open.

"After you dashed to his rescue, Bull said that Luis had picked up Angelica's gun after Bull shot her. It was Luis who shot Javier."

"But . . . how do we know Bull was telling the truth?"

Hannah shrugged. "I guess we don't know for sure. I can't imagine why he would lie about it in that spot. Luis didn't argue the point."

"Sure," Paulo hesitated, "but what if Bull figured out that it was a setup and guessed that Luis was wearing a wire? What if he wanted to incriminate Luis?"

"Then he's the smartest criminal on the planet. But it doesn't matter now. He's dead, and so is Luis. Between the two of them, they killed Angelica and Javier. It's over."

* * *

AFTER SETTLING PAULO in a folding chair in front of a low concrete wall ten yards beyond the finish line on the running track, Hannah found Dru and tugged on his sport jacket sleeve, interrupting a conversation he was having with one of the uniformed officers. "Detective, we have a date with a camera crew."

"I'm busy," Dru shot back coldly.

"We had an arrangement."

Dru turned from the officer and pointed a finger into Hannah's face. "We also had an arrangement about your drone not dipping below 200 feet. Remember that?"

"Yes, I do. It was an accident. The drone operator made a mistake." Hannah returned Dru's angry gaze, not blinking.

"I don't believe that horseshit for a minute. Go find somebody else for your sound bite."

"I only have one question, Detective. How does it feel to have taken out Javier Estrada's murderer?"

Dru snapped his head around to see Terry, holding his camera. He shot a witheringly angry look toward Hannah, then composed himself, knowing he was being recorded. "It feels good to have Angelica Monroe's murderer, as well as the man who helped him. Reggie Millen was a drug dealer and a thug. We're always sad when anybody gets killed during a police operation, but I think justice is served in this case as to both murders—Angelica Monroe *and* Javier Estrada."

"Are you happy to get a confession before the shooting?"

"I can't say anything about the investigation. Suffice it to say that two men are dead and it's likely the case—cases—will be closed."

* * *

PAULO BALANCED HIS LAPTOP on the thin wall and tapped out his story, ignoring the throbbing pain in his leg. Hannah and Terry set up for their live shot. Terry had identified a location on the level concrete a few yards away from Paulo's makeshift workspace. It was perfect, with the buzzing of police activity still prominent in the background to frame the shot. Terry had a terrific eye.

Hannah sat cross-legged on the cool ground, making revisions to the on-air text she had already drafted before the night's activities began. She had not anticipated two dead participants, but that was a minor detail in the story about the police solving the Angelica Monroe and Javier Estrada double murder. That was how the copy was going to read. She was not going to let anyone at the studio edit out Javier's connection.

She finished the revisions on her phone before William Wilson arrived. Hannah had alerted him that there would likely be a big story breaking in lower Manhattan after midnight and that he should be ready for a live shot. Nevertheless, Wilson arrived grumpy rather than excited.

"What's this all about?" he asked accusingly. He expected Hannah's story to fall short of being sufficiently important to justify getting him into his on-air suit at such a late hour.

"I've got somebody else who can do the live report if you're too busy." Hannah handed Wilson her phone, open to the text of the story.

The reporter scanned the first paragraph, then looked up. "No shit?"

"No shit, Sherlock. You up for it?"

"Oh, hell yes!" Wilson, now enthusiastic, read through the copy, then asked, "How long is the video clip?"

"About twenty seconds, and it's dynamite. It will be on every network that's willing to pay the rights fee by morning."

"Can I see it?"

"No, Robert is still editing, but it will be ready soon. I'll show it to you after you do your stand-up, then we'll do a few more for the morning shows. But, trust me, it's exceptional. All the lead-ins will say that it's disturbing and difficult to watch and will advise viewer discretion."

"Pure gold," Wilson gushed.

Robert's voice came through the speaker on Hannah's phone. "Hannah, we're ready. Video is twenty-two seconds."

"Great. Get it ready. We have an embargo on this for a few more minutes." She walked away toward Paulo's encampment.

* * *

WHILE HANNAH WAS briefing William Wilson, Paulo finished his story. The article focused on the murder of Javier Estrada and included specific information from Luis's taped confession. Paulo narrated his readers through the series of events, beginning with Javier happening on the scene when Angelica Monroe was in distress at the hands of Reggie Millen and ending with Millen—or possibly his accomplice—shooting Javier.

Paulo noted that the information was based on the first-hand account of Luis Torres, who later cooperated with police in the investigation, and was confirmed by audio recordings of the meeting between Torres and Millen, as well as by police sources and independent witnesses who were not named. Torres died during a sting operation, despite efforts by the NYPD to safeguard him. Although he was wearing body armor, during a hand-to-hand fight, Millen's gun went off, shooting Torres in his unprotected neck. He died at the scene.

Paulo did not mention the intervention of a drone operated by a tech from ACN. There was no point creating a side issue that would distract from the main story. He omitted the details about Angelica being a dealer in Reggie Millen's drug operation. He also left out the part about Javier being shot with Angelica Monroe's gun.

At 1:13 a.m., Paulo used his phone as a wi-fi hotspot and uploaded his story to the *LES Tribune* website. This time, he was confident Clarence would not object.

* * *

HANNAH STEPPED BEHIND the camera and pulled out her pack of Virginia Slims. Two lonely white cylinders rolled around inside. She popped one from the box and lit up, inhaling deeply while she watched Wilson prepare for his spot. Her nerves were frazzled after the day's unimaginable events. Blowing out a stream of blue-gray smoke, she closed her eyes and listened.

Terry flicked on the lights, mounted on a telescoping stand. Hannah heard Robert in her earbud count down to going live. It was one-thirty in New York, but the network was live globally. Viewers on the west coast were getting this at the half-hour mark of their ten o'clock news.

The next day, the recorded clips would run at the top of every hour. The video would run on every channel and on every news website. Hannah could see Wilson's face in the camera frame as she listened to her words being broadcast live and captured forever.

"Tonight, New York police officers shot and killed Reggie Millen, a known drug dealer with a lengthy criminal record. Police have confirmed that Millen shot Angelica Monroe and Javier Estrada in a double murder last Friday night in Washington Square Park. An NYPD task force was on the scene when Millen met with an accomplice, Luis Torres. The two men fought on a soccer field in lower Manhattan. Millen shot and killed Torres, then threatened approaching officers with a gun. The officers shot and killed Millen. ACN has exclusive video of the events, taken from a drone-mounted camera above the scene. These images are graphic and may be disturbing for some viewers . . ."

* * *

AT 3:05 A.M., HANNAH sent Paulo two thirty-second clips from the ground-level cameras near the soccer field. They were not the best of the clips she had, but there was a limit to how much video ACN wanted to post on its website on the first day. Hannah wanted Paulo to have some exclusive images to accompany his story. By 3:15, Paulo had embedded hyperlinks to the clips in his story on the *LES Tribune* website.

He was sitting on an examination table at St. Mary's Hospital. The ER doctor had stitched up his entry and exit wounds and given him injections to fight infection and to ease the pain. On a television mounted in the corner, he watched the drone camera images on CNN without any sound, marveling at the speed with which the video got distributed—for a fee.

That Saturday, Paulo's article on the *LES Tribune* website garnered more than double the highest number of views in the history of the paper.

Chapter 52 — Breaking News!

Friday

A T NINE O'CLOCK FRIDAY MORNING, Paulo went live at the ACN studio on 12th Avenue in an interview conducted by William Wilson. Paulo was exhausted after Friday's events, including being assaulted on the street. He had not slept much before his first interviews, which were all Zoom calls except for one old-school telephone link.

His cell phone had first buzzed at six o'clock, which was, apparently, the unofficial earliest time it was acceptable to call a source for an interview. He had promised Hannah before leaving the soccer field that he would do a live segment with Wilson in the morning. He had not figured that it would be his fifth interview.

Wilson looked fresh and chipper, which surprised and impressed Paulo. Maybe he was getting too old for the all-nighters. He focused on the questions and allowed Wilson to lead him through the entire sequence of events, starting with Luis contacting him and offering to make a deal with the police in exchange for his testimony.

Paulo became frustrated when Wilson deflected every attempt Paulo made to talk about Javier Estrada, rather than Angelica Monroe. Wilson never asked a question that would allow Paulo to talk about why Angelica was in the park a week earlier to meet with Millen. It was clear that ACN wanted to keep the discussion focused on the dramatic events of the night before on the soccer field.

Paulo wore sweat pants because he couldn't get anything else over his bandages. When asked why he ran onto the soccer field in the middle of a police operation, Paulo gave his stock response. He had worked on it while lying awake in the hospital. "I had arranged the police operation, with help from Hannah Hawthorne and the American Cable News network, after Luis came to me and volunteered to cooperate. I thought the police had not properly protected Luis. After he and Millen started fighting, I ran toward them to encourage the cops to move in. I obviously didn't expect Millen to turn his gun on me."

"Well," Wilson said solemnly, "you are a braver man than I, and a terrific reporter."

When the interview ended, Paulo spent several minutes with Hannah inside the sound-proofed interview room, while ACN returned to its normal programming.

"You did great!" Hannah gushed. "I can't believe the last twenty-four hours."

"Thanks. I got the distinct impression that your interviewer was steering me away from talking about Javier."

"Yeah. I know. Sorry about that. It's the network's preference on the story." She motioned toward his injured leg. "Are you still in a lot of pain?"

"Yeah. I have some pain meds, but I'm trying not to use them."

"Make sure you get a Tetanus shot."

"Thanks, Mom," Paulo deadpanned.

Hannah punched him lightly in the triceps. "Don't tease me for caring. It was stupid of you to rush off to save Luis, but it was brave. I admire your passion. You could teach me a few things about being a great journalist."

Paulo leaned on a crutch, shifting from side to side awkwardly. "My passion nearly ruined my paper. It didn't help Javier, and it didn't help Luis. I got beaten up and shot for my efforts. My advice is to not follow my example."

"Don't downplay your articles. They showed anybody who was paying attention how biased we can be about White girls automatically being tragic victims and Latino former gang members always being villains."

"Yeah, but was anyone listening?"

"I was," Hannah said softly.

They shared a melancholy sigh. Then, Hannah said, "If Luis hadn't come to you for help, we probably never would have known the truth about what Javier did, and how he died. Your articles told his story. That's worth something."

Paulo looked down into Hannah's eyes. "Thanks."

Hannah took a step back and gently clasped Paulo's hand. "I tell you what; from now on, I'll try to care more about the truth, and you can be a little more practical. We'll both get into less trouble."

Paulo squeezed Hannah's hand, then released it. "It's worth a try. You can start with your follow-up pieces after last night's tour-de-force."

"I have a meeting in a few minutes with my boss to talk about that."

"Maybe you can tell me how that goes over lunch later?" Paulo raised both eyebrows involuntarily as he posed the question.

"You mean, like a business briefing?"

Paulo couldn't tell if Hannah was not getting his message or if she was playing coy. He didn't know her well enough. "I'd say that our joint reporting venture is over, now that the story is put to bed. So, I was thinking of it more as a . . . social thing."

"Like a date?"

Now he was sure she was playing with him. "Yeah, Hawthorne, like a date. Don't make me beg."

Hannah put her hand on Paulo's bare forearm, above his crutch, making his pulse quicken. "Sure. I'd love to. How about at Rosie's at twelve-thirty?"

"Great. I should be wrapped up on all these damned interviews by then."

"Don't complain. You're a star."

"A reporter isn't supposed to be the story."

"In this case, think of it as everyone else needing to cite your work. You're the one who has all the inside information—and the one who got shot during the melee."

"Thanks." He covered Hannah's hand with his own, then quickly released it. "I'll see you later."

* * *

HANNAH SHUT THE DOOR to Dave Butler's office and collapsed into a chair opposite his desk without being invited to sit. That was a first for her. She figured that, with her story topping all the most-viewed charts and her drone video going globally viral, she had the most leverage with her boss she would ever have.

"That's some nice work, Hawthorne," Butler said, actually looking up from the rundown sheet for that day's programming.

"Thanks, Dave. I had a lot of help. And I'd like to talk to you about the coverage. You know I've been telling you how Javier Estrada—"

"Let me stop you, Hawthorne—Hannah. I know where you're coming from. You want to tell the whole story, blah, blah, blah. It's noble and journalistically right and proper. But this is television, not *The New York Times*. We've got an audience to feed."

"I'm trying to tell a better story!" Hannah slapped her palm on the wooden arm of her chair.

"Better? Who knows what that means." Butler paused. "I tell you what, Hannah, I'm totally fine with the story of how Javier Estrada came upon Angelica Monroe in the park being accosted by this guy, Millen, and how he tried to help her. Millen shot her, then chased down Javier, along with his right-hand man, Luis Whatever. They caught poor Javier and then beat him and killed him so he couldn't be a witness. That's a great story."

Hannah pressed her lips together and took a deep breath through her nose. "It is a terrific story. You want me to tell it without mentioning that Angelica was there in the first place to get her supply of drugs from Millen, or that Javier was shot with her gun."

"Exactly. That's exactly right. A pretty reasonable compromise, don't you think?"

"I think it's bullshit," Hannah slumped back in her chair, "but I know it's the best I'm going to get, so I'd better take it. Am I right?"

"Exactly right," Butler tapped his pen three times in quick succession on his desk blotter like a drummer on a snare.

"Fine. Do you want follow-up interviews?"

"Not unless you can find something that's better than what you already got, which I doubt. You're good, Hannah. We're going to make a quarter-million on the rights fees from the drone video and the other clips. We're going to release a new angle from the street-level cameras every twelve hours as long as they keep biting. Keep up the good work."

Hannah rose, but didn't turn to leave. "Hey, Dave, before I go. I really don't think Connor should get in trouble because of what he did, bringing the drone down on the shooter and violating the police rules. He's not going to get fired, is he?"

"Fired? Hell, no. Fired? He's going to get a bonus. That video is gold and he did a fantastic job with it. I don't give a damn about the police rules. How often are we going to be in that kind of position, huh? Probably never again. So why worry about next time? Like I told the kid, 'get us the best images you can get and don't worry about anything else.'"

"You told him that before the shoot?"

"I did. Besides, he was trying to prevent the other guy from getting shot, so he was being a hero, along with getting that fabulous video. You should like that—it's like what you would do."

Hannah closed her eyes and waited a beat. "Connor created a situation where Luis got shot at close range in the neck, instead of at a distance in the chest, where his body armor could have saved him. I thought Connor was doing it on his own, but you're telling me you *encouraged* him to break the rules and fly into the scene. That instruction may have cost Luis Torres his life."

Butler waved a hand in the air dismissively. "I suppose you could look at it that way, but nobody could have known how it was going to play out. He's a dead drug dealer and a thug. Didn't he confess to shooting the other guy—the basketball player?"

"No, Dave. He didn't. Reggie Millen said Luis shot Javier Estrada, but that claim can't be confirmed."

"It doesn't matter. It's just as well they're both dead, although a trial would have been big news." When Hannah didn't state her agreement, Butler said, "It's over, Hawthorne. Move on. Don't shed any tears over this lowlife. It won't bring him back and it won't do you any good. They're a dime a dozen."

Hannah walked slowly to the door, breathing in long, slow cycles. She stood at the threshold and said, "I'm going to think long and hard about what you just said." She walked away, leaving the door open behind her.

Chapter 53 — The Next Act

THE MONDAY AFTER THE SHOOTOUT, Dru and Mariana got the ballistics report back on the .45 recovered from the 6th Street soccer pitch. It contained Reggie Millen's prints and was a match for the gun used to kill Angelica Monroe.

"Reggie was apparently not smart enough to ditch his gun. If there had been a trial, it would have been a slam dunk," Dru observed.

"I'm glad that at least the *LES Tribune* story made sure Javier wasn't forgotten."

"Does it bother you that we'll never know whether it was Millen or Torres who killed him."

"Not really. They're both guilty. I'm guessing the commissioner isn't going to release the audio from Luis's wire, huh?"

Dru shook his head. "I doubt it. There won't be a trial, obviously. I don't think the department wants to acknowledge the immunity deal, and there are certainly political reasons not to talk about Angelica having a gun with her the night she was murdered."

"I guess folks will have to rely on the press reports."

Dru let out a derisive guffaw. "The press always gets it wrong."

"Yeah. Usually. Sometimes they don't have all the information. I guess, it's better that way." Mariana paused and glanced around the bullpen. Nobody was paying them any attention. "I never thanked you for having my back when Zimmerman and that dolt deputy commissioner were on me about the Merriman complaint."

"Sure. You needed it. You could have used it two weeks ago, when you made the complaint. I didn't agree with what you did. I was actually pretty pissed off, as if you couldn't tell."

"My immense powers of deductive reasoning did pick up on that, partner."

"Yeah. Well, I understand why you did it. I didn't want to get involved in a race-based complaint. I didn't see any percentage in alienating the uniforms. And I never did hear anything I thought was a slur or a racist comment."

"You didn't hear any racist comments during this investigation, either. Does that mean there was no racism involved?"

"Touche," Dru conceded. "Would that officer have beaten Merriman so brutally if he had been a White brat from the suburbs in a polo shirt? Probably not. I took the easy road. I didn't want to deal with the shit we would get from the officers and the union. You got the guy suspended. If the case sticks, he'll get fired for sure if there's ever another incident. And I backed you up on the excessive force."

"Yeah, like that was controversial."

"I'm sorry I didn't support you on the racism charge. You were right. If we have to testify at the arbitration hearing, I'll back you up and say I agree with your opinion."

Mariana hurled a skeptical look at her partner. "It would have made more of an impression if you had called him out on it at the time. Your first instinct was to protect the officer and close your eyes to what was really happening."

Dru pressed his lips together and sucked in a breath through his nose. "I know. I guess I need to open my eyes a little wider."

Before the conversation could continue, Sully's voice snapped them both back into the present. "Cook! Vega! Get in here for a minute. Please."

Inside the captain's office, the conversation was brief. Sully was happy that the cases were closed. There were two dead suspects. Millen killed Torres, and the cops unquestionably had good cause to use deadly force on Millen. Good outcome. All the publicity for the department was positive. The cops did their job. Justice was served. Innocent citizens could walk into Washington Square Park again without fear – or at least without more fear than normal when entering any New York City park at night.

Dru and Mariana got congratulations from the other detectives. George Mason walked over to Dru's desk. "If I was on the kid and you were on the girl, it might have gone differently. Glad you were on both." They even got a pat on the back and congratulations from the unit's senior detective, Mike Stoneman.

They had fifteen minutes to bask in the glow before an officer approached Dru's desk with a case folder. "Captain says you're assigned to this one, Detective."

"Yeah," Mariana said. "Always another murder."

* * *

DISTRICT ATTORNEY TRUITT CONCEDED that Luis's associates had qualified for immunity based on the confession

Bull made on the wire, even if there would never be a trial or a conviction.

Enrique was the victor in a brief struggle for control of the drug distribution operation. However, with the narcotics squad laser-focused on students distributing drugs at local colleges, the volume of Enrique's operation fell substantially short of Bull's business. Still, the sharks were easily recruited, the supplies were transferred at new meeting locations unknown to the police, and the students involved guarded their identities and participation carefully, not wanting to mess up their bright futures. Not surprisingly, students still wanted to score their weed without leaving campus and without showing an ID. It was still a thriving business, although a few of the sheriffs had to be laid off in order to preserve the profits for the rest. Since the police had no list of the sheriffs, they never noticed that a few had disappeared.

* * *

HANNAH PITCHED A SERIES of follow-up stories about Javier Estrada, chronicling his transformation from youth gang member to star basketball player and future college athlete. These would be in addition to the in-depth story about how Javier, the Good Samaritan, lost his life after coming to the rescue of Angelica Monroe. Despite Dave's assurances that Hannah could work on those stories, he found reasons to kill each one. The talking head she wanted to use for one was needed for other reports. Hannah was needed for a different breaking news story. Another producer went on leave and Hannah had to cover their projects. The budget was tight and couldn't support a "non-essential" human interest story. Then, finally, the Javier Estrada story was "old news" and nobody cared anymore.

Two weeks after the shootout at the 6th Street soccer pitch, Hannah got a call from a headhunter offering her a job in the video journalism unit of *The New York Times*. After Dave's last rejection, she packed up all her research, notes, and the original Luis Torres confession video, all of which she hoped to turn into a book someday, then quit.

* * *

PAULO WROTE SIX ARTICLES about Javier Estrada, which were loved by everyone in the neighborhood who knew and missed him. Unlike his story about the soccer-pitch shootout, other media outlets ignored his follow-up pieces. The viewing and reading public was apparently not interested.

He spent a month developing a proposal for a book or a movie about the whole story. The pitch included the true story of Angelica's involvement in the drug trafficking operation and how Javier Estrada was murdered with Angelica's gun. He was not successful finding a publisher that wanted to pick up the project.

While Paulo was writing and Hannah was butting her head against the ACN editorial policies, they were both crazy busy. They had lunch the day after the shootout, during which they were both exhausted and began nodding off after one mimosa each. Paulo then suggested dinner for the following Friday, which Hannah accepted, but it never happened. They were friends on Facebook and followed each other on Twitter and Instagram. They exchanged many text messages, but they could not seem to coordinate a meet-up. Whenever they bumped into each other at a news event or press conference, they exchanged hugs and agreed to keep trying.

* * *

IN THE WEEK FOLLOWING the soccer pitch shootout, the memorial for Angelica Monroe set up around the Hangman's Elm in Washington Square Park disappeared. NYU maintenance workers cleared away the dead flowers and burned-down candles. An organization supporting homeless children gathered the stuffed animals, cleaned them, and provided them to needy kids.

The trustees of NYU debated whether to commission a plaque to be placed near the elm to memorialize Angelica's death. A few trustees pointed out that some news reports suggested Angelica's involvement in drug distribution on campus, which was hardly something the university would want to glorify. A few others noted that reminding students about a murder only a few hundred yards from dorm buildings might not be a great idea. In the end, NYU did not erect any memorial, but did include a picture of Angelica and an *in memoriam* statement in the commencement program that year, and again the year she would have graduated.

The gun control advocacy groups did not hold any more rallies around Washington Square Park. The fact that the police caught the killer, albeit killing him in the process, removed most of the wind from the sails of the protesters. Angelica Monroe was no longer the proper poster child for the gun control movement.

* * *

LARS JOHANSSEN GRADUATED from medical school and accepted an internship at a hospital in Miami. After Reggie Millen was identified as Angelica's killer, nobody cared about the identity of the person who was, for a few days in April, the man everyone wanted to find. Lars never returned to The Scampering Squirrel.

* * *

AT THE ANNUAL CEREMONY where the broadcast journalism fraternity handed out kudos to their own, ACN's coverage of the soccer-pitch shootout and the Angelica Monroe/Javier Estrada murder won the award for breaking news coverage. Dave Butler accepted the award and praised the team, singling out Connor Osbourne, the drone operator who had captured the most-viewed video of the year. He mentioned Hannah Hawthorne's name among several others who worked on the story. Hannah was not invited to the gala, since she had left the company.

The awards ceremony was hosted by Taylor Espinoza, a Pulitzer Prize-winning fiction author who had begun their career as a print journalist. In remarks after the ACN team won its award, Espinoza called out the local reporting done by Paulo Richardson at the online paper the *Lower East Side Tribune*. It was, they said, a shining example that small, independent papers could still break news and write outstanding stories.

Espinoza addressed the most outstanding reporters in the country. "The truth was right there in front of us all along. Most of us didn't see it because we didn't want to look. We'll all have to think about that the next time."

Chapter 54 — There's Always Another Murder

DRU AND MARIANA DUCKED under a string of yellow crime scene ribbon and entered the courtyard of a public housing project on 155th Street in Washington Heights. Exiting the creaky elevator, the dimly lit hallway smelled of beer and stale cigarettes. Faded carpeting with an interlocking diamond pattern led to a mud-colored stain in front of apartment 2C. Inside, the tangy stench of blood emanated from a lumpy white sheet on the hardwood floor. The medical examiner had not yet arrived.

"What's the report?" Dru asked the officer who was first on the scene.

"White female age twenty-five. Neighbors say her name is Evalyn Stegman, which checks with ID in a purse. Looks like a gunshot. Three neighbors say they heard yelling, which was not unusual for this apartment, and a bang that could have been a gun. Ms. Stegman had a boyfriend, according to the neighbors. Carlos Cortez, Black man, six-four and two-sixty. We're running his background now. We have a bulletin out looking for him with instructions to treat him as armed and dangerous."

Dru thanked the officer and walked over to the body. Lifting the sheet, he contemplated the placid face of a young woman with short dark hair and blue eye shadow. In another context, she might have been asleep. "Nice to have one that's pretty easy, eh?"

Mariana peered over Dru's shoulder and said, "Seems that way. But things aren't always what they seem, right? Remember Angelica Monroe."

Dru meandered to the window, gazing out at the traffic oozing down Broadway. "Yeah. I won't forget."

[The End]

Thank you for reading *The Other Murder*. I truly enjoy hearing from readers about their reactions to my characters and stories. I welcome critical comments and suggestions that can help me improve my writing and urge every reader to **please leave a review**. Even a few words will go a long way and I will be grateful. Post on Goodreads, Amazon and/or BookBub to let other readers know what you think. And feel free to send me an email directly at www.kevingchapman.com to tell me your thoughts about this book.

And please tell your friends (and book club leaders) about this book. As an independent author, I need all the word-of-mouth plugs I can get. Keep reading books by indie authors; there are a lot of great writers out there just waiting for you.

Kevin G. Chapman
December 2023

About the Author

Kevin G. Chapman is, by profession, an attorney specializing in labor and employment law. He is a past Chair of the Labor & Employment Law Network of the Association of Corporate Counsel, leading a group of 6800 in-house employment lawyers. Kevin is a frequent speaker at Continuing Legal Education seminars and enjoys teaching management training courses.

Kevin's Mike Stoneman Thriller series, five full-length novels (so far), features NYPD Homicide Detective Mike Stoneman. The series includes *Lethal Voyage*, winner of the 2021 Kindle Book Award, and *Fatal Infraction*, winner of the CLUE Award as the #1 police procedural of the year. You can preview the series by reading the award-winning short story, *Fool Me Twice*, available free on most ebook retailer websites or you can get it directly from Kevin's website.

Dead Winner, published in 2022, was the Blue-Ribbon winner of the CLUE Award for the best suspense/thriller of 2022.

Kevin has also written a serious work of literary fiction, *A Legacy of One*, originally published in 2016, which was a finalist for the Chanticleer Book Review's Somerset Award for Literary Fiction.

Find Kevin on Facebook (Kevin G. Chapman Author) and at his website: KevinGChapman.com.

Book Club discussion questions for *The Other Murder*

1. How do you feel at the end of the book about Hannah? Is she the same career-driven producer she was at the beginning?
2. Did Paulo do the right thing publishing his story exposing Angelica as a drug buyer? Should he have left it alone? Should he have included that she was dealing?
3. How would you evaluate the value of the whole truth and whether to concentrate on Javier's story rather than Angelica's?
4. Have you observed race-based bias in television news coverage? Do you think it's legitimate for networks to prioritize viewership and ratings over reporting things their viewers don't want to hear?
5. Was Dru guilty of failing to call out racism, even without evidence? Do you think he will act differently the next time?
6. Was Mariana too focused on racism, rather than staying objective?
7. How do you think Dru and Mariana will do as partners in the future? (Would you like to read another story with them as the lead characters?)
8. Do you think Luis was telling the truth about what really happened?
9. Has reading this story changed how you perceive/believe what you see on broadcast news reports?

If your book clubs would like to read *Righteous Assassin*, book #1 in the Mike Stoneman Thriller series, please contact me for information about how your group can get discounted or free copies of the ebook and/or audiobook to get you started. Send me a note via my website at www.kevingchapman.com or by email at Kevin@KevinGChapman.com.

AUTHOR'S NOTE & ACKNOWLEDGEMENTS

As always, I must credit my wife, Sharon, for supporting me throughout my writing process, including those times when I wasn't sure how far to take this story.

I also thank my brilliant editor-daughter, Samantha (Samanthachapmanediting.com) whose willingness to tell me when I was being insensitive (or inadvertently racist) focused the story and helped me avoid disastrous blunders . She's the editor that every author wants. And kudos again to my cover designer, Peter from bespokebookcovers.com. Peter did a wonderful job creating this eye-catching cover. Also kudos to Jiawie "Peter" Hsu from Fotolux in Princeton Junction, NJ for making me beautiful prints for my publicity posters.

My beta readers provided me with invaluable perspectives and ideas as the book was in development. Thanks so much to, Roxx, Matt (M.C.) Thomas, Gayle Wilson, Jerilyn Schad, Kay Barton, Sue Martin, and the amazing Joanna Joseph. Everyone contributed something to the final product that would not have been there otherwise.

I also thank my intrepid band of Typokillers, who combed over the finished manuscript and rooted out the last few errors, large and small, to make the final text as clean as it can be. (But, if you find a flaw, please let me know so I can fix it.) All authors should use the typokillers. Thanks to Carole Poissant, Gayle Wilson, June Gaber, Kay Hagan-Haller, Nancy Harrison, Wayne B, Judy Johnson, Fred Casiello, Jerilyn Schad, Lynn Feinman, and Nancy Lee.

For this book, I also needed a group of sensitivity readers to help me temper my old-White-guy ignorance of what dialogue or story points that would have been inadvertently offensive. I, obviously, wanted to raise serious issues in this story, but I would have lost credibility if I had stumbled into gaffes that I didn't see due to my own cultural ignorance. Thanks to John Fraire, Neff Rodriguez, Phil Van Itallie, Mildred Stegman, and Jenna Kettenburg for their insight and support. If there are any insensitive or offensive dialogue or text here, it is either intentional or, if inadvertent, the fault is entirely my own.

I also thank all my newsletter subscribers who volunteered their names for use as characters in the book. Coming up with real-sounding names is more difficult than you might think. Using actual names (or parts of them) from my readers spares me the angst of fabricating names (mostly).

Other novels and stories by Kevin G. Chapman

<u>The Mike Stoneman Thriller Series</u>

Righteous Assassin (Mike Stoneman #1)
Deadly Enterprise (Mike Stoneman #2)
Lethal Voyage (Mike Stoneman #3)
Fatal Infraction (Mike Stoneman #4)
Perilous Gambit (Mike Stoneman #5)
Fool Me Twice (A Mike Stoneman Short Story)

<u>Stand-alone Novels</u>

Dead Winner
A Legacy of One
Identity Crisis: A Rick LaBlonde Mystery

<u>Short Stories</u>

The Car, the Dog & the Girl

Visit me at <u>www.KevinGChapman.com</u>

9 781958 33919